ROYAL MURDER
MYSTERIES

ROYAL MURDER MYSTERIES

Raymond Lamont-Brown

Weidenfeld and Nicolson
London

Published in Great Britain by
George Weidenfeld & Nicolson Limited
91 Clapham High Street
London SW4 7TA

ISBN 0 297 81071 5

Photoset by Deltatype Limited, Ellesmere Port
Printed in Great Britain by The Guernsey Press

Contents

Illustrations

Acknowledgements

The author would like to pay tribute to the inspiration and help he has received from the works and researches of the following, to whom grateful thanks are due:

William Rufus: To the Estate of Hugh Ross Williamson (1901–78) for short line quotes from 'The Death of William Rufus' in *Historical Whodunits* (Phoenix House, 1955).

Princes in the Tower: Short quote from Desmond Seward's *Richard III* (1983); to London Weekend Television for a perusal of the script of the Channel 4 production of 'The Trial of Richard III'.

James VI's Close Call: To the editor and publishers of *New Civil Engineer* for a sight of the paper 'Guy was certainly not joking' (1987) and for quotes of the research by Dr Sidney Alford.

The Dauphin: Grateful thanks to Mr Alain Lucas, Acting Assistant Director of the Ministry of Education and Information, National Archives and Museum Division, Mahé, Republic of Seychelles for help in tracing papers referring to the supposed Louis XVII, Mr Pierre Louis Poiret.

The Duke of Cumberland case: To the Estate of Maj. Sir John Richard Hall (1865–1928) for quotes from the Cumberland case in *The Bravo Mystery* (1923).

Napoleon: To Ben Weider and David Hapgood for the sequence of the search by Dr Sten Forshufvud to find evidence that the French Royal Family brought about the death of Emperor Napoleon Bonaparte. Their research is by far the best and most original in recent years on the supposed murder theories concerning Napoleon and the author pays full tribute to the help rendered by their text *The Murder of Napoleon* (1982).

Prince of Condé: To the Estate of Sir Arthur Salusbury MacNalty (1880–1969) for quotes from his paper 'The Death of the Duke of Bourbon' (1955).

Russian Imperial Family: To Robert K. Massie for short line quotes from *Nicholas and Alexandra* (1968), and to Anthony Summers and Tom Mangold for short line quotes and a study of their conclusions in *The File on the Tsar* (Gollancz 1976); and to Michael Thornton in his conclusions on the 'Anastasia Case'.

Ludwig of Bavaria: Thanks to the Historical Association for permission to quote from *The Historian* No. 7, Summer 1985; and to the author of 'The Death of King Ludwig II of Bavaria', Ms Jeanne Handzic, for generously allowing the quotes to be made.

Boris III: To the Estate of Sir George William Rendel (1889–1979) for quotes from *The Sword and the Olive* (1952), and for the inspirational original research in Stephane Groveff's *Crown of Thorns*.

Introduction
The Royal Killing Game

Whenever she appears in public HM Queen Elizabeth II is in the gravest danger, for she is the greatest potential prize on the international terrorists' list. Those most geared-up for her assassination are the IRA. Almost every month the anti-terrorist officers of British Intelligence receive whispers of plots to murder the Queen. In recent times the IRA have shown themselves capable and willing to assassinate royalty, for on the morning of 27 August 1979 they blew up the 79-year-old Earl Mountbatten of Burma aboard his fishingboat *Shadow V* near the harbour of Mullaghmore, Eire. Why they chose that day and that time is likely never to be known, but it is certain that they have a royal assassination hit-list with each member of the House of Windsor having a points rating to suit the occasion the IRA choose to celebrate with a royal death.

The IRA claimed responsibility for the explosion of 7lb of gelignite on 9 May 1981, the day Elizabeth II opened the oil terminal at Sullum Voe, Shetland. The Queen had walked within two hundred yards of the cache earlier that morning. On 4 July 1966, when the Queen was in Belfast, a seventeen-year-old youth, John Morgan, threw a block of concrete at her car, denting it; and on 13 June 1981 the Queen was attacked by another teenage youth, Marcus Simon Sarjeant, who fired blank shots at her during the Trooping of the Colour. Sarjeant was charged under Section II of the 1942 Treason Act. The Queen later remarked, 'Life must go on'.

Irish terrorists, called *Fianna Uladh,* were foiled in a plot against Prince Charles in 1959, but during April 1974, while serving as a lieutenant on a course aboard HMS *Jupiter*, at Portland, Dorset,

HRH was involved in a serious assassination attempt. Around two o'clock in the morning, Prince Charles was woken by a racket in his sitting room at the Royal Navy Barracks. HRH opened the connecting door from his bedroom and was pounced on by an armed assassin. The noise of the fight brought Detective Chief Inspector Paul Officer running in just in time to avert the attacker – a demented lieutenant at the Naval base – from hitting Prince Charles over the head with a chair.

On Wednesday, 20 March 1974, while returning home from an engagement with Captain Mark Philips, the Princess Royal was subjected to a kidnapping attempt which could have resulted in her murder. Her deranged assailant, 26-year-old Ian Ball, slewed his white Ford Escort in front of her car in the Mall. Ball fired several shots and wounded her detective, Inspector James W. Beaton, and her driver. Ball, who was charged with attempted murder, averred that his motives had been £3 million ransom money and a compulsion to draw public attention to what he saw as a lack of facilities for the insane on the NHS.

Taking pot shots at royalty – whether it is a well-aimed stone or a more lethal pistol-shot – has happened regularly since Egbert (827–39) founded the Saxon-Danish dynasty. It was not until the sixteenth century, however, that these attempts at royal discomfiture began to be officially recorded with any diligence, save of course, for the murder of St Edmund, the Saxon King, in 870. In 1584, for instance, the Welsh spy, William Parry, crept into Elizabeth I's garden at Richmond with the intention of killing her. Court records tell us that when Parry first set eyes on the Queen he was unable to carry out his intention. By then, perhaps, the Queen had become more phlegmatic about the evil intentions of some of her subjects; when a shot from a would-be assassin hit one of her bargemen as she sailed off one day, she gave the bleeding fellow her handkerchief with the utterance: 'Be of good cheer, for you will never want. For the bullet was meant for me.'

George III was the first reigning Hanoverian to sustain two major assassination attempts. On 2 August 1786, while he was alighting from his carriage at St James's Park, one Margaret Nicholson tried to stab him. She was overpowered, arrested, tried and declared mad. The second attempt was on 15 May 1800, whereon an ex-soldier,

James Hadfield, shot at George III at Dury Lane Theatre; Hadfield was also certified insane.

The seven attempts on Victoria's life are recorded in Chapter X, but her daughter-in-law was attacked in 1875. Alexandra, Princess of Wales, was struck by a splinter of glass when a stone smashed the window of her railway carriage as she passed Eton. Even though the headmaster of Eton was convinced that it was not the work of one of his pupils, but the work of a local town hooligan, he conducted a full inquiry; no culprit was found. It was to be some years before a member of Victoria's family was attacked again.

In 1900 when the royal train had stopped at Brussels on its way to Copenhagen, a sixteen-year-old tinsmith's apprentice, Baptiste Sipido, rushed from the gathered crowd and pushed a pistol muzzle through the window of the carriage and fired at point blank range at Edward, Prince of Wales. Sipido, who professed to the authorities that he had great sympathy with the Boers, was released on parole and disappeared shortly afterwards. HRH was unperturbed and commented only, 'The poor fool'.

Some twenty-five years were to pass before the newspapers of the time could record another attempt on British royalty. In 1925, while at Melton Races, the Prince of Wales was attacked by a shawled woman wielding a hatpin. Although she drew blood, Edward took it all in good part saying that very often someone might stick a pin in him or punch him. 'They could not get satisfaction from killing the House of Parliament, whereas I am both handy and responsive' he later commented. Ten years later, on 16 July 1936, while riding down Constitution Hill, London, on his way back to Buckingham Palace after presenting new colours to the Brigade of Guards in Hyde Park, Edward (then King Edward VIII) had a loaded gun thrown at him by a deranged Irish journalist called George Andrew McMahon, the alias of Jerome Bannigan. The gun hit the hind leg of Edward's horse and the King whispered to his brother, the Duke of York: 'We'll know in a minute if it's a bomb.' McMahon was sentenced to twelve years imprisonment with hard labour, charged with 'intent to alarm His Majesty'.

Although another Duke of York, Prince Andrew and his new wife were disturbed by an abortive attempt to attack them during their visit to the United States in 1987, the royal princesses have fared better at potential assassins' hands: although Princess Alexandra had a wooden chair thrown at her at SE London Juvenile Court in the 1960s, by a boy who had just been sentenced to a term in Wormwood Scrubs for felony.

In an age of 'warts and all' biography the re-examination of family papers brings to light some startling royal revelations. A recent disclosure was the accusation that George V was killed by his doctor, Bernard, Viscount Dawson of Penn. Those beautifully simple words, released by Dawson at 9:25 p.m. at Sandringham House, to herald the King's demise – 'The King's life is moving peacefully to its close' – take on a more sinister irony when it is suggested that the King's end was hastened to catch the morning papers. As a matter of clinical routine Dawson noted down that he accelerated the King's death so that the first news could be carried, not by the evening papers, but by the morning editions and especially *The Times*.

Among the thousands of murders, assassinations and attempted homicides that have taken place in Europe during the last one hundred years or so, none are more peppered with twisted testimony than those associated with royalty. It is a subject that is evergreen. Recently the late Princess Grace of Monaco was the implicit subject of a novel which made even more 'revelations' about the circumstances of her death in a car 'accident' in 1982. The book, by US crime reporter Leslie Waller, has as its heroine, Faith – a film star who marries a prince – being murdered by the Mafia because she wrests the casino of the principality from the governance of the Cosa Nostra. The novel is claimed to add a new slant to the allegations about Princess Grace's death that were made in the 1987 biography *Grace: The Secret Lives of a Princess* by James Spada.

Modern historical scholarship has done a great deal to clarify the history of royal murders of the past. We can be sure today, for instance, that Edward II's custodians Sir John Maltravers and Sir Thomas Gurney had the King murdered in 1327 at Berkeley Castle, as Ranulph Higden in *Polychronica* averred: *Cum vertu ignito inter celanda confossus ignominiose peremptus est* (He was ignominiously slain with a red-hot poker thrust into his anus). For such an act, while bringing about the poetic justice for his supposed sodomy, would leave the body unmarked for its viewing by 'abbots, priors, knights, burgesses' as attesting death by natural causes.

The royal fabric of any country is tinged with assassinations and murder, and this book will show that France was to supply more than one famous incident. On 16 January 1858, *The Times* of London, for instance, quoted an 'Express from Paris' on 'The Attempt to Assassinate the Emperor'. It appeared that at 8.30 on the evening of 14 January 1858, the Emperor Napoleon III – the son of Napoleon Bonaparte's brother Louis – and his wife were driving to a gala performance at the Opera; they were accompanied by their *aide-de-camp* General Roguet, with an escort of Lancers of the Guard. The Opera stood in Rue Lepelletier, Paris, and by it was a narrow alley, known as the Passage Noir leading to the Boulevard des Italiens, wherein was lurking the Italian conspirator, Felice Orsini and three accomplices. As the imperial carriage slowed in front of the steps of the Opera an explosion rocked the streets. A few seconds later another explosion erupted, then a third and the awning of the Opera door crashed down.

Glass fell like hail as the horses screamed in pain and bolted, and into the darkness of the street a thousand operagoers cascaded onto the thoroughfare – 156 people were hurt in the attempt, of whom twelve died. As the Empress opened the carriage door she faced an assassin; the police pounced and the Empress descended into the street, her white dress spotted with blood from a facial wound. The Emperor sustained a gashed nose but was otherwise unhurt.

Orsini's bombs, which had been made in Birmingham, rocked Europe and damaged Anglo-French relations. Later, Eugenie noted (recorded by Agnes de Stoeckl in *When Men Had Time to Love*, 1953) to friends that when the bomb went off, she felt in the secret compartment of the carriage for one of the two loaded pistols which were kept there, to find that the servant whose job it was to place them there had forgotten them – she declared that if she had been armed, when the assassin approached the carriage, she would have shot him. Napoleon III lived to a natural old age of sixty-five to die in exile in England in 1873.

This book is designed to show how new evidence is continually coming to light on the royal murders and assassinations of decades ago, and the content has been chosen to show cases with particularly special factors. For instance, the death of William Rufus was perhaps the best contrived of all the royal regicides; the Princes in the Tower case is a classic unsolved royal crime and it is as emotive today as it ever was with academics taking fiercely opposed sides. In the murder of Lord Darnley (called Henry, King of Scots) more than one faction was involved and both Protestants and Catholics wanted his death, and government involvement was more than clear in the Gunpowder Plot to blow up Darnley's son James VI and I. In the case of the Dauphin of France it was a supposed government killing that covered up a possible escape plan organized by the Committee of Public Safety. Today too, it is thought that Sellis, the royal Duke of Cumberland's valet was murdered and did not commit suicide, but the reader must say why, but note for the first time on record that the King's physician was publicly accused of a cover-up.

Many monarchs have had murders placed at their personal doors, Ivan the Terrible, Peter the Great, and Philip II of Spain are three famous examples, but were there many more privy to murder? Was Louis-Phillipe, for instance, privy to the murder of the Prince of Condé, and did the French Royal Family pay for the murder of Napoleon? Others like Ludwig, King of Bavaria, and Crown Prince Rudolph of Austria may have been killed by their families; only the reader can judge.

Raymond Lamont-Brown
St Andrews, 1990

1

The Violent Death of William Rufus

WAS THE KING A SATANIC SACRIFICE OR A POLITICAL MARTYR?

The inscription is stark and simple: 'Here stood the oak tree in which an arrow shot by Sir Walter Tyrell at a stag glanced and struck King William the Second, surnamed Rufus, on the breast of which he died instantly on the second day of August anno 1100.' In these few words, on the Rufus Stone (set up approximately a quarter-mile to the north of the A31, and three miles south west of Cadnam, by Lord John Delaware in 1745) there is recorded a royal mystery which is as enigmatic today as it was when its events evolved on that summer evening nearly nine hundred years ago. The stone in the sun-dappled glade, trampled around by tourists, does not do justice to the strange stories of satanism and political jockeying that unfolded on the sudden death of England's second Norman king.

King William II, whose auburn hair and florid sneering face earned him the nickname in his own lifetime of 'Rufus', meaning 'the Red', was a rapacious debauchee whose disgusting habits shocked his court. Even his former tutor, the Archbishop Lanfranc of Pavia, was reluctant at first to perform the sacred ceremony of coronation, so unworthy he thought the king – or at least that is what the biased monk Eadmer of Christ Church, Canterbury, would have us believe in his *Vita Anselmi*. Even so, William Rufus had the qualities necessary for a ruler in this harsh, violent and turbulent age. He had his father's great energy and ruthless determination, and was skilled at getting people to do his will. William Rufus was a strict disciplinarian and he was always 'in the thick of it' when campaigning. And this stammering monarch was subject to violent rages which led to much verbal abuse of those who displeased him. His personal courage was undoubted and his pursuance of the embryo chrivalric code of the day was exemplary, as is well-attested in contemporary anecdotes. This led to the court being made a magnet for military adventurers from all over Europe. Chroniclers speak of the knights in William's retinue as raping and plundering wherever they went on a *carte blanche* from the ungainly and portly king.

Such celebrated scholars as A. Freeman have concluded that William Rufus was homosexual, noting the fact that there are few references to him having mistresses and having no known children. And to the monkish chroniclers of the time, Rufus was lecherous, blasphemous and gave rein to 'everything that was hateful to God and to righteous man.' Rufus undoubtedly had an open contempt for the church and for his ministers. He made wealth by failing to appoint new bishops and abbots to vacant positions, thereby placing the funds due to them in his own coffers, all managed by the King's illiterate and unscrupulous crony Ranulf 'Flambard' (so called because of his ambition) elevated in 1099 to the rich ecclesiastic prize of the see of Durham. Because of such default the see of Canterbury went unfilled for four years after the death of the good and wise Lanfranc in 1089. It was only when an illness brought William Rufus to the realization that he might be dying that he briefly repented his actions and appointed Anselm of Bec as Archbishop (this was a short lived occupancy as Anselm was soon driven into exile). So the monastic chroniclers uniformly gave William Rufus a bad press and it is to them that we must return for contemporary witness . . . bearing in mind that they were strangely reticent on William's death for a man they openly despised.

By Norman custom on the death of William I, the Conqueror, the Duchy of Normandy was given to his eldest son Robert, and the Conqueror's newest possession, England, was given to his third son, William. Eventually the Conqueror's will was carried out and King William II was crowned at Westminster Abbey on Sunday 26 September 1087. The terms of the will divided the loyalty of the Anglo-Norman barons and many of them rebelled with William

Rufus's uncle, Bishop Odo of Bayeux, Earl of Kent; but these barons were defeated by the King with the help of English magnates recruited on false promises. William Rufus's most notable achievement was the securing of Cumbria from Scots King Malcolm Canmore in 1092 which added to his successful territorial expansion into Wales.

Strange to tell there was a kind of dress rehearsal for William Rufus's death in May 1100; Richard, the bastard son of Duke Robert, was killed in the New Forest. Orderic Vitalis records that Richard was struck accidentally and killed instantly by an arrow aimed at a stag by one of his companions. It was no real surprise to the clerics though, that William Rufus was struck down in a violent way; was it not heaven's disapproval for a life of cardinal sin?

At first the king's death was generally assumed to be an accident. There was no official enquiry and no attempt to seek out or punish the offender. Today we cannot pin down exactly how the accident occurred for details are sparse in the strictly contemporary accounts set out for example, in *The Anglo-Saxon Chronicle*. This chronicle says: 'In the morning after Lammas, King William, when hunting was shot by an arrow by one of his own men. . . .' Yet two men amongst the group of writers who began to flourish in the reign of Henry I believed they could offer more detailed accounts, although they were writing two decades after William II's death. One was William of Malmesbury and the other Orderic Vitalis who was certainly hostile to William. William of Malmesbury records graphically the events of that day in 1100 in his *De Gestis Regnum Anglorum*:

> After dinner [*the king*] went into the forest with a small number of attendants. Among these the most intimate with the king was Walter surnamed Tirel, who had come from France attracted by the liberality of the king. This man alone remained with him while the others were widely scattered in the chase. The sun was setting, and the king drawing his bow let fly an arrow which slightly wounded a stag which passed before him. He ran in pursuit, keeping his gaze rigidly fixed on the quarry, and holding up his hand to shield his eyes from the sun's rays. At this instant Walter, forming in his mind a project which seemed good to him, tried to transfix another stag which happened to

come near him while the king's attention was otherwise occupied. And thus it was that unwittingly and quite unable to prevent it . . . he pierced the king's breast with the fatal arrow. When the king received the wound he uttered not a word, but breaking off the shaft of the arrow where it stuck out of his body he fell to the ground, thus accelerating his own death. Walter immediately ran up, but finding the king unconscious and speechless, he leapt quickly on his horse and escaped at full gallop. Indeed there was no one to pursue him. Some connived at his flight; others pitied him.

Writing in his *Ecclesiasticae historiae libri tredecim*, Orderic Vitalis notes that William Rufus's younger brother Henry, with an entourage of noblemen and hangers-on, deliberately fanned out in the woods to take up position and wait for stags:

When the king and Walter de Poix [*ie Walter Tirel*] had taken up stations with a few companions in a grove, and eagerly awaited game with their weapons ready, suddenly a beast ran between them; the king moved from his place and Walter released an arrow. It grazed an animal's hairy back but glanced off and struck the king who was standing within range. He immediately fell to the ground, and without more ado, alas, he died. A dreadful clamour echoed through the woods at the death of a prince.

The king's body incidentally, it appears, was neglected for several hours, but was later conveyed to Winchester on a charcoal-burner's cart for burial beneath the cathedral tower. When the tower fell down seven years later, it was deemed to have done so because the cadaver was unworthy of such a resting place. William II lived in a superstitious age and the mode of his death was interpreted as divine judgement for his wickedness. But there were many since who believed that William II was given a decidedly mortal push into eternity.

Over the years historians have set out four main avenues for the reasons for William's death:

Walter Tirel deliberately loosed the fatal arrow; William was assassinated by the order of his brother Henry; William was killed through the machinations of his brother Robert; The king was slaughtered as part of a satanic cult.

Let us first examine the most startling of the four reasons for William Rufus's death – that he was killed because of an association with satanism.

In his book *Historical Whodunits* (1955) the writer Hugh Ross Williamson put forward the strange theory that William Rufus had been killed because he was chosen as a sacrificial victim of a fertility cult; a cult which such anthropologists as Margaret Murray (*The Witch Cult in Western Europe* 1921) averred had survived in Europe under a thin veneer of Christianity. According to this theory an anointed king was deemed an incarnate god, capable of great powers of fertility and divination. Should such a person (or a substitute) be ritually slaughtered, the crops and animals would be abundantly fertile for a period thereafter for the sustenance of mankind. Margaret Murray further averred (*The Divine Kings of England* 1954) that William Rufus shared these pagan beliefs of the extant, 'half-Christianised populace', and sought his own death when he felt his divine powers were being weakened. In *The Arrow and the Sword* (1947), Hugh Ross Williamson went further in an attempt to skein together a theory which linked William with the Catharists' cult (gnostic heretics who menaced church and society from the tenth century and who believed in ritual suicide), when he may have learned through his friendship with William IX of Aquitaine; and the 'Nature Ritual' supposedly practised and expounded by Prince Bledri of Wales. So Hugh Ross Williamson and others saw William Rufus as the Anglo-Norman 'devil' ritually slaughtered 'on the morrow of "the Gule of August", the great "witch" festival'. Ross Williamson further averred that the theory 'explains the conflicting accounts of the event – those of the rhymers and romancers who conveyed the true significance of it to posterity, and those of the monks who, understanding it no less clearly, made every effort to represent it merely as the vengeance of Heaven on a wicked and blasphemous ruler.'

To those who believed that witchcraft was a reality before the two Dominican friars, Heinrich Kramer and James Sprenger, manufactured the supposed rites of witches in *Malleus Maleficarum* in 1486, the theory is attractive. Yet, can it be substantiated by historical evidence?

First, the chroniclers agree that William Rufus was disparaging of the church and its administrators. He is likely to have been cynical about the pastoral clergy and was certainly thought of as a heretic in some ecclesiastical circles. In no way is that indicative though of William Rufus believing in a secret cult of satanists, or that he saw himself as a sacrifice. If that were the case, William Rufus would likely have been more explicit about his beliefs in order to mortify and scorn the clergy further. If this had been a reality, it would have been known by the clergy and used to further blacken the king's name. Henry certainly is not recorded as believing this – if he had, then he too surely would have used it against his brother. There is no evidence either that William had anything to do with the Catharan sect – they did not venture into England until some seventy years after William Rufus's death.

What Margaret Murray and Hugh Ross Williamson do is to disregard the basic rules of the use of historical research material. For instance Ross Williamson says: 'The various accounts of the death of Rufus abound in touches which convey its true significance. It is consummated in the depths of a forest at sunset on the site of a pre-Christian holy place. He stands under (or the arrow glances from) an oak, the Royal tree. His slayer stands under an elder tree, the tree of doom, which traditionally is both the tree of the Cross and the tree on which Judas hanged himself. The king partakes of a kind of last sacrament of herbs and flowers. In most of the accounts he is slain by an arrow loosed by his intimate, Tirel, after Tirel's hesitation and the king's command, "Shoot, in the Devil's name, or it will be the worst for you." ' The dialogue incidentally is supplied by Ross Williamson without any source. Williamson further belabours the occult point by saying that the soubriquet *rufus* was significant, 'For the colour of blood, has always and everywhere been the "witch" colour.'

Williamson's theory is based on chronicles of various dates and varying veracity. For instance, we know that it is Geoffrey Gaimer, the twelfth-century chronicler of Geoffrey of Monmouth in his *Lestorie des Engles* who writes of the tree lore and the herb communion; but Gaimar was writing a metrical romance in French with much poetic licence. The king's comment about shooting came from Henry Knighton's *Chronicon* written in the fifteenth century, and the Worcester monk 'Florence of Worcester' in *Chronicon ex Chronicis* mentions that William Rufus died near a ruined church and links it with divine providence to make a point. So the Williamson theory is not based on good historical research but is fanciful in the extreme.

Considering the second option that William was killed by the order of his brother Robert, we must study Robert's character. Robert Curthose (so named for the *courte heuse* – short breeches – he wore) was irresolute and gullibly incompetent; and his Normandy duchy was reduced to anarchy after William the Conqueror's death. Robert was a loser, yet William Rufus did have some kingly qualities besides the recklessly courageous military attitude he struck. Because he was a successful ruler, plus the fact that he held a coveted kingship, William was a target for Robert's jealousy which in a violent age often led to murder. Robert rebelled against his brother and to cut a long story short he was outwitted and defeated and decided to go on a crusade to the Holy Land to expiate his sins. So, although Robert did have the support of some barons, he did not have a real powerbase in which to pursue any wished elimination of William, and if he had had this powerbase, he had neither the gumption nor the expertise with which to carry it out.

As to the third option, that William Rufus was killed by the order of his brother Henry, what of that? Undoubtedly Henry had a very strong motive for murder. The fourth son of the Conqueror, Henry bynamed Beauclerk because of his greatly over-played scholarship, was a gratuitously cruel man; he was as untrustworthy as his royal brothers, but outdid them in avarice – and, Henry was likely to have been a murderer already. Had he not personally pushed the rich merchant, Conan, to his death from the castle tower at Rouen?

Henry had been born in England – a fact he held to give him a greater claim to his father's throne by European custom, by which rule he deemed William Rufus a 'usurper' – and had only a real chance of ascending the throne of England if William Rufus's death occurred by the end of August 1100. By then his elder brother Robert (declared William's heir) would have returned from his crusade, and, unlike Henry, Robert had a chance of a legitimate heir to succeed him.

We know that Henry was among the seven lords who rode with William Rufus on that fateful day. On receiving the news that William was dead, Henry rode to Winchester, seized the Treasury and put into action what seems to be a well-planned schedule. The next morning, 3 August 1100, Henry held an impromptu council, was elected king by members of the Witen and rode to London. There on 4 August he held a court to which he summoned Maurice, Bishop of London; on Sunday, 5 August, the Bishop (in the absence of the Archbishop of Canterbury) consecrated Henry who was then crowned king by Thomas, Archbishop of York, at Westminster Abbey.

Today we see a great deal of circumstantial evidence that suggests a conspiracy to murder. Henry wanted the throne of England and William was in the way, and a hunt would be an ideal place for a murder to look like an accident. There Henry, too, would plausibly have his accomplices about him, and the events after William's death went too smoothly to believe that there had been no plan. No time was wasted in declaring Henry king, and there was no opposition. Henry had around him all the men necessary – like William de Breteuil, keeper of the Treasury – to put the coup into action.

Now, how do Tirel's actions fit into the scheme of things? We learn from the chroniclers William of Malmesbury and Orderic Vitalis, that Walter Tirel, Lord of Poix, in Normandy, loosed an arrow that accidentally killed the king. Is it really plausible that a skilled huntsman such as Tirel, would loose an arrow, fully knowing that he would be firing into the line of his fellow hunters (by this time the stag was amongst the huntsmen?) How convenient it was for the arrow to 'accidentally' strike the king in the chest.

It is interesting to note too, that Geoffrey Gaimer records that it was the other archers who said it was not Tirel's arrow that killed the king, yet Tirel did flee. Did he flee to escape reprisal? Certainly his path to the coast was unimpeded. Was he a convenient perhaps willing scapegoat? For the rest of his life he maintained his innocence, and even went so far to say that he was not even in the same part of the forest as the king – this was recorded by Abbot Suger of St Denis in his *Vie de Louis VI le Gros*.

If Tirel was lying throughout, he was either a paid assassin, or murdering for his own gains. He had married Alice de Clare, whose brothers Gilbert and Roger were Henry's men and were present in the hunting party on that day. In short time Alice's uncle, William Giffard, was appointed Bishop of Winchester, the richest see in England. All of Alice's brothers ultimately benefited from Henry's largesse. It seems a very strange coincidence that Gilbert de Clare (he had already had had two attempts at plotting against William Rufus) was present at the death; had a family who gained by the death; was by Henry's side in the fast-moving events after the killing; and was the brother-in-law of the man deemed to be the assassin. Did Tirel sacrifice himself for Clare advantage?

If Tirel was not lying, what then? It is more than possible (whether or not William's death was an accident) that Tirel was accused and blackmailed into fleeing in order to deflect the blame from say, another member of Henry's party. His quick flight (he was a stranger to Hampshire), and a rapid embarkation for Normandy (a ship had been arranged?) remain surprising. Further, Tirel's lands in Normandy were not confiscated as one would have expected had he really been guilty.

Of all these theories this latter one remains most plausible, namely that William Rufus's death was arranged and carried out by the de Clares on behalf of Henry Beauclerk. This theory shows that the conspiracy to murder may have been the best contrived regicide ever.

2

The Princes in the Tower

THE MOST FAMOUS ROYAL MURDER OF ALL TIME

Born at Fotheringay Castle, Northamptonshire, on 2 October 1452, King Richard III, the eleventh child of Richard Plantagenet, 3rd Duke of York, and the tough-minded Lady Cicely Neville, has gone down in history as the wicked-uncle *par excellence*. Because of the professional hatchet job done on him by the Tudor propagandists of Henry VII and Henry VIII's reign, aided and abetted by William Shakespeare, Richard appears in history as an evil monster. His detractors have him plunge a dagger into the hapless Lancastrian King Henry VI; they have him the slayer of his brother George, Duke of Clarence; the poisoner of his wife Ann Neville; and the murderer of his little nephews. Richard died on the Field of Bosworth in battle with Henry Tudor on 22 August 1485 and was buried in the Grey Friars Abbey, Leicester; his reputation was to become so foul that he was later disinterred and his bones thrown in the River Soar.

Richard's terrible aura remained for decades until historians began to question the Tudor historians, like Sir Thomas More, whose *History of King Richard the Third* (1543) Shakespeare had quarried, and the Italian historian Polydore Vergil whose character assessment of Richard appeared in *Anglica Historia* (1543). The first questioner in print was Sir William Cornwallis the Younger who circumspectly issued his thoughts as a 'Paradox' in *A Brief Discourse in Praise of King Richard the Third* (1616). Sir George Buc, James VI and I's Master of the

Revels prepared a full-scale siege on the tradition in his *History of the Life and Reign of Richard the Third* in 1646. Forty years later William Winstanley set the ball rolling for a real rehabilitation of Richard in his *England's Worthies* which was given acceleration by the English writer Horace Walpole, 4th Earl of Orford who published his *Historic Doubts on the Life and Reign of Richard III* in 1768.

Undoubtedly Richard was put on the road to more public rehabilitation by the distinguished novelist and playwright Josephine Tey (Elizabeth MacKintosh) in her novel *The Daughter of Time*. Therein, using the character of a detective sifting through the evidence on Richard's supposed murder of his nephews, Miss Tey found Richard innocent. Today that innocence is emphasized by the 'Richard III Society' who hold regular meetings and lectures on the Ricardian story.

Several modern historians look upon Richard as a cruelly wronged man. Indeed his letters reveal him to be an attractive and cultured nobleman, and there is a very strong impression that he was a country gentleman at heart rocketed onto the political stage by circumstance. Furthermore it is undoubted that he was a man who trusted others too easily. Up to his apparent seizure of the crown he was a man of valour and uprightness in his dealings, although he was a true Plantagenet with talent for intrigue and ruthlessness (the latter should be assessed though in a medieval context and not a modern one).

Only eight years old when his brother was proclaimed king as Edward IV, Richard, Duke of Gloucester, showed himself to be a loyal and loving brother. Richard married Ann Neville, the widow of Edward, Prince of Wales – Henry VI's only son – in 1472; and a son, Edward, was born in 1473. Richard's brother, George, Duke of Clarence, had married Ann Neville's sister, Isabel, in 1469. The marriages caused a rift between the brothers as George was anxious to retain the lands of his father-in-law (Richard Neville, Earl of Warwick). Even so there is nothing to suggest – before More and Vergil's accounts – that Richard of Gloucester had any murderous proclivities at all.

Concerning the first three murders of which Richard stands accused by the Tudors – those of the Lancastrian king Henry VI, Richard's wife Ann Neville, and Richard's brother, George, Duke of Clarence – the following can be said:

Born at Windsor Castle 6 December 1421, Henry VI of the House of Lancaster became king when he was eight months old. Throughout his life he was blighted by a recurring mental affliction and his reign was pure tragedy. He comes down to us in history as a pathetic figure. Most of his reign was concerned with the third stage of the Hundred Years War, and the beginning of the War of the Roses. He was deposed by the House of York, restored as a puppet king in 1470, and deposed again in 1471. Henry VI died on the night of 21 May 1471 in the Tower of London; as the Yorkist author of *The Historie of the Arivall of Edward IV in England* put it, of 'pure displeasure and melancholy'. Historians agree that there is little doubt that the Yorkist king Edward IV ordered Henry VI's murder. When Henry's bones were exhumed in 1910 his hair was found to be matted with blood and his skull showed a violent end.

Writing in the 1490s, Dr John Warkworth, Master of Peterhouse, Cambridge, accuses Richard of Gloucester of murdering Henry, Richard 'being then in the Tower'; but that is no proof that Richard had a hand in the murder. Again, writing in 1502 Polydore Vergil accuses Richard of murdering Henry VI's son after the Battle of Tewkesbury (1471, where Edward IV defeated the army loyal to Margaret, wife of Henry VI), but this totally unsubstantiated accusation may be dismissed as gossip from the Tudor propaganda package.

Of Richard's wife Ann Neville, there is again no proof that he poisoned her in the Palace of Westminster on 16 March 1485, as Tudor chronicles aver. It is clear from contemporary sources that their marriage was happy and Richard's love and respect for her seem genuine. It is likely that Ann was consumptive and would be given the potion of the day for this very infectious disease, namely a mixture which included arsenic. If Ann died of arsenical poisoning, her physicians would be to blame not Richard.

As to the Duke of Clarence, he was arrested on Edward IV's orders and placed in the Tower on a charge of treason. His trial was conducted in January 1478; and he was found guilty of conspiring against his brother. Clarence was condemned to death. Before he could be officially executed, Clarence was murdered in the Tower, as tradition has it by drowning in a butt of Malmsey wine. All the time Richard of Gloucester had opposed Clarence's execution and was overcome with grief at his brother's death. Once more there is no evidence at all that Richard murdered his brother as is accorded by Tudor hearsay.

The murder of Edward, Prince of Wales, the uncrowned Edward V, and his brother, Richard, Duke of York – known to history as 'The Princes in the Tower' – remains the classic unsolved royal murder in history. Many modern historians generally look upon Richard as misrepresented for the story of the murder is put together from very few bits of source material, basically manuscripts like the *Second Continuation of the Crowland Chronicle* (the chronicle of the monks of Crowland Abbey, Linconshire, 1459–86) and the scholarly Roman Dominic Mancini's eyewitness description, for Angelo Cato, Archbishop of Vienne, of Richard's usurpation of 1483 called *De Occupatione Regni Anglae per Riccardum Tercium*. So we are concerned with a very brief part of Richard's life and may construe the certain facts of the case as follows.

Edward, Prince of Wales, was born in 1470, the son of King Edward IV and his second wife, Elizabeth Woodville. When Edward IV died in 1483 and the Prince of Wales became Edward V, the new king's heir was his brother Richard, Duke of York, then aged ten. On his deathbed, Edward IV had named his trusted brother Richard as Protector of the Realm during the minority of Edward V. This move had dismayed the boys' mother and her family (all looked upon at court as grasping upstarts), who determined to keep the young king firmly under their own grasp. Richard of Gloucester was equally determined to retain control and made the first move.

In May 1483 Richard intercepted the young king's party on their way to Ludlow and Edward V was taken shortly afterwards to the Tower of London, then a royal residence as well as a fortress/prison. Even so, Richard expressed complete loyalty to his nephew, but the chroniclers now began to indicate that Richard, Duke of Gloucester set in motion his resolution to be king himself.

Slowly Richard of Gloucester did sweep away opposition: Lord Hastings, Edward IV's Chamberlain, was executed without trial (he had refused to aid Richard in his aims) as were the queen's brother Anthony Woodville, Earl Rivers, and her son, Sir Richard Grey. The Archbishop of York, the Bishop of Ely and Lord Stanley – all members of the Council – were imprisoned; but later Richard's leniency was extended to them. On 16 June Edward's brother, the Duke of York, was conveyed to the Tower; Richard now had both boys firmly under his protection.

Over the next few weeks the two boys were seen playing and shouting 'by sundry times' in the garden of the Tower, reports the *Great Chronicle of London*. But after that they disappear from the public eye – for ever.

If Richard, Duke of Gloucester, was the real murderer of the boys what were his motives? In the simplest terms, should Richard's claim to the throne be defective then the existence of the boys would be a threat to him. On 22 June 1483, Dr Ralph Sha preached a sermon at St Paul's Cross, stating that Edward IV's sons were bastards. This statement was made on information given by Bishop Robert Stillington of Bath and Wells that King Edward had 'solemnly plighted his troth' to one Lady Eleanor Butler, daughter of the Earl of Shrewsbury. To many that was deemed as binding as a marriage itself and that Edward was consequently not free to marry Elizabeth Woodville, the boys' mother. Consequently too the marriage was null and void and the children illegitimate. Others, of course, looked upon the marriage as perfectly lawful. But, as a result of Sha's sermon, Richard was offered the crown and he was proclaimed king as Richard III on 26 June.

Some historians like M. R. Myres, believed that Richard's hand was now forced. Indeed how could Richard be secure until he nullified the power of the Woodvilles, whose chief dynastic and political assets were the boys? Furthermore, with the boy king still alive, Richard's claim to the throne was weak and taking into consideration that a coalition of Yorkists and Lancastrians was forming to support Edward V, Richard had to act. By September 1483 too, reports began to circulate that the boys were dead, and rumour was rife in Europe that Richard had actually murdered them. Richard knew of these rumours – the court was always rife with gossip – but strangely he never produced the little princes to refute the rumours.

In the most recent biography of the king, *Richard III: England's Black Legend* (1983), Desmond Seward states that 'nothing of importance in Richard's defence has been found for a century'; and, 'the few discoveries in recent times have all confirmed that he was violent and ruthless'. Seward develops his case against Richard. He underlines the 'black legend' that surrounds Richard's reign, which he calls 'the unhappiest in English history' and notes Richard's unpopularity and state of emotional tension and insecurity; but none of this is in itself unusual in one who has seized the throne.

Seward believes that the 'decision to kill the princes may even have been taken before Richard seized the throne', but the likes of the *Crowland Chronicle* say that it was only by autumn of 1483 that Edward IV's sons were rumoured as dead (Richard was crowned on 6 July 1483). Certainly by early September the boys' mother, with Humphrey Stafford, Duke of Buckingham and Dr John Morton, Bishop of Ely, and others, were putting forward Henry Tudor, as Pretender to the Throne and schemed to have him marry the sister of Edward V – so at the very least they *believed* that Edward V was dead, or they *knew* it.

Based on the testimony of one Philippe de Commynes, Seward noted that the date of *circa* 15 August is given for the murders. Commynes however in his *Memoires II* adds some confusion; first, he says that Buckingham killed them. So therein, Commynes cites the two main culprits in history and helps pose the royal mystery.

Both the *Titulus Regius* (1486 passed after Bosworth by Henry VII's parliament) and the *Crowland Chronicle* accused Richard III of the murder, but neither was impartial. Nothing substantial was publicly apparent until 1502 when Sir James Tyrell of Gipping (then awaiting execution for his part in the plan to put the Yorkist Pretender, the Earl of Surrey, on the throne) and his servant John Dighton 'confessed' to how the princes died. Tyrell was deemed to have been entrusted by Richard III to kill the boys, says Thomas More, and Tyrell acted with the collusion of Sir Robert Brackenbury of Selaby, Co. Durham, the Constable of the Tower of London. Thereupon the actual murder was done by John Dighton and one Miles Forest 'a fellow fleshed in murder beforetime'. The mode of murder was smothering. The murderers then buried the bodies 'at the stairfoot, meetly deep in the ground under a great heap of stones'. Thomas More notes that Brackenbury ordered a priest of his household to bury them in a 'secret . . . burial place' at a later date. It must be remembered at this point though, that Sir Thomas More's version of the murder is full of errors and bespotted with unauthenticated imagination.

In 1674 when workmen were demolishing a staircase in the White Tower, they discovered a wooden chest in which were found the bones of two children. Charles II ordered that the bones (those left by the souvenir hunters) be interred in a regal Wren urn in the Henry VII Chapel at Westminster Abbey. When the urn was opened in 1933 the skeletal remains were examined; they were found to be from cadavers of youngsters of around twelve and ten – the ages of the princes in 1483; this opinion was given by the distinguished anatomist Professor W. Wright. In the 1950s the findings were re-examined, but opinions were contradictory as to sex and the age of the bones.

Thus is the story of the two unfortunate princes presented from Thomas More's manuscript, but what of the others who had reason to see the princes dead? In this question history cites two possible contenders, Henry Tudor and the Duke of Buckingham. Henry Tudor was born at Pembroke Castle, 28 January 1457, and was to become King of England after defeating Richard III at Bosworth. The son of Edmund Tudor, Earl of Richmond and the Lady Margaret Beaufort, Henry was a direct descendant of Edward III. Henry's claim to the throne, however, was doubtful and was based on civil war and disorder; indeed his mother's descent from Edward III's son, John of Gaunt, was contestable in terms of bastardy. On 18 January 1486 Henry Tudor married Elizabeth of York, eldest daughter of Edward IV and established the Tudor dynasty.

Humphrey Stafford, Duke of Buckingham, was also a descendant of Edward III and was Richard III's cousin. At first he sided with Richard and then gave his support to Henry Tudor. Buckingham and Henry's possible involvement in the murder of the two princes was to be examined in a fascinating piece of historical presentation.

In 1984 London Weekend Television set up *The Trial of Richard III* as a production for Channel 4. The programme was devised and produced by Richard Drewett and formed a remarkable piece of television. The intention was to present the case of murder of the Princes in the Tower, and establish Richard's guilt or innocence therein, before a modern judge and jury within a studio setting. The late Lord Elwyn-Jones of Llanelli and Newham was the presiding judge, and a jury of twelve was chosen from 'ordinary members of the public without any specialist interest in or knowledge of medieval history'. Richard (represented by an empty desk) was to be prosecuted by Mr Russell and defended by Mr Dillon – two eminent barristers who, for ethical reasons, used pseudonyms.

The witnesses for the prosecution in the case were academic historians, while the witnesses for the defence were by and large a mixture of amateur historians and academics. The judgement on Richard was to be assessed on 'the balance of probability' of guilt or innocence.

'The Trial' began with the charge that: 'King Richard III did, in or about the month of August 1483, in the Tower of London, murder Prince Edward, Prince of Wales [*in reality Edward V*], and Prince Richard, Duke of York'.

The defence barrister entered a plea of 'not guilty' for Richard and Mr Russell opened the case for the prosecution by setting the historical scene within the background of the War of the Roses; that civil struggle between the rival dynastic houses of York and Lancaster, both of whose protagonists were descendants of Edward III, who had allowed his family to marry with his nobles, thus complicating hereditary claims to the crown. Then Mr Russell showed how Richard disinherited the two princes on the charge of bastardy, murdered them and remained completely silent about their fate.

The prosecution then set out to prove five things:

That the two princes *were* murdered in the Tower.
That Richard III had *the* motive to kill them.
That Richard III had ruthlessly *killed others*.
That no killing of the boys could have been possible, *without* Richard's knowledge.
That Richard III was *believed* by his contemporaries to have murdered the boys.

Counsel for the prosecution showed that if Richard wished to achieve power he had to eliminate the Woodvilles. Counsel guided witnesses through all of the events from the incarceration of the Princes in the Tower to Richard's coronation. Their testimony underlined that Richard, Duke of York, was Edward V's true heir and that if Richard of Gloucester was to be king, the princes had to be killed to stop them becoming the focus of rebellion. Counsel showed too that by now Henry Tudor had shown his interest to marry Queen Elizabeth's daughter and that the Tudors and the Woodvilles now combined to seize the throne themselves. In underlining Richard's motives, testimony showed that Henry Tudor also had a strong motive to kill the princes if he wanted the throne himself – if the princes stood between Richard and the throne, they also stood between Henry and the throne; counsel did not elaborate on this point. Buckingham in the meantime had espoused the rebellion against Richard and was defeated and executed.

In reply, defence counsel showed that Richard was considered to be a 'good man' certainly by 1483 and no more of a dissembler or schemer than anyone else at the court. It was also emphasized that it was not unusual for the princes to be in the Tower; as a palace all the kings processed from the building to their coronation.

Further evidence examined gave modern medical opinion about certain aspects of the skeletal remains found in 1674. Dr Jean Ross, Senior Lecturer in Anatomy at Charing Cross Hospital Medical School averred that through modern analysis that at the time of the death the bones might have been of people younger than the two princes, but the teeth and jawbones discovered were consistent with coming from children of about twelve and ten and indicated consanguinity. But there was no proof of cause of death, or that the bones were male.

Opening the case on behalf of the defence, Mr Dillon emphasized that for every point posed by the prosecution there was a plausible and sincere opposite view. The defence made the point that Tudor tradition painted Richard black and Henry VII white; and how, for instance, even official portraits of Richard were later tampered with to show deformity, thus highlighting the 'monster' image of Richard. The defence called an archivist witness to discuss and show how the pre-contract marriage between Edward IV and Lady Eleanor Butler was important and valid and that it did legally bastardize the princes – by the conventions of the time – and clearly gave Richard legitimate precedence; with the inference that he had no need to kill the boys.

The defence's final witness, Ronald Potter, chairman of the Richard III Society was called to give a balanced picture of Richard the man, and to consider the part played by Humphrey, Duke of Buckingham, Constable of England. Buckingham, from his position in the state, had every opportunity to kill the princes, cause Richard difficulties therein, and claim the throne for himself through his descent from Thomas of Woodstock, Duke of Gloucester, son of Edward III. In the event Buckingham changed sides and played a part in the attempt to put Henry Tudor on the throne and was executed at Salisbury.

Evidence showed that when Henry VII came to the throne after Bosworth there was no contemporary accusation of Richard's supposed murder of the princes. Neither did the Tudors produce any bodies. It was only seventeen years later that Tyrell made his 'confession' and, even then, Henry VII made no reference to it.

It now fell time for the two barristers to sum up the case for and against Richard. The prosecution emphasized that Richard must have known about the death of the princes. They were totally in his power. His friend was the Constable of the Tower and Richard had a clear motive to murder them. The bones discovered were found where people said the princes had been buried. Richard had slowly and ruthlessly eliminated those who stood in his way to the throne; he had murdered before. Rumour and record of the time, the prosecution averred, had clearly condemned Richard.

The defence noted that the evidence against Richard was circumstantial and largely hearsay. Contemporary accounts are conflicting; again many of the 'opponents' of Richard acted strangely. Take the case of Elizabeth of York, daughter of Edward IV and Elizabeth Woodville. Henry VII married her ultimately, but her mother (i.e. Richard's opponent) had *willingly* given up her daughter into Richard's care. If the princes were a threat to Richard's path to the throne, then so was Elizabeth their sister; but Richard left her alone. It must be remembered that Henry VII later used the same methods of murder that Richard was accused of in the liquidation of the last surviving Plantagenet male.

It is moot to note that the chroniclers of the day all offered the point of view of the people of the south and the court; there is no northern version of Richard's life and times, and his household in the north. The Tudors did manipulate historical record to smooth Henry VII's path. Again the 'bones evidence' is indecisive. What is more, others like Buckingham did have legitimate access to the tower – and these were killing times. There is no contemporary enquiry into Richard's supposed guilt, and strangely, if the Tudors really knew the answer they never exploited it.

All of these points made, the judge summed up and the jury retired to assess their verdict; and that verdict was *not guilty*.

The story of the murder of the 'Princes in the Tower' is likely to be debated again and again. What may be taken as accepted is that through the jockeying for the throne, Edward V's dethronement was accelerated, and for that Richard III was responsible – but that alone.

3

Murder at Kirk o'Field

DID THE QUEEN OF SCOTS ORDER HER HUSBAND'S
ASSASSINATION?

Mary Stuart, Queen of Scots, daughter of James V of Scotland and Marie de Guise-Lorraine, and great-granddaughter of Henry VII of England, had several reasons why she might attempt to murder her husband. She had fallen out of love with the treacherous, debauched and weak Henry Stewart, Lord Darnley. Had he not been of the number who entered her chamber at the Palace of Holyrood the night of 9 March 1566 and who murdered her faithful secretary David Riccio in her presence? With pistols and knives the pregnant Mary had been threatened and forced to watch helpless while the brave lords butchered her servant. And now there was the child, soon to ascend the throne as James VI. Mary strongly suspected that Darnley was conspiring against her life and the life of her child in his keenness to rule alone. Indeed, Darnley was a dangerous man, but it must be remembered there is nothing in Mary's biographical record before 1566 to suggest that she had criminal tendencies.

Henry Stewart, Lord Darnley, elder son of Matthew, 4th Earl of Lennox, and Margaret Douglas (daughter of Queen Margaret Tudor by her second husband the 6th Earl of Angus) had been born in England in 1545. Consequently both English and Scottish royal blood ran through Darnley's veins and he had a claim, in his own right, to both the English and Scottish thrones.

One contemporary described Darnley, Earl of Ross and Duke of

Albany, as 'an agreeable nincompoop', and another described him as 'more like a woman than a man, for he was handsome, beardless and lady-faced'. Although weak and morally worthless, Darnley had won the heart of Mary Stuart – who described him as 'the lustiest and best-proportioned long man' she had seen – and she married him, her second cousin and three years her junior, on 29 July 1565.

Even though they ruled as 'King Henry and Queen Mary' it was impossible to give Darnley a real share of authority and his jealousy smouldered. His petulant arrogance alienated the nobility, yet they used him for their purposes. Thus Darnley was amongst their number when David Riccio was murdered, for Darnley was as jealous as the nobility of the little Italian's supposed influence with the queen. Mary was to retain a burning unforgiveness for Darnley's part in Riccio's murder.

Mary Stuart, a passionate and attractive woman, with courage and devotion to her principles had one grave character fault. She lacked sound judgement in politics and religious affairs and was a dreadful judge of character. It seems that soon after Riccio's murder she was reconciled with Darnley and their only child was born on 19 June 1566. A few months later they were estranged again.

In spite of her growing loathing of the syphilitic Darnley, Mary's unerring lack of judgement saw her on 20 January 1567 riding out of Edinburgh to bring back the sick Darnley from Glasgow, to the house called Kirk o'Field at Edinburgh. There Darnley remained until between Sunday and Monday 10 February 1567 a vast explosion blew Kirk o'Field to rubble. The body of Darnley was found lying strangled in the garden of the ancient house.

That Darnley was murdered is quite irrefutable; it was no accident. But murdered by whom? Today it is clear that there were three groups of people who would have gained by having him dead. First, Mary herself. She incontestably knew of the constant danger in which she was placed. Again she knew for certain that Darnley was conspiring against her; she noted as much in a letter to her Ambassador in Paris, Archbishop James Beaton, that it was 'openly bruited' that Darnley 'by the assistance of some of our nobility' was set to kidnap the infant James and rule during his infancy. Mary was contemplating divorcing Darnley, and did have discussions on the subject with her advisers. But for a Roman Catholic monarch like

Mary such a way out was fraught with difficulties. There was no guarantee that the Pope would agree; there was no guarantee that her divorce would be accepted by fellow monarchs; and she ran the risk of bastardizing her heir.

Yet, in the face of her son's future, and the possibility of his violent death she may well have deliberately indulged her disposition to be naively clement and pardoned, on 24 December 1566, her scheming lords for murdering Riccio. The pardoned and the waiving of banishment increased the number of Darnley's enemies able to frequent the court. If Mary was contemplating a direct hand in Darnley's murder, she needed allies; the Protestant politicians did not want to see Darnley restored to ascendancy with the queen; she encouraged them further by financial incentives in 1566. By restoring the jurisdiction of the Archbishop of St Andrews she had someone on hand to perform a divorce, thus making Darnley's murder not an act of treason (as he would no longer be king).

Secondly, then, among those who wished to see Darnley hustled into the hereafter were the Scottish nobles who had everything to gain and were willing to back any side which put gold into their pockets and advantage their way. They hated and suspected Darnley. He had changed sides after Riccio's death, had betrayed his fellow assassins and had caused the scattering of the nobility. James Douglas, 4th Earl of Morton, for instance had been one who had been dismissed as Chancellor; but now he was back in Scotland after exile and he was the head of the powerful Douglas clan. Also there was James Stewart, Earl of Moray, the illegitimate son of Mary's father James V, by Margaret Erskine, wife of Robert Douglas of Lochleven. He had been foresworn the crown by an accident of birth, so he too had an axe to grind. Hovering too was the bold, swashbuckling Border adventurer James Hepburn, Earl of Bothwell, hereditary Lord High Admiral of Scotland, who was deemed by many to be already having an affair with Mary. Darnley dead would free the Queen for marriage.

The third group which would have readily involved themselves in Darnley's murder were the European monarchs who had a vested interest in Scottish political affairs. Elizabeth I of England was in close contact with the Earl of Moray, as leader of the Scottish Protestants; Elizabeth wanted a friendly nation along her northern border and preferably Protestant. In Europe there were His Catholic

Majesty, Philip II of Spain, Charles IX of France and the Pope, all anxious about Scotland's future religious role in Europe, and all unwilling to see her step aside from Catholic influence. In his vacillation, now supporting the Catholics, now the Protestants, Darnley made himself a prime candidate for assassination.

During January 1567 there was a meeting between the Earls of Morton and Bothwell at which, both were subsequently to claim, that the other had brought up the need for Darnley's assassination. It is undoubted that Mary knew about the plots and in going to Glasgow to fetch Darnley she believed that she could successfully monitor the plots and perhaps persuade Darnley to a divorce without wrangle or ultimate bloodshed. Or, at the very least, she might persuade Darnley to go into exile (he had, in fact, threatened to do this in 1566). These plans would be undoubtedly easier if Darnley was under Mary's eye close to her capital rather than in Glasgow where he was dominated by his scheming father, the Earl of Lennox.

The nobility interpreted Mary's moves differently. They believed she was anxious to be rid of Darnley and was bringing him close at hand for the final coup. At this point it is worth contemplating that it is one thing to acknowledge and prove by the contemporary letters and comments of the day that Mary knew about the murderous scheme concerning Darnley; but, it is quite another to conclude that she was a party to that murder.

On 31 January 1567 Darnley arrived at his lodgings, Kirk o'Field, a resting-place he had chosen himself; indeed Mary had wanted to take him to Craigmillar Castle, to the south of Edinburgh. Darnley was lodged in what was called the Prebendaries' Chamber, which was part of the domestic buildings associated with the early sixteenth-century collegiate church of St-Mary-in-the-Fields (bynamed Kirk o'Field). The lodging was situated pleasantly enough on a small hill overlooking the Cowgate, with gardens around. The house was of two storeys, with a turnpike stair and separate bedrooms one above the other for Darnley and the queen. Mary's room was directly under Darnley's and there was a presence chamber, a kitchen, vaulted cellars and two garde-robes. Darnley's room had a gallery which projected from the face of the house and probably this rested on the old town wall, with a drop below. The buildings connected with Kirk o'Field were later converted into the College of King James, now the

University of Edinburgh. The hall of the Senatus occupies the site of the Prebendaries' Chamber.

In piecing together the events, the evidence and the conclusions of Darnley's murder, it is necessary to realize that what happened cannot be ascertained with absolute certainty. The evidence we have to hand today is, to say the least, untrustworthy. The depositions of those who played a minor role in the events, the testimony of the witnesses and the activities of those who carried out secondary duties were either extracted by torture, or fabricated, or were doctored to protect the noble conspirators, or were tailored to shield those in political power. It was necessary too, to focus all the blame on Lord Bothwell, who by then had fallen out with his former associates. The whole truth too was subject to a contemporary political and historical re-write which has clouded the truth as it comes down to us.

Mary's part in bringing Darnley to Edinburgh, by the by, may have been precipitated by her pregnancy – pregnancy with a child that could clearly not be Darnley's – so a public reconciliation was necessary.

The sequence of events leading up to Darnley's death developed thus:

1-7 February 1567: Mary and Darnley seem to have cohabited in a friendly way. Darnley even dissemblingly discussed with her, or so Mary's secretary Claude Nau later attested, his fears concerning attempts on her life; adding with self-righteous horror that even he had been advised to kill her. On Wednesday 5 February and Friday 7 February, Mary slept at Kirk o'Field; otherwise she slept at Holyrood Palace, visiting Darnley daily with her entourage. Darnley himself had few supporters around him. So the later suggestion that he was plotting to kill Mary at Kirk o'Field scarcely holds water. His supporters were greatly outnumbered by Mary's and he would hardly have had gunpowder placed directly under a bedroom in which he languished.

Sunday 9 February 1567: Preparations were made for Darnley to be moved to Holyrood. In the city it was a day of feasting and carnival. During the morning the marriage of the Queen's attendant Bastian Pages took place at Holyrood followed by a midday meal. In the evening too, there was a banquet, given by the Bishop of the Isles, for Moretta, Ambassador from Savoy, who was about to be recalled. At around 21.00 hours, Mary and her retinue rode up to Kirk o'Field and spent the rest of the evening with Darnley. Lords Bothwell, Huntly, Cassilis and Argyll played dice while Mary chatted pleasantly to Darnley on that cold snowy evening.

Mary remembered that she had promised Bastian that she would attend his marriage dance at Holyrood, and returned to the palace where she spent the night, much to Darnley's petulant objection. As she mounted her horse at Kirk o'Field Mary noticed the Earl of Bothwell's former page Paris, and remarked with surprise: 'Jesu, Paris, how begrimed you are.' She rode back to Holyrood by way of the Canongate, attended the marriage dance and retired to bed just after midnight.

Testimony concerning Darnley's last few hours rests upon his father's account. The Earl of Lennox describes a pathetic, lonely, young man (Darnley was only twenty years old) reciting the Fifth Psalm with his servant: 'Give ear to my words, O Lord, consider my meditation.' He called for wine and commanded that 'great horse' be got ready at five o'clock for his planned return to Holyrood Palace a mile and a half away down the hilly streets. Darnley then retired for the night. Taylor, his valet, slept in the same room and two more servants slept in the gallery. Below, two grooms were also in attendance.

As Darnley was now asleep, the scene of action changed and the account of what led up to Darnley's death comes from the evidence of the servants of the Earl of Bothwell; evidence it should be remembered that was extracted under torture and mental duress.

Somewhere along the line the Earl of Bothwell had discussed with his kinsman, John Hepburn, the practicalities of killing Darnley. Originally it seems that certain of the nobles (Maitland, Argyll, Huntly, Morton, Ruthven and Lindsay were named) were to each supply two underlings for an attack on Darnley in Kirk o'Field. As time went by this was considered too hazardous, and gunpowder was thought the best mode of death. Keys to Kirk o'Field were obtained and gunpowder – supposedly supplied by Bothwell – was secreted in Kirk o'Field under the king's bedroom. This was done while Mary was visiting Darnley. The story that Mary commented to Bothwell's servant, Paris: 'Jesu, Paris, how begrimed you are', would seem odd, for if she knew about her husband's planned murder, she would hardly call attention to the fact that Paris's face was black with gunpowder.

That is the story as it has come down to us from the 'official sources', sources which were never out of the control of Mary's brother, James Stewart.

Bothwell meanwhile had ridden down to Holyrood with Mary's entourage. He changed and returned to Kirk o'Field to light the fuses. At the house he was joined by a party of Douglases who surrounded the king's lodging.

Monday 10 February 1567: At 02.00 hours an enormous explosion was heard all over Edinburgh. People in the houses around Kirk o'Field flooded into the Cowgate and Friars Wynd. Kirk o'Field had been reduced to a pile of débris. On that section of the town wall that had backed onto the house, a servant was seen calling for help. Down below in the gardens corpses began to be discovered. First a groom then Darnley and his valet, William Taylor. Both were naked except for nightshirts. Beside them a chair, a rope, a dagger and a furred cloak. An old woman who lived in a cottage nearby came up and attested that she had heard Darnley cry out: 'Pity me, kinsmen, for the sake of Him who pitied all the world!' As a closer examination was conducted it was seen that both bodies had the marks of strangulation rather than the effects of explosion wounds.

Had something frightened Darnley? Scared him so much that he had fled into the icy February morning clad only in his nightshirt? Had he lowered himself into the garden in a chair, helped only by his servant? Fleeing perhaps from the smell of burning fuses, had he escaped only to fall into the hands of the Douglases?

It is further curious why the conspirators waited so long after Mary's departure to fire the gunpowder, also the destruction of the house was not consistent with gunpowder explosions, but of a mine. If the house was 'undermined', as the Earl of Moray later attested, who had planted it? Why was Darnley not just poisoned? Was a mine meant to kill Darnley *and* Mary and their suite? Indeed the militant Protestants might have been involved as there was an heir to the throne who could be directly influenced should the parents be killed.

Soon after the discovery of the cadavers, Mary was informed of the assassination. In a letter to Beaton in Paris she expressed horror and amazement at the murder, as she emphasized that it was only by the merest chance that she herself had not slept the night at Kirk o'Field. She told the archbishop that the murderers would 'shortly be discovered' and punished. In reality however, she did not pursue and punish the murderers. Within three months of the event she had married one of the chief suspects. Indeed it was only when Darnley's father pressed her that she allowed a private indictment against the Earl of Bothwell. Bothwell was acquitted. In marrying Bothwell, Mary explained, she had made a virtue of necessity. Few were convinced.

The events which immediately followed the assassination of Darnley may be summarized rapidly. There was a show trial in which Bothwell was acquitted. He then abducted Mary (possibly with her consent) and obtained a divorce from his wife. On 15 May 1567 Bothwell and Mary were married; the news shocked and dismayed even her strongest supporters. Indeed this action was so fatal to her reputation that it was ultimately the marriage which lost her the throne and not the murder of Darnley. Mary was now faced by a confederacy of nobles and the combined forces of Mary and Bothwell met the confederates at the battle of Carberry Hill. The queen was beaten and surrendered on 15 June 1567; she was imprisoned at Lochleven Castle and compelled to abdicate in her son's favour on 24 July. At Lochleven she miscarried of twins.

On 2 May 1568, Mary escaped from Lochleven and supporters flocked to her aid; but she was defeated again at the battle of Langside on 13 May. She fled through the south west of Scotland and four days after the battle she crossed the Solway and sought asylum in England.

By the end of 1568 enquiries took place at York and Westminster to determine whether or not Mary should be restored to the Scottish throne. Although there were other factors to consider, a fundamental plank of the enquiry was what part did Mary play in Darnley's murder? The enquiry at York got under way on 4 October 1568 and commissioners representing Mary, the Scottish Regent, the Earl of Moray, and Queen Elizabeth were present.

Not much was achieved at York, as Moray was the only one with a clearness of thought and singlemindedness of purpose; at all costs he wanted to keep Mary out of Scotland. The commissioners re-assembled at Westminster on 25 Novemebr. Much of the 'evidence' against Mary was enshrined in the controversial eight Casket Letters, the originals of which vanished without trace in 1584. Their appearance goes thus. The Earl of Morton asserted that his servant had found the documents is a silver casket on 20 June 1567 at a house in Potterrow, Edinburgh; by this time the Earl of Bothwell had fled. The casket is supposed to have contained letters, professedly written by Mary and Bothwell; some French sonnets; a signed but undated promise by Mary to marry Bothwell; and a marriage contract between the two. The documents were produced by Moray at York and at Westminster. It was alleged that they were written in Mary's hand. She denied the provenance of the documents and was never allowed to see the originals. The genuineness of the Casket Letters has always been doubted. Modern scholarship tends to the view that they were forged, and forged by men in a hurry to supply 'evidence' to condemn Mary.

When the evidence had been collected, Elizabeth I charged half a dozen earls to consider the narrative of data presented at York and Westminster. The enquiry being, of course, entirely political and not judicial. Their verdict was 'not proven', and no sentence was passed, yet the commission led to Mary being imprisoned for life in England and ultimately to her execution in 1587.

Looking at the facts, the notion is very strong that Mary wholeheartedly *wished* for Darnley's death, and her nobles were in no doubt that she would *approve* their actions, whichever ones it was who assassinated Darnley. Mary herself had a horror of violence and did not wish to know the actual murder plans; but it seems irrefutable today that she must have known they were proceeding. Mary did obviously help the conspirators by bringing Darnley from the protection of his kinsmen the Lennoxes in Glasgow to within their grasp in Edinburgh, and today we can say that although Mary did not order her husband's death she did nothing to warn him, or raise a finger to save him and in this she aided and abetted those who did murder him.

Looking now at the advantages and disadvantages of the events, who was the most likely to benefit? Undoubtedly Mary's half-brother Moray. Only after Mary was safely under lock and key at Lochleven did the Casket Letters appear. Moray was his sister's deadliest enemy. He never forgave that his illegitimacy denied him the throne. He was behind every plot against Mary. He had tried to stop Mary's marriage with Darnley (he had taken them both prisoner). When this failed he organized the murder of Riccio. Moray played the politics of the situation all ways; he played on Darnley's jealousy and on Bothwell's lust for the queen. And, he was very careful not to be present when any of the skulduggery came to fruition. As the richest man in Scotland he could buy action and abroad he had powerful friends in Queen Elizabeth and her able minister William Cecil, Lord Burghley.

Moray had hoped that Kirk o'Field would eliminate both Mary and Darnley; when it did not – for there seem to have been too many fingers in the pie – he had to implicate her. But all his work was to no avail. He only sidetracked the course of history. During his regency of Scotland Moray made many enemies amongst both Mary's supporters and among rival nobles, especially the Hamiltons. It was through a scion of this house that he met his end; Moray was murdered at Linlithgow on 23 January 1570 by James Hamilton of Bothwellhaugh, while the sister he tried to murder languished in English captivity for seventeen more years until the beheading axe gave her rest.

Incidentally, two other Scottish monarchs had fallen to assassin's blades. James I (r. 1406–37) was assassinated by Sir Robert Graham at the Dominican friary at Perth. And James III (r. 1460–88) was almost certainly murdered by obscure assassins during the final skirmishes which ended the Battle of Sachieburn.

4

James VI's Close Call

IF ONLY GUY FAWKES HAD WAITED A BIT LONGER,
HE MIGHT HAVE SUCCEEDED IN KILLING THE KING.

Early in the morning of 5 November 1605, Guido (Guy) Fawkes of the City of York, a mercenary and fanatical Catholic, was discovered in a cellar under the Houses of Parliament with 36 barrels of gunpowder, a tinder box and slowmatch, with the clear intention of assassinating James VI and I, his queen, his heir, and his Parliament. For the ensuing 390 or so years, historians have pored over the events to try to discern what actually happened. Indisputably the famous Roman Catholic plot, a part of the plan it was recorded, to re-establish the Roman Catholic religion, was thwarted by an anonymous letter being received by the thirty-year-old Catholic William Parker, 4th Baron Mounteagle on 26 October 1605. In the letter Mounteagle read: 'My Lord, out of the love I bear to some of your friends I have a care for your preservation; therefore I would advise you, as you tender your life, to devise of some excuse to shift of your attendance at this Parliament; for God and man hath concurred to punish the wickedness of this time. And think not slightly of this advertisement but retire yourself into your own country where you may expect the event in safety; for, though there be no appearance of any stir, yet I say they shall receive a terrible blow, this Parliament, and yet they shall not see who hurts them. This counsel is not to be condemned because it may do you good and can do you no harm, for the danger is past as soon as you have burnt the letter and I hope God will give you grace to make good use of it, to whose holy protection I commend you.'

The motivation for such an assassination has been made very clear by such historians as E. W. Brayley and J. Britton in their *The history of the ancient palace and the late Houses of Parliament at Westminster* (1836): 'This most sanguinary project seems to have been the result of the desperation and despair to which Catholics were reduced by the unrelenting severity of the government under Elizabeth, and the disappointment of their hopes of redress after the accession of James I'. This despair was doubled by the growing influence of the Protestant merchant class which now superseded the supremacy once enjoyed by the Catholic landowners.

Mounteagle took the letter to Robert Cecil, Earl of Salisbury, the Secretary of State, who showed it to the king, although he, Salisbury, showed open scepticism of the letter's authenticity. The hyper-superstitious king, however, ordered a check of the Houses of Parliament, 'especially under the rooms', on Monday 4 November, but nothing dangerous was found, except a servant pilings logs and coal in the cellars. It seems that when the king was told of the 'servant Johnson's' presence and that he was a minion of Thomas Percy, he remembered that Percy was a well-known papist activist declared to be 'ill-disposed to the monarchy'. Consequently a second search was authorized led by Sir Thomas Knevet, and this time Johnson (really Guy Fawkes) was discovered with the gunpowder and means to ignite it. Fawkes was arrested and under 'duress' (torture on the rack) he revealed the plan and incriminated the main conspirators. By 31 January 1606 those who remained of the conspirators, as some were killed during the ultimate arrests, were bestially hanged, drawn and quartered in the Old Palace Yard, their butchered bodies hung on the gates of London and their heads upon poles on London Bridge.

In 1987, the magazine *New Civil Engineer* commissioned a top explosives expert, Dr Sidney Alford, to examine the Gunpowder Plot, as the conspirators' plan is remembered, and give his scientific opinion as to the possibilities of the plot having ever been successful. It seems that the conspirators went for 'total overkill'; and filled the cellars under Parliament with 25 times as much explosives than was needed to demolish the building. It is important to remember that the present House of Commons is totally different in design and construction to the building of Fawkes's day, which burned down in 1835. *The Antiques of Westminster* (1807) by John Thomas Smith describes the cellar as 77ft x 24ft x 10ft and running almost under the whole length of the House of Commons. Probably the cellar was not vaulted, but had large wooden beams which formed the ground floor.

Looking at all these factors Alford noted: 'Even if the amount of powder available has been overestimated by one order of magnitude, it is unlikely that the wooden floor above, however resilient, would have survived recognizably intact. The entire floor would have lifted and broken up, the beams cracking at their mid-points, and the boards separating and splintering. The blast would then have reached the upper floor (upon which the intended victims were seated), closely followed by large pieces of timber travelling at velocities of perhaps 100 metres per second.

'Though white smoke would have made visibility nil to anybody falling back into the remains of the building, some light would have been provided by sparks and flame from burning wood and coal, and by the combustion of the explosion gases in the inrush of air'.

Alford then assessed the most reliable description of the amount of gunpowder used. This description had been given by Salisbury himself at 'two hogsheads and 32 small barrels, all of which [*Fawkes*] had cunningly covered with great store of billets and faggots'. Alford gauged that this would amount to 2500 kg of gunpowder; allowing for the gunpowder being of inferior quality only some 100 kg would have been needed for the job involved. Alford made some close assessments of the power of seventeenth-century gunpowder and noted that it was only half as powerful as today's manufacture and that the saltpetre in Fawkes's mixture would have positively attracted water moisture if left. Alford said: 'A major source of saltpetre in the early 17th century was the encrusted salt deposits scraped from the cellar walls, originating from rotting organic waste. The alternative was urine-impregnated earth and refuse and wood ash. Such material was likely to be heavily contaminated with sodium and ammonium nitrates which are both markedly more hygroscopic and, unless the saltpetre was recrystallized quite meticulously, would yield gunpowder with a tendency to become significantly damp if stored in a humid environment. Since it is improbable that such a quantity of powder could have been insinuated in a cellar at once, the effect of lingering so close to the Thames in unlined barrels would have been to reduce the burning rate significantly.' Alford reasoned that Guy Fawkes, who seems to have had some mining experience, would know of this and that he would retain at least one barrel of dry powder by him to prime the rest.

A contemporary picture of the cellar under the Houses of Parliament shows the barrels of gunpowder heaped in one corner. Alford felt that Fawkes would have been better served if he had piled the barrels at the centre of the cellar where the roof was most vulnerable. The fact that the cellar had been used for coal storage would have been an added advantage said Alford: 'If it were sufficiently friable, the coal dust would then ignite, prolonging the pressure pulse generated by the gunpowder, and increasing the pushing effect of the total explosion. Firewood, on the other hand, being of lower density and tending to splinter when subjected to explosion, would more usefully be put to its intended purpose, and placed above the barrels'.

It is certain that Fawkes planned to ignite the gunpowder using a lantern and 'a reliable ignition source'. Alford noted that a traditional powder train would have been useless: 'On a damp cellar floor this would have been subject to extinction, generated an excessive amount of smoke prematurely, and the danger of a spark shortcircuiting the train would have presented a fearful risk of the operator being hoist by his own petard'. Indeed Guy Fawkes is reported as having been found with a slowmatch – 'a length of hemp or cotton rope boiled in a solution of saltpetre or wood ashes, and then dried'. One yard of this would have given eight hours of fuse time, allowing him ample time to escape across the Thames to Lambeth.

Alford calculated that Fawkes's explosion would also produce a huge amount of deadly carbon monoxide and led to the conclusion: 'Any survivors of the explosion, not killed by the blast, flame, or flying debris, would have further to survive projection out of an upper window or over the walls or, alternatively, dropping back among the burning rubble into an atmosphere which would have killed a healthy man within a few minutes'. So as far as Guy Fawkes was concerned his efforts were in earnest and if he had tarried a bit longer and used a shorter fuse he might have been successful. But what if the explosion was a non-starter from the beginning?

The idea that the whole Gunpowder Plot was a government ruse was discussed very early on. For instance, one English correspondent was observing this on 10 December 1605: 'Those that have practical experience of the way in which things are done hold it as certain that there has been foul play and that some of the [*Privy*] Council secretly spun a web to entangle these poor gentlemen'. Historians have repeatedly suggested that when Mounteagle took the letter to Cecil that it was no surprise for the Secretary of State, for Cecil was expecting it, and that it was Cecil who had set-up Mounteagle in what historian Hugh Ross Williamson described as 'the most spectacular "frame-up" in British history'. Indeed, Mounteagle was to be rewarded by a £700 pension per annum for life, the equivalent of some £80,000 in today's spending power, a small price to pay for destruction of the Roman Catholic powerbase. Cecil had succeeded where his father, William, Secretary of State to Elizabeth I, had failed. Plots to assassinate Queen Elizabeth were regularly 'discovered' by William Cecil's agents and were all spurious as historian Martin Hume has pointed out:

> The accusations that have been repeated by nearly every historian from Elizabeth's time to our own of widespread and numerous plots to assassinate the Queen are to a large extent unsupported by serious evidence. Pamphlets and broadsides, professing to give the whole story of the various murder-plots, were numerous and have formed the basis of our historical relations for three centuries; but they were written in nearly every instance with political or party aspect and, from the nature of the case, were necessarily based upon an imperfect or partial statement of facts.

In truth the Cecils had been toying with a 'gunpowder plot' as early as 1587, and in modified form they used it in the Des Trappes Plot to compromise the French ambassador; indeed the ambassador received a government apology for the débâcle and was encouraged to treat it as a joke. But, any plot involving gunpowder would be guaranteed to drive the cowardly, slobbering sot James VI and I to react hysterically, as his father Henry Darnley had been blown to kingdom come.

Scholars, then, believe that this is how Cecil managed to bring the plot to fruition using Mounteagle. Most of the 'conspirators' were blood relatives, or connected by marriage: the leader Robert Catesby, the planner Thomas Wintour, the financial sponsor Robert Wintour, Francis Tresham, and Lord Mounteagle, who were all first cousins. John Grant was brother-in-law to the Wintours, who were also connected to Robert Keyes and Ambrose Rookwood by the maternal branch of the family. John and Christopher Wright's mother was of Wintour stock, and Thomas Percy, cousin of the Earl of Northumberland, was the Wrights' brother-in-law. Guy Fawkes had gone to school with the Wrights; Thomas Bates was Catesby's servant, and Sir Everard Digby was a Catesby family friend. All were fanatical Roman Catholics with the vital touch of recklessness that would get them involved with a conspiracy for the faith.

The Victorian historian S. R. Gardiner in *What the Gunpowder Plot Was* summed up the 'official account' of the plot as it had been circulated by Robert Cecil:

In February 1604, King James banished all Catholic priests. Immediately, a Catholic named Robert Catesby proposed to a few of his friends a plot to blow up King, Lords, and Commons with gunpowder at the opening of Parliament.

The King had two sons, Henry and Charles, and a little daughter, Elizabeth.

Catesby, expecting that the two Princes would be destroyed with their father, intended to make Elizabeth Queen and to take care that she was brought up a Roman Catholic.

Guy Fawkes, a level-headed soldier, was summoned from Flanders to manage the scheme.

The plotters took a house next to the House of Lords and began to dig through the wall to enable them to carry the powder into the basement.

The wall, however, was nine feet thick, and not being used to mason's work, they made little progress.

In the spring of 1605, James increased their anger by reimposing fines on the Catholic laity.

Soon afterwards their task was made easier by the discovery that a coal cellar which reached under the floor of the House of Lords was to be let.

One of their number, Percy, hired the cellar and introduced into it barrels of powder, covering them with coals and billets of wood. Parliament was to be opened for its second session on 5 November, and during the preceding evening Fawkes went to the cellar with a lantern, ready to fire the train of powder in the morning.

One of the plotters, however, had betrayed the secret.

Fawkes was seized, and his companions were pursued.

All the conspirators who were taken alive were executed and the persecution of the Catholics became even more vicious than ever.

Other historians have averred that there *was* a genuine plot which, somehow, was intercepted by Cecil's agents. Instead of arresting the conspirators straight away, Cecil aided and abetted them in a number of ways, and carefully removed all evidence of his own machinations. To support this contention certain questions were asked by scholars:

Why was Parliament's prorogation postponed twice? Was this to make sure that the conspirators had the gunpowder in place and that Cecil's agents knew the exact whereabouts of each conspirator?

How did the conspirators obtain the gunpowder? Gunpowder was very difficult to come by as it was a government monopoly and not available on the open market.

How did the conspirators come to hire the cellar next to the Houses of Parliament from a government official? The official, Whynniard, conveniently died on the morning of 5 November. Was he silenced by Cecil's agents?

Why were the brains of the conspiracy shot out of hand? Of all the conspirators Robert Catesby and Thomas Percy were shot and never brought to trial. Did they know of Cecil's conniving, or helping the plot, so that they had to be silenced? Their killer was given a pension.

Why were conflicting stories issued about the exact place of Guy Fawkes's arrest? Was this a part of Cecil's dissemination of misinformation?

Why was it that the servants of Rookwood and Keyes, their landlady, and several people with no connection to the plot, were all arrested *before* the plot's discovery, and examined personally by the Lord Chief Justice? Was this last minute information-gathering by Cecil? Most curious of all, why was Mounteagle – ostensibly the hero of the piece who saved the royal family – totally removed from all official versions of the plot?

As to the anonymous letter to Mounteagle, this was Cecil's official excuse to act, so was it necessary to log it into the state archives, for it is interesting to note that other peers had been advised to absent themselves before the letter was delivered to Mounteagle at his mansion at Hoxton. Every one of the peers warned/advised was important to Cecil's and the government's present and future plans. In his book *Guy Fawkes*, Father Francis Edwards, sets out to plausibly prove that the anonymous letter was in Cecil's 'disguised' hand. To make sure that the world knew about the letter, the document was published in the *Kings Book*, the official government account of the plot, and copies of it were sent to the ambassadors at foreign courts, and other public people.

The Gunpowder Plot has an organizational crudity about it and more than a strong suggestion that it could not have progressed as far as it did without government connivance or even assistance. James VI and I is likely not to have known about the connivance, but he and his family might have been successfully assassinated if Guy Fawkes had been a more efficient explosives expert. For Cecil could have been hoist on his own petard if any government mole amongst the conspirators had played a double game.

5

The Assassination of Henry IV of France

A DEATH BLOW BY A 'SINCERE CHRISTIAN' HELPED
FRANCE FORGE A NEW NATIONHOOD.

In the year of Our Lord 1610, on Friday 14 May to be precise, the supreme court of justice in France, known as the Parliament of Paris, was in session in a hall of an Augustinian monastery at the Quai des Augustins on the left bank of the Seine near the Sorbonne. As the afternoon session droned on the members were interrupted by the usher to the session striking his mace on the floor. Minutes later the King's advocate-general, Louis Servin, informed the members of the wounding of His Most Christian Majesty Henry, King of France and Navarre by an assassin's knife. The shocked assembly hastened out of the council chamber, each member bent on satisfying himself of the exact details of the event.

The King's advocates rushed to the palace to ascertain what had happened to find a stunned court unable to comprehend what had occurred. But soon the events were pieced together from firsthand reports. Between two and three in the afternoon, the king had ordered his coach to be brought, as he wished to confer with his chief finance minister, Baron de Rosny, Duke of Sully, in the Arsenal. To this end Henry left the Louvre accompanied by the dukes of Montbazon and Epernon, several marshals and a few courtiers, but, by the king's own command, no bodyguard. In order to see the events of the afternoon, and particularly the preparations for the entry of Queen Marie de Medici into Paris, Henry had drawn back the leather curtain of his carriage. At a gallop the coach turned into the Rue de la Ferronnerie, which ran alongside the huge Saint-Innocent cemetery, but soon it slithered to a halt behind a cart loaded with wine and another loaded with hay which were blocking the narrow street. While the footman went ahead to see how the congestion could be relieved the king studied letters with the courtiers in the coach with him. Suddenly a man leapt onto the wheel of the king's carriage and plunged a knife into Henry's chest. 'I've been stabbed,' he shrieked as the assassin plunged in the knife again. Jolted into action one the king's household, Saint-Michel, made to hack down the assassin with his sword, but was stopped in doing so by the Duke of Epernon. Soon the coach was turned and the party returned to the Louvre; the king was dead on arrival.

The procurator-general to King Henry in the *Chambre des Comptes* (the Audit Office), Jerome Luillier, who was also Henry's councillor and personal adviser, left an eyewitness account of the king's return to the Louvre: 'I was attending the King's council which was in progress directly beneath the Queen's antechamber, when the Chancellor and members of council left the room in great alarm and agitation. The Chancellor went upstairs with the presidents Jeannin and de Vic. I followed them and saw these gentlemen go in to see the Queen. M. de Vic and I went further on into the dressing room of the King used when he slept alone. There on the bed we saw the dead body, fully clad, with his doublet unfastened to reveal his bloodstained shirt. Nevertheless, prayers were being said over him by Cardinal de Sourdis, flanked by Boulongne, the chaplain, and M. de Vic. These three, together with the Queen's first doctor, de Lorme, were repeating the hortatory prayers customary when a person is at the point of death. But the poor King was dead already.'

An autopsy was done on the king, and the report issued on 15 May 1610 refers to a four-inch wound on the left side between the axilla and breast across the second and third ribs, running along the pectoral muscle, but without penetrating the chest cavity. The autopsy, compiled by eighteen of Henry's physicians and thirteen of his surgeons, continued, 'We were unanimously of the opinion that this wound was the sole and immediate cause of death.' It seems that the rest of the king's body was intact.

Henry's assassin was immediately arrested after his strike, and soon after the king had been rushed back to the Louvre, the assassin was taken to the nearby Hôtel de Retz for his own safety as the angry crowd which had assembled shouted for his blood. Within the hour the tall, strongly-built, red-haired assassin, now identified as the unmarried 32-year-old François Ravaillac from Angoulême, was interrogated and subjected to torture by the order of Marshal La Force. Next day Ravaillac was taken to the Conciergerie on the Ile de la Cité, where his interrogation continued.

Ravaillac's interrogators were anxious to reveal whether he had acted alone, or as a member of an organized plot. All through his interrogation — even under torture — Ravaillac insisted that he had acted alone. Even so his questioners were not convinced that someone of stature at court was not behind the assassination, but they curiously did not keep Ravaillac in solitary confinement during his incarceration in the Hôtel de Retz and it is said that he was visited by a Jesuit royal confessor, one Père Coton; there is a strong hint, therefore, that Coton may have warned Ravaillac to hold his tongue concerning any fellow-conspirators. By this time informers supplied the extra background that Ravaillac was a penurious barrister who when young had been received into the religious Cistercian Order of the Feuillants as a lay-brother. Many Feuillants were activists in the Holy Catholic League which was a coalition organized in 1576 by the Duke of Guise to suppress the reformed religion in France, by denying civil and religious liberty to the Huguenots, and particularly to prevent the future accession of the Protestant Henry of Navarre to the French throne. In truth Ravaillac had had the habit of the Feuillants taken away from him as he had confessed to seeing 'visions'; the Order held a healthy distrust of visionaries. After this Ravaillac had tried to join the Jesuits but had failed. Ravaillac now repented to his interrogators of his 'evil crime' but maintained that he had done it for God to rid God, and France, of the 'heretical' Henry, promoter of the Edict of Nantes of 1598 that had given Protestants religious liberty in France. It seems too, that Ravaillac had made two previous attempts to murder Henry but had been thwarted.

The Ravaillac incident brought forth an epidemic of would-be regicides with informers confirming several supposed attempts being plotted on the life of the new king Louis XIII. These attempts can be dismissed as 'the familiar wave of imitations which often follows "sensational" crimes or suicides' as Professor Roland Mousnier has put it. Today scholars admit that there were several Roman Catholic groups who desired, expected and prepared plots for the murder of Henry IV of France, but only one group had the ubiquitous network of information gathering, subterfuge and expertise to successfully carry out such an assassination and leave hardly any trace of their machinations — the Jesuits, members of the fanatical Society of Jesus, an order of priests founded in 1534 in Paris by Ignatius Loyola, Francis Xavier and others, to defend the Roman Catholic Church against opposition and propagate its faith amongst the heathen.

One important informant of history who points the finger at the Jesuits (aided by the fanatically Roman Catholic Spanish court and the exiles of the Holy League in Spain) was Pierre du Jardin of Rouen, Sieur de La Garde. He was imprisoned for a while because he publicly accused the Jesuits, but his public memorandum on his beliefs is dated 1619 and rests in the *Bibliothèque Nationale*. A soldier of fortune who saw service in the guards' regiment in Provence, Savoy, and Venice, La Garde monitored the machinations of the Jesuits. While in Naples (then Spanish territory), La Garde averred that he had become acquainted with one La Bruyère, and through him met prominent Jesuits like Father Alagon who made it plain that he was the recruiting agent (for the Spanish court and the Jesuits) of any man who would assassinate Henry IV — he offered the commission to La Garde.

La Garde asked for time to think about the commission of regicide, and meanwhile enjoyed the 'feasts and banquets by various hosts, including a certain Charles Hébert, secretary of the late marshal de Biron'. While at table one night the party was joined by a richly dressed man who was obviously well known to, and welcomed, by the company. La Garde noted that this man was a courier for (he later found out) the Duke of Epernon, who was subsequently a love of Queen Marie de'Medici, Henry IV's treacherous wife. Next day La Garde had a further interview with Father Alagon who asked if he had decided on taking the commission. La Garde parried the question and asked the best way to kill the king. The Jesuit suggested that the best time would be to shoot the king while he was out hunting. In the event, La Garde excused himself, fled to France, and acquainted

Henry IV with what he had found out. So, if La Garde is to be believed, the French refugee colony in Naples which was in close contact with the Spanish court and the Jesuit fanatics, had been plotting to kill Henry since 1602. Just as intriguing as the memorandum is a statement, again held in the *Bibliothèque Nationale*, in which La Garde testifies that the man he had seen at the Hébert dinner party was Francois Ravaillac!

On 27 May 1610, after almost two weeks of interrogation and torture, Ravaillac was declared guilty 'in fact and in law of the crime of high treason'. He was condemned to publicly repent at the door of Notre-Dame, and thence be conveyed to the place of execution at La Place de Grève. Ravaillac's public execution — including hideous torture, followed by being drawn and quartered by horses linked to his limbs — was bestial in the extreme. The house in which he was born was razed to the ground, his parents were exiled on pain of death should they return, and his siblings were forbidden ever to use the name of Ravaillac again.

Today most historians see Ravaillac as a religious fanatic bordering on the insane, and, if he was chosen as an agent of their plans by the Jesuits, they chose well, as Ravaillac never gave them away even under the most excruciating torture. These days scholars generally absolve the Jesuits of having any knowledge of (or part in) the assassination of the tyrannical Henry III of France by the Dominican monk Jacques Clement in 1589, but undoubtedly the Jesuits had the greatest motives to assassinate Henry IV. He was undermining Roman Catholic power in Europe and Jesuit influence, and the Jesuits were afraid that he might act as a focus of a Protestant army against the Pope and his chief agent His Most Catholic Majesty Philip II of Spain; indeed, had not the Jesuits been expelled from Paris in 1595 and had not Henry declared war on Philip in the same year? To the Jesuits then Henry's assassination was God's work and a fit end for a king who had been excommunicated (by Pope Sixtus V in 1585).

Even so there are those who believe that Ravaillac was acting for himself. As Professor Roland Mousnier of the Sorbonne has put it: '. . . it was France [*Raviallac*] repudiated, the France he had meant to strike down in the person of Henry IV, the absolutist, Gallican, patriotic, nationalist France, whose sovereignty constituted a threat to Pope and Emperor.'

6

The Murder of the Dauphin

DID THE FRENCH HEIR TO THE THRONE ACTUALLY
ESCAPE THE FRENCH REVOLUTION TO DIE IN EXILE
IN THE SEYCHELLES?

Louis Charles, Duc de Normandie, was born on Easter Sunday, 27 March 1785, second son of Louis XVI, King of France, and his wife Marie Antoinette. When Charles's brother, Louis Joseph, Compte de Provence, died of pulmonary tuberculosis in 1789, four-year-old Charles became Dauphin and heir apparent to the French throne of the Capet-Valois-Bourbon dynasty. The story of this bright, intelligent, highly-strung little boy is one of the most tear-jerking in history. With his parents the terrified child endured the journey from Versailles to Paris surrounded by the howling revolutionary mob and was abruptly taken from his parents' loving arms to be perverted, brutalized and terrorized at the hand of the leftist revolution. According to the official version of the story Louis Charles was dragged through disease, solitary confinement and neglect to his death, a far more cruel fate than the public guillotining of his father (and mother) in 1793, whereupon the boy became Louis XVII to the Royalists at the age of eight.

The story of the sufferings of the French royal family are shrouded in mystery. All through the Reign of Terror – the most violent epoch of the French Revolution dominated by Robespierre and the Committee of Public Safety 1793–94 – there had been many schemes to rescue the royal family from their Paris prison of La Temple. After the execution of Louis XVI and his wife there were weekly plans to rescue Louis Charles and his sister Marie-Thérèse-Charlotte. Long before the official announcement of the death of Louis Charles there had been widespread rumours that he had escaped from prison and that a substitute had been left in his place. The behaviour of the Revolutionary Government, both before and after Louis Charles's death, lent much credence to the rumours. Subsequent events added fuel to the rumours and it is said that in the early 1800s there were no less than fifty pretenders to the throne of France, all claiming to be the Dauphin. The story of Louis Charles's supposed rescue and later life have been the theme of many romances with Regnault-Warin's *Le Cimitière de la Madeleine* (1800) being perhaps the most famous.

The events leading up to the deepening of the mystery of the murder of the Dauphin are simple to relate. During August 1792 the Royal Family were transported to La Temple prison and incarcerated in *la Grande Tour*: today the site of the medieval tower is the park of the Place du Temple. The Dauphin slept in his father's room and during the day the king helped Louis Charles with his lessons. On 21 January 1793 Louis XVI was executed and his queen, Marie Antoinette, proclaimed her son to be Louis XVII. The young king developed a feverish illness, with a pain in his side; it is thought that he probably had developed an attack of pleurisy with effusion, which is an early indication of pulmonary tuberculosis which had already carried off Louis's Charles's elder brother and a young sister, Sophie. Marie Antoinette nursed her son devotedly, but his health was undermined.

Outside La Temple the revolutionaries were nervous; Prussian and Austrian troops were at France's borders, and on 30 June 1793 the Committee of Public Safety learned from agents that General Dillon was planning to rescue Louis Charles by force and publicly proclaim him as king. As a result Louis Charles was removed from his protesting mother and handed over to the drunken pervert Antoine Simon to make him *un bon citoyen de la République*.

The Dauphin's new tutelage was brutal; he was beaten, given too much to drink and taught to swear and sing revolutionary songs, and mouth obscene calumnies about his mother. The cruelty of Simon and his wife is likely to have been exaggerated by the Royalist writers, and it seems that the coarse couple eventually began to become fond of their royal charge. Indeed Simon suggested to the Committee of Public Safety that he should adopt the Dauphin as his son and teach him his own trade of shoemaking. In time, however, rumours of plots to free the royal family grew and Simon so feared for his life should the Royalists succeed that he asked to be relieved of his guardianship. The Committee of Public Safety agreed and from 19 January 1794 the Dauphin was guarded only by members of the Revolutionary Council.

At this point – the departure of Antoine Simon – the subsequent fate of the Dauphin becomes mysterious. On 19 January 1794, at 9 o'clock the Council members relieved Simon of his duties and issued a certificate that Louis Charles was alive and well. From that date until June 1794 there is no official record of Louis Charles. In the prison room above, his sister Marie-Thérèse (called Madame Royale), and his aunt Madame Elizabeth (Louis XVI's sister) no longer heard the Dauphin singing or shouting. The young princess was to write: '. . . on 19 January we heard a great noise at my brother's, which made us conjecture that he was leaving the Temple, and we were convinced of it, when looking through a hole in our sunblind, we saw many packages being taken away. On the following days we heard his door open and, still convinced that he was gone, we believed they had put below some German or foreign prisoner, whom we baptized Melchisedec to give him a name.'

Of his fate during those 'missing' six months the French historian M. A. De Beauchesne has speculated that Louis Charles was placed in a room (which had been that of Jean Baptiste Clery, Louis XIV's valet) with a door nailed up and plated with iron; his food was slipped to him through a barred wicket gate. Discounting this, the writer G. Lenôtre, said that the 'sealed room' theory just did not hold water as he had found documents to prove that, even if Louis Charles was in Clery's room, he would have access to a suite of connecting rooms. Again, Lenôtre quoted papers that seemed to indicate that windows were reglazed and heating pipes were lengthened *dans la chambre du petit Capet*.

Whatever the reason little was seen of the Dauphin. It would appear that the two Revolutionary Commune members responsible for the royal prisoners, Hébert and Chaumette, contemplated removing the relic royal family to a safer place should there be a movement against the Revolution. Chaumette was later guillotined by the revolutionaries as a suspect royalist sympathizer, and Hébert perished on the scaffold too during the Terror, but before their demise they seem to have lost all interest in the Dauphin. And Simon who visited La Temple quite regularly, did not ask for '*petit Capet*', nor did he see him. *Could it be that all three knew that the Dauphin was not there?*

Robespierre himself visited La Temple and was petitioned by Madame Royale with the note: 'My brother is ill. I have written to the Convention to obtain medical attention for him. The Convention has not replied. I reiterate my request.' On 27 July 1794 Robespierre himself fell foul of the Revolution and Citizen Barere, in the Convention, put forward the unlikely story that Robespierre had removed the Dauphin with a view to restoring him as king and marrying Madame Royale. In reality Citizen Paul Barras found the ill Dauphin in La Temple and interviewed both the sick child and his sister. It is important to note that he did not see the sick child and his sister *together* and there is no way of knowing at this point that the child was the Dauphin. Barras recommended to the Committee of Public Safety that the child's insanitary quarters be cleaned; that he be given medical treatment, and that the 24-year-old Creole, from Martinique, one Laurent, be appointed as guardian.

Strange to tell, although Laurent was Barras's *protégé* in full knowledge of Barras's recommendations and the orders of the Committee of Public Safety to relax the strict regime of the Dauphin, he parried all of Madame Royale's requests to see her brother and ordered all of Antoine Simon's papers on the Dauphin to be seized. G. Lenôtre argues that soon after his appointment as guardian Laurent realized that the young prisoner in La Temple was not the Dauphin, and with Barras's collusion kept the fact quiet, assuring Madame Royale that her brother was being well cared for.

Laurent tended the boy regularly and fed him personally taking his meals from the servants outside the boy's room. He continued to make excuses if anyone who had known the Dauphin well asked to see him. Even when the Revolutionary Convention began to be concerned that rumours of the royal family's escape were circulating widely in Paris and sent two members of the Committee of Public Safety to La Temple to confirm the royal family's presence, Laurent took them to see Madame Royale (she herself confirmed it in her journal), but there was no corroboration that they ever saw the boy prisoner. If the boy in La Temple was not the Dauphin, this would certainly account for Laurent's not allowing his sister, or any who might have known him before imprisonment (and that included a few members of the Committee), ever seeing him.

On 8 November 1794, Laurent was joined as custodian by the 38-year-old son of a Parisian upholsterer, one Gomin, a quiet, kindly man who did his best to make the boy prisoner's life more comfortable with toys, flowers and books. Gomin, it appears, lived until 1841 and was interviewed by the historian M. A. De Beauchesne who told him the pathetic story of how '*le petit garçon*' had gathered flowers from a chink in the masonry during a rare visit for fresh air at the top of *la Grande Tour*. On his way down, the boy had placed the flowers outside one of the prison doors. Gomin presumed that the Dauphin believed the door to be his mother's prison – it had long been the Dauphin's habit to bring his mother flowers from his garden at the Tuileries before their arrest. If Gomin's tale was true then the boy certainly was the Dauphin.

It is known that the boy in La Temple suffered from tuberculosis; he suffered from attacks of fever and exhibited tumours on his limbs. The Committee of Public Safety sent three deputies, the *ci-devant* Baron Jean Baptiste Harmand, J. B. Charles Mathieu, and J. Reverchon to review the Dauphin's health, and in 1841 Harmand published an account of his visit to the Dauphin which had taken place on 19 December 1794. Taking into consideration that Harmand was writing for a royalist audience his testimony is probably acceptable.

Harmand said that the Dauphin refused to speak to them although they tried to get him to converse for over an hour. Harmand said: 'His face never altered, he never showed the slightest emotion or even surprise. In fact he treated us as if we had not been there.' Even so the boy's incarceration in solitary confinement may have caused him to lose the power to express himself. Indeed the housepainter Etienne Lasne, who took over from Laurent as custodian in April 1795, recorded that he had only heard the boy speak once; on the other hand Gomin testified that he had spoken with the Dauphin many times. Laurent incidentally became *Chef du bureau de la justice et de la police* and died in 1807, but left no testimony of his time at La Temple. Out of the visit, however, there grew the rumour that the Dauphin had been substituted by a deaf mute. It is interesting to note that the trio ordered Laurent to bring Madame Royale down to see her brother; Laurent once more disobeyed adding fuel to the substitution story for neither Harmand, nor Mathieu, nor Reverchon knew the Dauphin by sight.

By now the Reign of Terror had ceased and France was negotiating with the European powers who had taken up a stance on behalf of Louis XVI. The question of the release of the royal children was raised and was debated by the National Convention, but while that was being done the Committee of Public Safety received the report on 5 May 1795 that '*la vie du petit Capet est en danger d'expiration*'. Consequently the Committee sent Dr Pierre Joseph Desault, the head physician at the Hôtel Dieu to examine the Dauphin in the presence of his jailers. The doctor had royalist sympathies and had narrowly escaped execution and the Committee did not fully trust him, but he was the best physician in France. Although his written report has never been found, it is known that Desault prescribed infusions of hops and massage for the Dauphin's swollen joints.

Strangely enough Dr Desault was taken ill soon after his last visit to the Dauphin on 29 May and died on 1 June. His two assistants Choppart and Doublet also died during the same week as the doctor, maybe of some epidemic disease; but, rumour spread that the doctor and his assistants had been assassinated because Desault had refused to poison the Dauphin. Some whispered too that he had threatened to expose the Committee's plans to kill the Dauphin, while others said the doctor had been silenced because he realized that his patient was not Louis XVII.

On Desault's death the Committee of Public Safety appointed Dr Pelletan to look after the sick child, and he was to write in 1817 that he had found the child well cared for by Gomin and Lasne. Pelletan's report shows that he diagnosed that the child was suffering from tuberculous enteritis and had him removed to more salubrious rooms overlooking La Temple gardens. During this time the child was visited by Commissioner of the Commune Bellanger who had been one of Louis XVI's architects; he is on record as having recognized the Dauphin and made a sketch of him. The evening of 7 June 1795 saw the boy take a turn for the worse. Pelletan was summoned and brought with him a colleague, Dr Dumangin. On 8 June 1795 around three o'clock the boy died.

Despite the strong rumours in France that the boy prisoner was a substitute for the Dauphin, the revolutionary government took a very strange course of action. The boy was not officially identified by his sister, nor by any other captive former courtiers. The historian Lenôtre emphasizes that 'every precaution was taken to make identification uncertain and to delay the announcement of the captive's death'. Even the jailer, Gourlet, who had been present when the boy died, was arrested and put into solitary confinement with the obvious inference that he was to be silenced. Dr Pelletan himself was detained for a while, and Lasne and Gomin carried on taking food and medicine to the child's room as if he were still there.

On 9 June an autopsy was made on the child's cadaver by Drs Pelletan and Dumangin, assisted by P. Lassus and N. Jeauroy, all of whom signed the subsequent report. That report showed that they had examined the emaciated cadaver of a male child of around ten years of age, which showed signs of extensive intestinal tuberculosis and that both lungs were adherent to the chest wall with indications of old pleurisy. The cause of death was given as a 'scrofulous affection of long standing'. The report also stated that the body was that of 'the late Louis Capet's' son. Dr Pelletan removed the boy's heart at the autopsy and took it away with him: he subsequently offered it to Louis XVIII who refused it. On the day of the autopsy the Committee of Public Safety announced the death within their own meetings; the fact was not released publicly until 12 June and this gave rise to a new set of rumours.

A formal identification of the body – if it was the Dauphin's – by Madame Royale, would have put an end to the procession of Dauphin 'pretenders'. Both Dr Le Conte (*Louis XVII et les Faux Dauphins* 1924) and De La Sicotière (*Les Faux Louis XVII* 1882) made a detailed study of the many claims of the pretenders and each one was seriously flawed in evidence. But it still remains possible that the Dauphin *did* escape, maybe to die soon afterwards, or live in exile.

None of those who knew the Dauphin well, it must be emphasized, was ever summoned, or allowed to see the child's cadaver, and, as Lenôtre commented: 'From them the body was hidden, to appeal to passers-by who had not seen the Dauphin for four to five years past, and to them was shown, in semi-darknesss, a shaven head, a sawed skull, or a covered face!' The official records show that the corpse was interred on 10 June 1795 in *La Cimitière de Sainte-Marguerite*, Paris, in an unmarked grave. According to a statement made by his widow, the gravedigger Betrancourt, in order to thwart future royal investigators, dug up the coffin and moved it to a location near to the church wall, but he died before the House of Bourbon was restored in 1814. In reality neither the restored Louis XVIII nor Charles X wished to give official consideration to finding the supposed dead Dauphin's body, in case he proved to be alive and appeared to claim his throne.

French historians quote two further exhumations. In 1846, Abbé Haumet, *curé* of Sainte-Marguerite caused an excavation of the place Betrancourt said he had buried Dauphin's body. A lead coffin was found containing the skeleton of a child's torso with limbs from another cadaver. The brain-pan of the skull had been sawn in two, and some locks of reddish gold hair still adhered to it. Drs Milcent and Récamier examined the bones and reported: 'These bones are those of a child confined in the Temple and whose autopsy was made by Drs Dumangin, Pelletan, Lassus and Jeanroy ... but it is absolutely impossible that this skeleton could have been that of a child of ten years and a few months; it can only have belonged to a young boy of 15 or 16.'

In 1894 a further examination of the bones – which had been sealed in an oak box by Abbé Haumet – was made at the official request of Mâitre Laguerre. Drs Backer, Bilhaut, Magitot and Manouvrier noted that they were looking at the bones discovered in 1846 and in particular they recorded 'the curvature of the ribs, "the lack of development of the thorax denoting a certain degree of rachitis" ' (*rickets*). This opinion was that the skeleton belonged to a boy of 16–18 years of age and could in no way have been that of the Dauphin. This report seems to underline the veracity of the story of the widow Simon.

French records show that Antoine Simon was executed with Robespierre in 1794, and in 1796 Madame Marie-Jeanne Simon, was admitted to a hospital for incurables in La Rue de Sèvres, Paris; there, and for the rest of her life, she regularly affirmed that the Dauphin had escaped. Her story went thus: On 9 January 1794, the Committee of Public Safety had sent a vehicle to La Temple to collect the Simons' belongings; on its entry the vehicle contained 'a wicker hamper with a double bottom, a pasteboard horse and several toys' for the young prisoner. From the pasteboard horse they lifted out a rachitic and deformed child obtained from the School of Surgery. This boy was substituted for the Dauphin, who was secreted under soiled linen in the double-bottomed hamper. Simon himself must have been in the conspiracy for when the sentries at La Temple challenged the vehicle and made to search the contents, Simon affected a rage – 'Do you wish to waste the republic's time examining my dirty washing!' They let him and the vehicle pass unexamined.

It seems too, that Marie-Jeanne Simon was visited in early November 1816 by Madame Royale (then la Duchesse d'Angoulême) and that Mme Simon told the duchess that '*mon Charles*' had visited her in 1802 (eight years after his supposed disappearance) in hospital. On the 16 November 1816 Mme Simon was visited by the police who frightened her into silence; on her deathbed, however, in 1819 she maintained that she had told the truth about the Dauphin's visit.

Although in public she accepted the story that her brother the Dauphin had died in La Temple, it is certain that Madame Royale entertained doubts. Any investigations she made had to be very discreet as her husband and cousin, the Duc d'Angoulême, was the son of Charles X, and who but for the revolution of 1830 would have succeeded as King of France.

Up to 19 January 1794 (when the Simons left La Temple) the Dauphin's movements were precisely discernible. After that date Madame Royale in her *Journal* notes that she ceased to hear his voice. From what she could cull from those who did see the tubercular child introduced as the Dauphin, she noticed that he exhibited a total change of character; from being a lively, intelligent, expansive and hypersensitive child, the boy had become apathetic and dull, slow-witted and taciturn. The Committee of Public Safety made some rather curiously thorough deflections to anyone trying to obtain information on the Dauphin's demise. They did not allow any who had known the Dauphin well to view the body; they delayed the public announcement of the death; the documentation of the death was irregular; and the former Royal governess Madame de Tourzel attested that when she had a surreptitious view of the prison register it made no reference to the death. Did the Committee of Public Safety know/doubt that the child they buried was Louis Charles, King of

France? If the remains exhumed by Abbé Haumet in 1846 and Maître Laguerre in 1894 were of the Temple Captive, *then they were not those of the Dauphin Louis Charles*.

On 8 August 1936 there appeared in *The Times* a letter from Miss Isabella Stirling appertaining to a possible solution to the Dauphin's disappearance. Miss Stirling averred that when on a visit to the Seychelles in 1861, one Captain Charles Stirling RN, commanding HMS *Wasp*, heard the story from the Civil Commissioner Georges Thompson Wade, that an old impoverished Frenchman 'with Bourbon features' had claimed, during his last days, to be the vanished Louis Charles. Today the Seychelles Ministry of Education and Information (National Archives and Museum Division) contains the papers referring to the claimant.

The man was Pierre Louis Poiret and shortly before his death he revealed to his family that he was Louis Charles, Dauphin of France, to whom his mother had knelt on that morning at La Temple when she declared him Louis XVII. His dying words were revealed by his new confessor Father Ignace who attested that Poiret had said: 'My God, My God, I am humiliated. At the moment of dying, a newcomer [*Ignace*] insults me to my face. I have only a few more minutes to live and I go before God, who will judge me. I repeat – I am the son of Louis XVI and Marie Antoinette who were killed in the revolution.' Poiret related further how he had been smuggled out of La Temple and had been placed in the charge of a cobbler called Poiret. After some considerable time he was smuggled out of Paris by royalists and taken to Dunkirk. There royalist supporters arranged for him to be shipped for greater safety to the Seychelles. All was done in the utmost secrecy.

Official records show that Poiret was about nineteen years old when he first appeared in the Seychelles. He is described as a quiet, unassuming but poorly educated young man (Marie Antoinette had always been concerned that her son showed little application to learning). He had sailed from Dunkirk aboard Admiral Linois's frigate *La Marengo* which was accompanied by *La Belle Poule*. Poiret was in the charge of a M. Aimé who treated him with great respect and deference. He was put ashore on L'Ile Poivre sometime late in the year 1804; after a protracted stay M. Aimé set sail for Mahé and is recorded as having arrived on 22 May 1805; Aimé was carrying letters of instruction to the Chevalier Quéau de Quinssi, then Commandant of the Seychelles.

While he was on Poivre it appears that Poiret was kept under close surveillance, but was given or attached for training to a cotton ginning factory. Poiret remained on Poivre for a number of years and made acquaintance with a Marie Dauphine, by whom he had two daughters. Some time after 1822 Poiret left Poivre for Mahé, and was given two land concessions, one at Cap Ternay and the other at Grand Anse (which he later surrendered). There he was supplied with slaves and settled down to grow cotton. The grants of land were authorized by the British Civil Agent, E. H. Madge with agreement of Chevalier de Quinssi as *Juge de Paix*. By this time Poiret entered into a relationship with another woman, Marie Edesse of Port Glaud, and by her had seven children; the names of his nine children all began with Louis or Marie in respect, it is said, of his parents. Poiret died of a gangrenous abscess in 1856 at the age of 70 and was buried at Bel Eau.

News of Poiret's death was given to the authorities by his negro *valet-de-chambre* who produced several pieces of silver plate bearing the arms of the Bourbons, four miniature paintings (of Marie Antoinette, Louis XVI, the Dauphin and Madame Royale), a gold dagger, and letters including a copy of one written by Poiret in November 1838 to Archduke Charles of Austria. Poiret had written: 'I am the son of Louis XVI and Marie Antoinette, the one believed to be under the ground for more than forty years and who wants to give notice [*several words missing*] since the separation of Papa and Maman in the Temple in 1792, which left Papa in the hands of the executioners. Then I was taken to Dunkerque [*several words missing*] I am doing physical work on one of the Seychelles islands. I hope to go back. When I see you, I will give you the news'. Poiret had sent his letters to his European relatives, including Charles X of France (his uncle) through Civil Agent Madge. It seems that for official purposes Madge was satisfied as to Poiret's identity.

Pierre Louis Poiret's last surviving child, his namesake as supposed Dauphin, Louis Charles Edesse died in 1913 and attested that Poiret had a red turkey-shaped mark on one of his shoulders, a birthmark some said that was also carried by Louis XVII.

The Royal Duke and the Valet

Rape, incest, debauchery, nothing was ever too bad to be said about the sons of George III and Queen Charlotte. Even in an age when sexual indiscretions were the norm rather than the exception they horrified polite society. The most consistently disliked in an unpopular Royal Family was the King's eighth child, the Duke of Cumberland. Only H. Morse Stephens gave Cumberland much of an impartial assessment in the *Dictionary of National Biography*. Most writers presented the royal duke as 'foul-mouthed' and an 'ill-mannered lout' as did Harold Kurtz in *History Makers*. Cumberland was even accused of fathering his sister Sophia's child; this was an unfair calumny as Cumberland was abroad at the time of conception – but that was the kind of reputation Cumberland attracted.

HRH Prince Ernest Augustus, Duke of Cumberland, was born at Queen's House, Buckingham Palace, London, on 5 June 1771. He was educated first by private tutors, and then at the University of Göttingen in Hanover. In 1790 he entered the 9th Hanoverian Light Dragoons and made the army his career; he saw active service in Europe and was severely wounded at Tournay in 1794, losing his left eye. On his elevation to the peerage in 1799, Cumberland took part in political debate in the House of Lords and espoused the Tory cause. This made him a target for the Whig pamphleteers and he was largely vilified publicly and in print by such as the Grenvellites whose vast network of high political intrigue led from its workbase at Stowe, the seat of Earl Temple (later the Duke of Buckingham and Chandos).

Cumberland's dreadful reputation was to colour public reaction when it became known that an attempt had been made to assassinate him in the early hours of Wednesday, 31 May 1810. The Duke claimed, went the official story, to have beaten off an attacker who was armed with a sharp sword. Soon afterwards the Duke's valet, the Italian Joseph Sellis, was found with his throat cut. The Whigs cried murder and pointed to the Duke as the culprit.

In reviewing the case today the first consideration may be given to the location of the attempted assassination. In 1810 the Duke of Cumberland was living in that set of apartments in St James's Palace which is commonly called York House. The entrance to the apartments is in Ambassadors Court, which in 1810 went by the name of Kitchen Court. The Duke's bedroom, which looked on to Cleveland Row, was on the first floor at the extreme west end of his apartments. Next to it was a dressing-room and a lavatory in which were two large walk-in cupboards. Besides the doors into the dressing-room and the lavatory, Cumberland's bedroom contained two other doors, one of which communicated with a sitting-room, known as the West Yellow Room, and the other with a narrow passage leading directly to the attendant's waiting-room. The ordinary entrance to this waiting-room was in the long gallery, facing Kitchen Court, from which both the main and the secondary staircases descended to the ground floor. At its eastern end the gallery was closed by a green baize door, which separated Cumberland's apartments from the adjacent rooms. Next to the waiting-room was a small bedroom for a servant, situated immediately behind the recess in which the Duke's bed was placed. It was always occupied by the valet on night duty and could be entered only from the waiting-room.

Visiting these apartments in the 1920s Sir John Hall, who had an interest in the case, noted this:

. . . in ordinary circumstances, [*Cumberland*] never used the door communicating with the servants' quarters, but would enter or leave his room by the door leading into the West Yellow Room. This was one of a suite of three drawing-rooms, looking on to Cleveland Row, the other two being known respectively as the

Ball Room and the East Yellow Room. Each of these rooms communicated with the other and each of them had a door giving access to the gallery. Beyond the East Yellow Room was a small room, described as an armoury, and beyond that again was a spare bedroom with a dressing-room, known to the members of the Duke's household as the 'summer' room. Leading out of the 'summer' dressing-room was a small dingy servant's room, of the same type as the one adjoining the Duke's bedroom, its solitary window, which looked on to the gallery, being high up in the wall above the bed. It was habitually reserved for Joseph Sellis, the Duke's Italian valet, who slept in it on those occasions when he had to accompany his master on a journey necessitating an early start.

The story of the attack on Cumberland that swept the clubs and salons of London like wildfire went as follows. About half-past midnight Cumberland returned to his apartments in St James's Palace, having dined at Greenwich, as President of the Royal Navy Hospital, and having attended a concert for the benefit of the Royal Society of Music. He retired to bed about one o'clock. The Duke's bed stood in a dimly lit recess behind which was a small room, in which slept the page in attendance, one Cornelius Neale. On the sofa lay the Duke's recently sharpened military sabre. Writing of the events in 1867 the Admiralty clerk turned historian John Heneage Jesse, recorded:

About half-past two o'clock in the morning, the Duke was aroused by a blow on the head, which was immediately followed by a second blow. His first impression was that a bat had got into his apartment and was beating about his head. The light of the lamp, however, gleaming on the sabre, he at once perceived the extreme peril of his situation and accordingly, following the first impulse of the moment, he felt for the bell-rope which usually hung over the head of his bed, but which, whether accidentally or designedly, had been displaced. The Duke, who had now received a third stroke, sprang from his bed and rushed towards the door of the apartment of the page in attendance; his assailant at the same time pursuing him. Fortunately he succeeded in opening the door, but not till he had received a wound in the thigh, and other injuries. The assassin having previously dropped the sabre, now made good his retreat in the darkness. A dent, which was subsequently discovered in the door, as well as the circumstances of the point of the sabre being bent, evinced how narrow had been the escape of the Duke. A picture near the door was found to be slightly splashed with blood.

By this time the household and Neale had been aroused, and the Duke pointedly asked for his valet Sellis. As Jesse further recorded: 'Sellis was discovered sitting half undressed in a reclining position, on his bed, with his throat cut from ear to ear. . . .' On a chest of drawers, near Sellis's bedside lay a razor, and a basin of water tinged with blood. . . . The inference would seem to be, said Jesse, 'that after having attacked his master, he had rushed back to his own apartment with the intention of washing the Duke's blood from his hands . . . but that the approach of the persons sent in search of him, told him that detection was inevitable and induced him to commit suicide in order to avoid the consequences of his crime'. It is interesting to note that Jesse records that it was one of the examining surgeon's opinions that Sellis's throat had been cut by a right-handed person, whereas Sellis himself was left-handed. Again throughout the subsequent investigation it was never averred that the Duke knew who his assailant was. The Duke calling for Sellis (with questions about his whereabouts) suggested that the Duke did not suspect who his assailant was. Or was it a cover-up by the Duke alarmed by the possibility of Sellis elsewhere in the building telling his version of an attack on him by the Duke?

The affair created an enormous sensation. In her *Autobiography* (1861) Ellis Cornelia Knight recorded: 'It was the fashion to go and see the Duke's apartments, which for several days were left in the same state as when he was removed. The visitors discovered traces of blood upon the walls. . . .' Cumberland of course had been taken to Carlton House by the Prince of Wales, his brother, some hours after the assault. The opening of the apartments to the public was an attempt by the Royal Family to 'soften public opinion'.

The legally presented facts of the case came out from the depositions taken from all the witnesses by John Read, the coroner and principal magistrate at Bow Street. He began his work at ten o'clock the next day (31 May 1810) following the incident. These depositions were set before the Coroner's Jury which subsequently sat in Cumberland's apartments at St James's. Although the jury was composed of Whig merchants from such areas as Whitehall and Charing Cross, and thus politically opposed to the Duke, he seems to have been given a just and fair hearing.

The depositions set out this scenario: Because the Duke was out, Joseph Sellis, the valet, was free for the whole evening. He did not retire early but was seen in the Duke's rooms by the under-butler, Thomas Strickland, who brought in the Duke's last night drink. When he returned the Duke was attended by Neale. Cumberland put on his padded night-cap and was asleep by one o'clock.

Cumberland was awakened some time between two o'clock and half past by a hissing noise and received a blow on the head with a sabre, which passed through the padding of the night-cap and inflicted a deep set of wounds. Unable to escape by the other side of the bed which stood against the wall, Cumberland leapt up and raising his arm to ward off a blow, received another severe wound which practically severed the fingers of his hand.

The Duke then staggered towards his page Neale's door shouting: 'Neale, Neale, I am murdered'. Leaving the Duke dripping blood, Neale ran into the bedroom brandishing a poker and tripping over the sabre discarded by the Duke's fleeing assailant. Cumberland instructed him to raise the alarm and summon the guard to seal off the entrances to the palace, and together they went off in search of the porter. Once back in the bedroom Cumberland found the sabre lying on the floor and recognized it as his regimental sword, the scabbard of which was found in the walk-in cupboard of his lavatory. The record of the attack in the *Annual Register* for 1810 notes that Sellis is thought to have hidden in the cupboard to await his master's return as his slippers were found there and evidence that someone had made themselves comfortable amongst the linen.

The conduct of events was now taken over by the Duke's housekeeper, Mrs Anne Neale, who summoned the King's physician Sir Henry Halford and the surgeon Mr (later Sir) Everard Home. All this time Sellis was missing, and hysterical rumour began to circulate that Sellis had been murdered. Mrs Neale was sent by Cumberland in search of the valet. Mrs Neale testified that she went to Sellis's room with the porter Benjamin Smith and a *jäger* (an attendant in huntsman's uniform), Mathew Graslin; they knocked and called to Sellis through the locked door. At this point there is no evidence that Sellis was in his room. Receiving no answer, Mrs Neale approached Sellis's room from another direction – the rooms in Cumberland's apartments were mostly interconnecting and she encountered locked doors which were not usually locked. On arrival at the door she 'heard a deep gurgling noise and the sound of trickling water'; whereupon she and the porter went away for more assistance.

Sergeants Creighton and Davenhall and four men of the Coldstream Guards returned with them and they found Sellis's room door now ajar. They entered and found Sellis dead with his throat cut from ear to ear; his head was almost severed and the blood was still frothing and running freely from his throat. This would suggest that death had come only a few minutes before. A razor with a white handle lay on the floor some two feet from the bed. Creighton retrieved the razor and placed it on the bedside table. It is interesting to note that when the soldiers arrived at Sellis's room the door was now ajar; it had been locked when Mrs Neale had called to him. Had a successful attempt on Sellis's life taken place only a few minutes before the soldiers arrived?

Completing his examination Surgeon Everard Home found the Duke's wounds to be serious, and to be more numerous than had been expected. Some of the head wounds were so deep that the brain was visible and he had one gash in his throat; his hand, left leg and right thigh were badly lacerated. By this time too, Cumberland's brothers had been informed and HRH Prince George of Wales arrived and was joined by HRH Prince Augustus, Duke of Sussex. It was Sussex who now took command of the proceedings to investigate the whole affair. Sussex immediately concluded that the attempt on his royal brother's life, 'had obviously' been done by a member of the household staff, for, every door and window which might have afforded entry and escape was locked, and a trail of blood led from Cumberland's room to that of Sellis.

The conduct of the official inquiry which lasted some six hours was carried out by the Coroner of the King's Household (purely an honorary post), the solicitor Samuel Thomas Adams of Great Russell Street, Bloomsbury. Adams summoned his jurymen (choosing local merchants and excluding the King's Yeoman who would normally have been represented in such an investigation) and Mr Francis Place, a tailor, was appointed foreman. As well as the seventeen jurymen present were Gill and Hodgson, Coroners for the County of Middlesex, Read the magistrate, Mr Bricknell, Solicitor to the Admiralty and to Cumberland. At Place's insistence four newspapers were represented and two surgeons from the Strand, Messrs Jones and Jackson. The inquest began in Sellis's room.

The jurymen and surgeons examined Sellis's corpse taking note of the large amount of blood on the bedclothes; there had clearly been no struggle. Water in the wash-basin was observed to have blood in it and blood was seen on Sellis's blue coat which was placed over a nearby chair; Sellis's neckcloth had been cut through by the razor. Those present made the assumption that 'the position of the body showed that Sellis had cut his own throat as he sat upon his bed, and had fallen backwards, while the razor had simply dropped from his hand to the floor where it had been found'.

The jury did not examine the Duke of Cumberland and only consulted an affidavit of his account of the affair. Without retiring the jurymen, with only one dissension, returned a verdict of *felo de se* (suicide).

The public was disappointed with the verdict and by and large most folk were convinced that Cumberland, although he had not killed Sellis himself, had given orders for the valet to be murdered. Some even said that Cumberland had faked an attack on himself and had then murdered the valet and raised the alarm. The extensiveness of Cumberland's wounds would make the fake attack theory unlikely. Most people, however, were convinced that the Duke had been attacked by someone.

Today there is no shred of evidence extant to implicate the Duke with a murder attack on Sellis. But the report of the incident in the *Annual Register* for the date, noted that Sellis had a wounded left arm. Was this self-inflicted, or had Cumberland first attacked him? No one knows. More factors still remain unsolved. What were Cumberland's assailant's motives? If Sellis attacked his master, why had he done it?

Described as being from a 'well-informed contemporary', J. Heneage Jesse quoted the words of Col Henry Norton Willis: 'I strongly suspect that the motives which actuated Sellis in his attempt to assassinate the Duke of Cumberland were the taunts and sarcasms that the Duke was constantly, in his violent, coarse manner, lavishing on Sellis's religion, who was a Catholic. This conduct, in addition to the part the Duke had notoriously taken to prevent the extension of entire toleration to that religion, appear to be very sufficient motives to indulge a bigot to commit the most desperate action.'

Again in July 1810 Col Willis made this diary insertion: 'Called at Carlton House. In going out saw Colonel McMahon [*Col John McMahon, Keeper of the Privy Purse and Secretary Extraordinary to the Prince of Wales*] who told me that the Duke of Cumberland had dismissed Captain Stephenson in a very harsh, severe manner; the cause as follows. Stephenson dined at the Prince's table in company, among others, with Mr Blomberg [*The Rev. M. Blomberg, Private Secretary to the Prince of Wales*]. Stephenson was asked if the Duke had on any occasions treated his servants cruelly or harshly. He replied – "No his conduct was much the contrary." He remembered, indeed some years ago, Sellis the assassin, being in the act of pulling off the Duke's boots, the latter gave him a kick which threw him; that this act, at the time, seemed to produce no resentment on the part of Sellis, who with the Duke and Stephenson all joined in the laugh.' Next day Blomberg related this story to the King at Windsor with some probable additions Jesse avers. The King felt that in talking about the Duke, Stephenson was disloyal and the officer was dismissed.

The relationship between Cumberland and Sellis and the characters of the two men became a matter of public speculation. Sellis had been in the Duke's employ for a number of years before the incident. There is evidence that Cumberland was kind to Sellis and his family, assuring for instance, that Sellis had his own apartments where he could live with his wife and family when not on duty. There are consistent references throughout the subsequent investigation of gifts and favours for Cumberland in particular. Of his three valets (the other two were Conelius Neale and James Paulet) Sellis was generally deemed the favourite. Cumberland and his sister, HRH the Princess Augusta, had stood sponsor by proxy at the christening of Sellis's youngest child. Nevertheless Cumberland was outspoken and irascible and the hot-headed Italian and the quick-tempered Duke may have had a love-hate relationship. Sellis had grievances too against Cumberland in that he averred that the Duke did not give the precedence that say, the Duke of Sussex gave his servant (who rode with Sussex in his carriage rather than on the box); and Sellis grumbled about deductions from his pay. Sellis too had grievances against the valet Neale, and accused Neale publicly and in print of cheating Cumberland. But these were master-servant and 'below-stairs' grievances which could have been mirrored in a thousand households in London. No . . . there had to be more.

In his own manuscript of the events, the jury foreman Francis Place set out murder motives which are worthy of scrutiny. Place noted that one important reason *why Sellis would want to kill his master* was 'because Sellis had found his wife Mary Ann in bed with Cumberland'. Again Place gave one important reason *why Cumberland would want to kill Sellis* in that Sellis was his sexual 'minion' and 'that the Duke killed him to prevent a threatened exposure'.

Although Cumberland ultimately weathered the storm of public scepticism over the verdict it was these two 'motives', highlighted by Francis Place as being common speculation, which cast a shadow over Cumberland for the rest of his life. All his future actions were viewed with suspicion.

In 1812, for instance, Henry White, the proprietor and editor of the Sunday newspaper the *Independent Whig* published an article under the pseudonym 'Junius', stating that Sellis was not his own 'executioner' and that the case should be re-examined. In the following Sunday's edition the paper published another article this time signed 'Pluto-Junius' (the pseudonym of the Whig rake and profligate S. C. Graves), libelling the Duke by saying that the scenario of Sellis's room had been so devised to make the incident look like suicide and that Cumberland was a sodomist. The scurrilous articles continued and the Duke was forced to take action against the *Independent Whig*, and on 5 March 1813 the case was heard before Lord Chief Justice of the King's Bench, Lord Ellenborough. White was found guilty and sentenced to fifteen months imprisonment and a fine of £200.

Later that year the *Annual Register* recorded a statement by Sir Everard Home (who had been called in to the Sellis case). Home considered it his public duty to state:

I went to his apartment, found the body lying on his side of the bed, without his coat and neckcloth, the throat cut so effectually that he could not have survived above a minute or two; the length and direction of the wound were such as left no doubt of its being given by his own hand, any struggle would have made it irregular. He had not even changed his position; his hands lay as they do in a person who has fainted, they had no marks of violence upon them, his coat hung upon a chair out of reach of blood from the bed, the sleeve from the shoulder to the wrist was sprinkled with blood, quite dry, evidently from a wounded artery, and from such a kind of sprinkling the arm of the assassin of the Duke of Cumberland could not escape.

The public were cynical and attributed Home's statement to the fact that he had been recently knighted.

Soon after this Cumberland left Britain for Prussia to pursue active service in the Napoleonic Wars. In 1815 Cumberland married his cousin Fredericka, the former wife of Prince Frederick William of Sohns-Braunfels, and of Prince Frederick Ludwig of Prussia; both previous husbands, the Whig gossipers speculated had been murdered by the new Duchess of Cumberland.

The Cumberland-Sellis case was to lie undisturbed, but not forgotten, until 1832. In that year a publisher called Philips issued the book *The Authentic Records of the Court of England during the past Seventy Years*. In the volume the Duke of Cumberland was again castigated as a sodomist and it was inferred that the Lord Chief Justice (Lord Ellenborough) had worked in collusion to interfere with the witnesses' testimony. The book cited a man called Joseph Loux (nicknamed 'Jew') as a material witness who 'was never called' to testify, and who averred that the Sellis suicide was murder and that Sir Henry Halford (the King's physician) had been an accomplice. 'Jew' it appeared had once served the duke as a footman.

Cumberland took legal advice from Sir Charles Wetherall (the High Tory Solicitor-General in Wellington's administration) on this new libel. The case was tried on 25 June 1833 before the Whig Lord Chief Justice Thomas Denman with Sir Charles representing the Duke. 'Jew's' story was found to be a complete fabrication and Philips was sentenced to six months (he actually skipped bail and fled the country).

1832 also saw the publication of *The Secret History of the Court of England from the Accession of George II to the death of George IV*. The authoress of the book was Lady Anne Hamilton (a daughter of the 5th Duke of Hamilton). Again it was another Whig inspired smear on Cumberland, and the book repeated 'Jew's' fabricated story . . . the volume was suppressed, but appeared over the years as an 'under the counter' collector's piece.

On the succession of Queen Victoria to the throne of Great Britain, Cumberland succeeded as King Ernest I of Hanover (the Salic Law debarred Victoria from ruling Hanover). As king, Cumberland made a popular though autocratic monarch and was widely and sincerely mourned by his people when he died at his palace of Herrenhousen on 18 November 1851.

Only Cumberland really knew what actually happened on the night of 31 May forty-one years before his death and he took that secret with him to his tomb. Today historians mull over the loose ends and inconsistencies of the Sellis case. For instance, there's the imputation that the normally left-handed Sellis's throat had been cut by a right-handed man; and what is more important, that Sellis's head was almost severed. In nine cases out of ten such a state of affairs would be impossible. A suicide tends to lean the head back to cut the throat, thus making it difficult to sever. Again, suicides do not usually have deep lacerations, but have several tentative cuts; generally too, the cuts are shallow.

Then there is the mention of the discarded neckerchief which was seen to have been cut through. Would not a suicide remove this rather than try to cut through the garment first? What is more, was Sellis strong enough to slice through his own neck? In his account of the case Sir John Hall in *The Bravo Mystery and other cases* (London, 1932), avers that Sellis was 'a small and weakly man'. If this is so, could such a man successfully attempt to assassinate a rugged, militarily trained man like Cumberland? Unless, of course, Sellis was fighting for his life? What if he were fighting off an attack by Cumberland, and his fiery temper carried him over into a state of human strength different from the normal?

The trail of blood from the Duke's bedroom, through the West and East Yellow Rooms and the Armoury to Sellis's bedroom could easily have been made by Sellis's body being dragged by. . . ? Cumberland with his horrific wounds could not have done it . . . but what about Neale whom Sellis had slandered? He could very well have murdered

Sellis for he left Cumberland for a while after the assault. Then there was the closed door. Could Sellis have been defending himself with the razor in his room? Was that what Mrs Neale heard outside the door? Or was the trail of blood actually Cumberland's . . . on his way back to the apartments to stage an 'I've been assassinated' scenario? We are told that Cumberland, badly wounded as he was, went off to search for the porter. And as to the bloody water in Sellis's room? Why would Sellis wish to wash his own hands? Did his murderer actually wash his hands? The room was witnessed as being relatively undisturbed so Sellis may have known any assailant and be taken by surprise.

Obviously these loose ends will never be tied up now. But a modern examination of the depositions and facts shows that Sellis is very unlikely to have taken his own life, but was more likely to have been murdered by a person or persons unknown.

8

The Killing of Napoleon

HAS TODAY'S FORENSIC MEDICINE UNCOVERED ONE
OF HISTORY'S GREATEST MURDER STORIES?

Six days before his death Napoleon Bonaparte made a strange request of his medical attendant, Dr Alexander Arnott (1771–1855), the English military doctor who cared for him in the last weeks of his life. 'After my death,' said Napoleon, 'I want you to open my body . . . I recommend that you examine my stomach particularly carefully; make a precise, detailed report on it, and give [the report] to my son . . . I charge you to overlook nothing in this examination. . . .' Did the former emperor suspect that he was being slowly murdered?

One man, Dr Sten Forshufvud, a Swedish dental surgeon from Göteborg, believed that Napoleon had been murdered and collected a dossier on the emperor who died in exile at 5.49 p.m. on 5 May 1821, at Longwood House, St Helena, at he age of 51 in the sixth year of his exile. For a long time Forshufvud had suspected that the French royal family were behind Napoleon's death. The key figure, he believed, was the Compte d'Artois (1757–1836), the younger brother of the ailing, childless French monarch Louis XVIII. The Compte was a fanatical hater of the Revolution and all its facets, and the focus of his hatred was the 'worst spawn' of the Revolution, *Napoleon usurpateur*. D'Artois, with his network of agents, was at the centre of many plots on Napoleon's life, but all came to nought as his agency was infiltrated by Napoleon's spies. The royal family of Bourbon had been put shakily back on to the throne of France following Waterloo, 18

June 1815 to be shoved off it again when Napoleon came back from exile; Louis XVIII had been restored on Napoleon's recapture after the Hundred Days. Yet, by 1815 it was still in the interests of the Bourbons to attempt to assassinate Napoleon and work for the reinstatement of the *ancien regime* of before the Revolution. Even so believing that the Bourbons had set up and paid for Napoleon's murder was one thing, how they might have done it was another. So Forshufvud began with the autopsy reports on Napoleon's cadaver and began one of the world's most intriguing historical detective cases.

The autopsy had been conducted the day after Napoleon's death by the emperor's personal physician, the Corsican Francisco Antommarchi (1789–1838), in the presence of six English doctors. Antommarchi opened the chest cavity and the doctors examined the vital organs; he removed the emperor's heart and opened the stomach. Once the doctors had finished their examination of the organs, the emperor was sewn up again, the executors having denied permission to examine the emperor's brain.

In due time the seven doctors wrote up their reports and none agreed on the cause of death. They did agree that there was an ulcer on Napoleon's stomach near the pylorus, that opening from stomach to intestine. Antommarchi recorded it as a 'cancerous ulcer', but the English doctors defined it as 'scirrhous portions leading to cancer'. So, medical history recorded Napoleon's death as *cancer of the pylorus*.

Napoleon's jailers breathed a sigh of relief. No political embarrassment would arise out of what had been officially assessed, and the English governor of St Helena, Sir Hudson Lowe (1769–1844), was able to report to London that everything was 'normal'. That was even though one of the English doctors, Thomas Shortt, reported Napoleon's liver to be 'enlarged'. Lowe was anxious to avoid such comments that would suggest hepatitis, a disease of health conditions, and the governor wanted no besmirching of Napoleon's treatment record at the hands of the English. The governor forced Dr Shortt to delete his comment from the official report (though Shortt openly commented on it once he had returned to England). But Hudson Lowe could not stop Antommarchi saying that Napoleon's liver *was* abnormally large and that he blamed the English for killing Napoleon because of exile in such a climate.

That was the first fragment of evidence logged by Dr Forshufvud, and he made a special note of a phrase in Napoleon's will. The will had been read out aboard the 500-ton storeship HMS *Camel* on 25 May 1821 by Count Charles-Tristan de Montholon (1783–1853), Napoleon's first executor. The *Camel* was taking Napoleon's suite out of exile and now in European waters the time had come to fulfil the dead emperor's last wishes. Forshufvud made a particular note of one of Napoleon's testament phrases: *'I die prematurely, murdered by the English oligarchy and its hired assassins'*.

Dr Forshufvud was an unashamed Napoleonophile, his home in Göteborg was packed with books about the emperor and pictures of Napoleon's life and times; Forshufvud's second passion was serology, the study of blood, and a related research area, toxicology, the study of poisons. Dr Forshufvud had studied all of the theories concerning Napoleon's death and believed totally that the emperor had not died of cancer. Anxious to find out what really had been Napoleon's cause of death, Forshufvud turned to the memoirs of Louis Marchand (1791–1876) who had been Napoleon's chief bodyguard and *premier valet-de-chambre*, who had been with him at St Helena from 1815 to 1821. The second volume of Marchand's memoirs had been published in the autumn of 1955, just at the time that Forshufvud had begun a serious examination of Napoleon's death.

As he had hoped Marchand detailed the day to day account of the last months of Napoleon's life in a way no other writer had. He described Napoleon's last illness, the symptoms, the reactions to medicines and how the body appeared, particularly its growing obesity. Forshufvud was fascinated, as Marchand was the only person who had been at Napoleon's bedside for most of each 24 hours. Marchand described how Napoleon alternated between insomnia and somnolence; he had severe odema (swelling) of the feet, and he lost his body hair. The Swedish dentist began to feel that Napoleon had been killed over a long period of time with repeated small doses of poison – probably the poison most difficult to trace at autopsy, arsenic. All the symptoms were there and Forshufvud remembered Antommarchi and Shortt's comments on the enlarged liver – *anyone suffering from arsenic poisoning would be expected to have an enlarged liver*.

The arsenical poisoning of Napoleon made the most sense. If the Emperor had died of cancer it is likely that he would have become emaciated. In fact Napoleon had become fatter, Marchand said so, and a glance at the later portraits of Napoleon showed this; and, *obesity is always expected in cases of arsenical poisoning.* Dr Forshufvud was satisfied that he had discovered Napoleon's real cause of death. For four years he put it out of his mind, but still he carried on with his study of Napoleon's life, particularly his last few years. Forshufvud could recite them backwards. . . .

The man who was the most successful general of the French Revolution, and who had been master of Egypt and France by the time he was thirty, had given France a new Golden Age. He had defeated the massed forces of the combined crowned heads of Europe, struggled with the British, lost his empire in Spain and Russia, had been imprisoned on Elba, escaped, won back his empire for a hundred days and lost it again at Waterloo . . . and all before he was 46 years old. On 9 August 1815, Napoleon had been transported to exile in far off St Helena aboard the Royal Navy gunship HMS *Northumberland.* Dr Forshufvud dentist knew Napoleon's every step of the way.

Time passed and by 1959 Dr Forshufvud was devoting as much spare time as possible to the study of the scholarly articles and biographies that were regularly written on Napoleon. His own belief that Napoleon was poisoned was an established fact in his mind and as he read he became more and more puzzled that, following Marchand's memoirs, no historian or medical writer had made use of the symptoms revealed therein in subsequent examinations of Napoleon's life.

One day he was reading the latest article on Napoleon's death, an article that rehashed all the old theories of hepatitis, cancer and so on, but which did not mention Marchand's revelations, and somewhat irritated Forshufvud decided that he would write the definitive examination of Napoleon's death. He began by reviewing all the known material on arsenic, its symptoms in a victim and its legal and murderous use in the eighteenth and nineteenth centuries. He studied every account of Napoleon's death and autopsy, building up a dossier of fact, opinion and comparison. First he set about proving that Napoleon had been poisoned, and then he projected to prove who he believed had done it.

Forshufvud carefully logged all of the symptoms of arsenic poisoning, noting how they duplicated those of many common diseases and often appeared contradictory. He isolated thirty main symptoms and noted that Napoleon had, in his last days, shown twenty-two of those symptoms. What he needed to do now was to test Napoleon's remains for arsenic. But how was he to do that?

Napoleon's cadaver had been buried in a valley on St Helena on 9 May 1821 and in 1840 it had been brought back to Paris and was interred under thirty-five tons of porphyry in Les Invalides. Forshufvd knew that there was no way that the French authorities would allow an exhumation order, or a further autopsy. But, as a toxicologist Forshufvud realized that there was one avenue open to him – the examination of Napoleon's hair. It was an established scientific fact that the body tries to expel arsenic through the hair, and methods of analysing hair for arsenic were now common knowledge amongst toxicologists. The dentist knew that following the eighteenth-century custom there must be samples of Napoleon's hair extant for many had been issued as keepsakes. Indeed Marchand had noted in his memoirs that he had brought back some of Napoleon's hair clippings for the Bonaparte family, and one such lock had been kept for his daughter.

Thumbling through the papers on hair analysis for arsenic poisoning Forshufvud was disappointed that he might have to find fully five grammes of hair for an experiment to take place. Certainly the Marchand keepsake would not have been as much as that? By chance the dentist came across the work of the toxicologist Dr Hamilton-Smith of Glasgow University, who averred in a scientific paper that only one strand of hair was needed for a conclusive examination. Forshufvud was elated. Could he persuade Dr Hamilton-Smith to analyse a strand for him?

The first step, however, was to find a strand of hair. So Forshufvud decided to write to the current representative of the Bonaparte clan, one Napoleon Louis Jerome Victor Bonaparte, Prince Napoleon, descendant of the Emperor's younger brother Jerome who had been created King of Westphalia in 1807 and who was a commander in Napoleon's Russian invasion and at Waterloo. To Forshufvud's delight, Prince Napoleon agreed to see him in Paris and the dentist travelled to the French capital. In the event Forshufvud was inexplicably stonewalled by the secretaries in Prince Napoleon's office and the dentist received the impression that the prince did not wish to open the subject of his ancestor's death. There were after all political reasons why the prince should remain aloof, for it was only in the early 1950s that Bonapartes had been allowed to live on French soil.

Forshufvud thought about his position for a while in his Paris hotel room. At length he hit on the idea of contacting Commandant Henry Lachouque, who had been a director of Les Invalides and who was the author of *The Last Days of Napoleon's Empire* (1966) and who had helped edit Marchand's memoirs. Lachouque agreed to a meeting, and Forshufvud outlined his research and the target of his quest for a strand of hair. Lachouque said that he had a lock of Napoleon's hair and from his private museum he produced a strand of reddish-brown, silky hair – a lock that had been transported from St Helena by Marchand. Forshufvud was overjoyed.

The Swedish dentist lost no time in sending the strand of hair to Dr Hamilton-Smith at Glasgow University's Department of Forensic Medicine. Dr Hamilton-Smith's answer confirmed that the *subject of the hair had been exposed to large doses of arsenic*. Forshufvud estimated that the registered dose was thirteen times the normal arsenic content which might have been picked up through environmental sources. But the dentist reasoned that one test was not enough; there would have to be more, and he would have to try and prove that the hair sample was Napoleon's. He decided to discuss his research with Dr Hamilton-Smith.

Sten Forshufvud met Hamilton-Smith at Glasgow in August 1960. Here the dentist learned of Hamilton-Smith's methods of testing poisons using the nuclear-bombardment technique, in which the hair sample had been compared with the known properties of arsenic. To further his professional relationship with Hamilton-Smith, Forshufvud revealed that the hair sample was from the head of Napoleon; Dr Hamilton-Smith was deeply shocked. Nevertheless he agreed to help the dentist further with his research.

The Swede now had to obtain more of Napoleon's hair so that Hamilton-Smith could test how the arsenic had been absorbed by the emperor's system. Was it a steady stream of doses, for instance, or a series of large doses? On his return from Glasgow, Forshufvud discussed with Lachouque his plans to test more of Napoleon's hair using Hamilton-Smith's methods. Indeed Lachouque agreed to make more strands available and made the necessary arrangements for Forshufvud to meet a group of interested government parties at the *Ministère de la Defense* office within the Hotel de Brienne at Paris; ironically the former Paris residence of Napoleon's mother, Letizia Bonaparte, Madame Mère. There Forshufvud met eight government representatives including two military doctors and an army pharmacist, Col Kiger. To them the Swedish dentist described his researches and detailed his future plans, and the group showed interest in Forshufvud's work and showed sympathy with his aims. Two days later Lochouque accompanied Forshufvud to see one Henri Griffon, head of the Paris police toxicological laboratory, a man recognized as a leading expert in arsenic poisoning. Griffon also showed great interest in the case and enthusiastically agreed to conduct experiments which could incorporate his own hair analysis technique. Lachouque supplied Griffon with more strands of Napoleon's hair.

In May 1961, Forshufvud rang Griffon from Göteborg to hear the results of his analyses. To his puzzlement and no little disappointment, Forshufvud was told that Lachouque had reclaimed the strands of the emperor's hair from the laboratory for use in an *exposition*. As Lachouque had possessed a full lock of Napoleon's hair, and would therefore not need a few extra strands, his reaction mystified Forshufvud, who in rapid time dismissed it as a trumped up excuse.

Immediately Forshufvud reasoned that pressure had been brought to bear on Lachouque to cease his co-operation. The French government, the Swedish dentist believed, had thought the prospect through; if Napoleon was murdered then it was most likely that it was by one of his suite, all Frenchmen. It would be a political and diplomatic hot potato to make such a finding public and it was obviously a prospect that the French government did not wish to contemplate.

So the French politicians had closed the door to further official research, thus Forshufvud had another try. He went back to his records. Napoleon's memoirist, Louis Marchand, had brought back several locks of Napoleon's hair, so Forshufvud would just have to find another source. Trying to discover the whereabouts of more locks of Napoleon's hair would be a very lengthy process so Forshufvud decided to make his researches known to as wide an audience as possible in the hope that someone would read about them and contact him. He collaborated with Hamilton-Smith and Anders Wassen, a Swedish toxicologist, and wrote an article for *Nature* magazine entitled *Arsenic Content of Napoleon I's hair probably taken immediately after his death*; the piece was published 14 October 1961 and struck gold almost immediately. Although the article was attacked by French Napoleon 'experts', Forshufvud was elated because he was contacted by one Clifford Frey, a French textile manufacturer from Munchwilen in Switzerland. On the telephone he told Forshufvud that he had read his article on Napoleon's death and had in his ownership a lock of the emperor's hair that had been in the possession of Napoleon's Swiss groom Abram Noverruz – who had once saved Napoleon from assassination by Mollot at Avignon – who had shaved hair from the emperor's head after death. Frey expressed willingness to allow Forshufvud to have some strands for testing, and that he could hand them over to the Swedish dentist on a business trip he was making to Hamburg. Forshufvud agreed to meet Frey in Hamburg. There he met the businessman and was soon travelling back to Göteborg with his prized sample of *cheveux de l'immortel Empereur*. Immediately he set about posting the sample to Hamilton-Smith in Glasgow.

In the end Clifford Frey took the sample of hair to Hamilton-Smith himself. While he waited for the results, Forshufvud prepared a detailed note of the movements of persons at Longwood House, St Helena, and jotted down all the witnesses' memories of the final seven months of Napoleon's life. He matched the descriptions of the emperor's condition with the known symptoms of arsenic poisoning. Forshufvud began to plot the actual occurrences of the symptoms to match them with whatever Hamilton-Smith might discover. Forshufvud noted that Napoleon had had bouts of reasonable health between his periods of prostration. He placed all these medical notes into sequence. The seven months of terminal illness had begun 18–21 September 1820, when, Forshufvud noted, acute poisoning symptoms first appeared. This led to a decline into death on 5 May 1821; the day after which the hair samples were taken.

Hamilton-Smith's results based on 140 separate tests of the hair sample showed a lesser amount of arsenic content than the first test, but even so it was *five times the normal amount*. He set his findings on a graph which showed that Napoleon was *not accidentally killed* by casual arsenic in the environment, but *by regular deliberate doses*. The graph incidence of doses plotted by the hair content analysis coincided with the acute poisoning symptoms chart that Forshufvud had already plotted. Forshufvud had now proved to his own satisfaction that Napoleon had been poisoned during the last months of his life. What he must do next was to find out when the poisoning began . . . was it begun earlier than Napoleon's six-year exile at St Helena? . . . and who was the administer-murderer?

The Swede returned to his files and decided to look at the histories of those who had known Napoleon well on St Helena. He turned first to the entries on Betsy Balcombe (1800–73). Napoleon had spent the first two months of his exile at St Helena in the Chinese Pavilion at 'The Briars', the home of William Balcombe (1779–1829), naval agent for the East India Company and subsequent food purveyor to Napoleon's residence at Longwood House during 1815–18. One of Balcombe's children was the 15-year-old Betsy who was taught French by Napoleon and with whom he had a flirtatiously playful relationship. Betsy had written a memoir of her friendship with Napoleon and had received a lock of his hair. Now Forshufvud made arrangements to meet Dame Mabel Balcombe-Brookes, the grand-daughter of Betsy's younger brother.

Dame Mabel had written to Forshufvud, having seen a mention of his article on Napoleon, and had agreed to allow the locks in her possession to be tested by Hamilton-Smith. She had in her possession two separate locks, one which the emperor had given Betsy Balcombe and one which had belonged to Fanny Bertrand, the wife of General Henri-Gratien Bertrand (1773–1844), the military engineer and grand marshal of Napoleon's palace at Les Tuileries; Bertrand had been on St Helena from 1815 to 1821. Forshufvud was delighted to have the locks to test as they were taken from the emperor's head around 1816.

Forshufvud met Dame Mabel for tea at the Grosvenor House Hotel, London, and he was able to inform her that the locks in her possession did show abnormally high traces of arsenic. He also reviewed the next steps of his enquiries. Dame Mabel had helped him to uncover an important piece of new evidence; the poisoning must have begun before 1816, so he could now rule out as suspects all those who came to St Helena after 1818; he also ruled out those who left before the final days of the emperor's life. Forshufvud told Dame Mabel that he was convinced that Napoleon's murderer had actually lived within Longwood House and that the extent of the poison needed to kill the emperor was no more than what could have been secreted in an envelope.

His publicity idea was to bring Forshufvud two more important samples of Napoleon's hair. One lock came to him from Col Duncan Macaulay of Arundel, Sussex, whose ancestor Rear Admiral Sir Pultney Malcolm, had commanded the St Helena squadron, 1816–17. The lock had been given to the admiral by Napoleon during the naval commander-in-chief's farewell call at Longwood House on 3 July 1817. The sample showed two to six times the normal ingestion of arsenic. Forshufvud believed that this was the earliest cutting of Napoleon's hair extant which showed arsenical poisoning, and that it proved conclusively that Napoleon had been poisoned within the first two years of exile, that is during 1816–17.

The next lock of hair came via the Napoleon buff Gregory Troubetzkoy in New York. This hair sample had been bought at auction in London along with a holograph page of the Emperor's memoirs. This hair was also examined by Hamilton-Smith who carefully noted that it had a high rate of arsenic content, almost double the Macaulay strands. It appears that the strands had been cut by Napoleon's barber, Santini, around 1816. So Forshufvud believed that Napoleon had been dosed with arsenic pretty regularly from around 31 July to 1 October 1816.

For some time Forshufvud had been corresponding with a Canadian Napoleonist called Ben Weider. The Canadian had been following Forshufvud's work and had been assessing the reaction of North American Napoleonists to the Swedish dentist's theories. Academic opinion seemed to be on Forshufvud's side in that the theory was plausible – outside of France and pro-French cadres in Canada that was! Weider decided to try and help Forshufvud overcome this French-based opposition and help him sift the evidence.

Together they studied Forshufvud's findings and discussed the differences between acute and chronic arsenic poisoning. Napoleon had suffered from the latter, and as it was a condition not really recognized until the 1930s they were able to see that contemporary doctors at St Helena, like Francesco Antommarchi and erstwhile ship's surgeon of HMS *Bellerophon* Barry E. O'Meara, would be unaware of the medical subtleties of the condition. They were convinced that the doctors themselves had not colluded on Napoleon's death.

Slowly they dismissed the theories then current on Napoleon's death . . . indeed some French sources did admit that Napoleon was poisoned but attributed it to:

The Fact that Napoleon used a hair cream impregnated with arsenic. This Forshufvud and Weider dismissed because cream would have produced a constant level of poison . . . in reality there were 'peaks and valleys' in the recorded effects.

That the curtains and the wallpaper at Longwood House contained arsenic. This referred to the dye 'Paris Green' (copper aceto-arsenite) used in fabric dyes. This they dismissed too as others would have been affected and this would have had the effect of constant poison levels.

That Napoleon used arsenic based tonic. Both Forshufvud and Weider knew that Napoleon refused to take medication, and in any case such a tonic was not used in France until the 1860s.

They also dismissed the 'liver abcess' theory of death put forward by Surgeon General Lieutenant Raol Brice in *The Riddle of Napoleon* (1937) as inconclusive.

Even so, could the two researchers be sure that the hair samples were Napoleon's? What they could be sure of was that the scattered sources – Australia, France, Switzerland, USA and so on – all produced hair from *the same person*. They were convinced that, as several samples of the hair had been passed down to descendants from those who had been on St Helena with Napoleon, that they were genuine.

They also looked at the question of why the poison was so protracted? Why did the assassin not polish off Napoleon with one large dose? Clearly the assassin did not wish to arouse suspicion and force an autopsy.

First Forshufvud and Weider excluded all those who did not actually live at Longwood House. While they could have poisoned the household they could not solely target Napoleon. That cleared all of the English staff. Then they eliminated those who were not present for the entire exile, for their tested evidence showed that Napoleon was poisoned only in the first, middle and last periods of exile. This exonerated the Napoleonic courtier Count Emmanuel Las Casas (1766–1842) who was only at St Helena during 1815–16; the artillery officer and aide General Baron Gaspard Gourgaud (1783–1852) at St Helena 1815–18; Dr Barry O'Meara; Albine de Montholon (c. 1780–1848), wife of the aide Major-General Charles-Tristan de Montholon (1783–1853); and Cipriani Franceschi (1757–1818), Napoleon's agent and major-domo at Longwood House, who although he had supervised Napoleon's food supplies had died three years before the emperor.

They also eliminated Henri-Gratien Bertrand, the military engineer and aide, because he did not live at Longwood House, and did not have the opportunity of administering poison. This left two main suspects: Charles-Tristan de Montholon and the valet Louis Marchand.

Forshufvud and Weider assessed the two main suspects from their extensive joint knowledge of the household of Napoleon. Louis Marchand had been the most loyal and the longest-serving servant; indeed Marchand's mother had served with Napoleon's household and the environs of the Emperor's suite was the only real home that Marchand had known. There was no reason at all to suppose that Marchand had any royalist connections. But, Count Charles-Tristan de Montholon *had* Bourbon associations; when Napoleon had abdicated to Elba, Montholon had curried favour with the Bourbons. In fact Forshufvud was able to prove that Montholon did not enter the Emperor's service until *after* Waterloo. *Was he a willing royalist plant given the task of assassinating the erstwhile Emperor?* Forshufvud now thought so. But why would Montholon accept being put into voluntary exile with Napoleon? There had to be a reason said Weider, and there had to be a real motive. Forshufvud was soon able to supply that too.

Montholon had, he had found out, embezzled a large sum of soldiers' pay, a criminal act that would have earned him a long term in jail and humiliation for the rest of his life, cutting off his playboy outlets and his royalist connections. So, reasoned Forshufvud, in exchange for a royal pardon, Montholon agreed to be the assassin . . . he even endured the fact that his wife Albine became Napoleon's mistress and probably bore him the daughter called Napoleone. So if they accepted Montholon as the Bourbon's assassin how had he administered the poison? Forshufvud reminded Weider that Montholon had been Napoleon's wine steward and that Napoleon always drank his own wine (*Vin de Constance*) from his own store . . . and Forshufvud remembered, every time that Napoleon had given anyone a gift of wine from his own store, the recipients had become ill.

Even so, Weider was not totally convinced that Montholon was Napoleon's assassin. Forshufvud patiently noted that the whole key to Napoleon's death lay in the last phase of the Emperor's life. That, said Forshufvud, was when the assassin stopped killing his victim and switched to having a physician administer the fatal doses. Now that Montholon had worked on weakening Napoleon's body, a medic would give the *coup de grâce* and no autopsy would show arsenical poisoning. Forshufvud now began a detailed reconstruction of the last days of the Emperor (1 January–5 May 1821):

1 January	Napoleon suffers from his last attack of the symptoms of acute arsenic poisoning. Montholon wrote (5 December 1820) to his wife that Napoleon was suffering from *maladie de langueur* (interpreted as cancer by the French government).
27 January	Montholon endeavours to get rid of Napoleon's doctor Antommarchi – a doctor in the pay of the Bourbons would 'falsify' any post-mortem needed.
30 January	Antommarchi reports that Napoleon is in a very weak state.
27 February	Napoleon's decline increases; much vomiting and weakness.
17 March	Napoleon suffers from 'icy chill' (a symptom of arsenic poisoning).
30 March	Napoleon seen by Dr Arnott who says that there is no cause for alarm.
2 May	Napoleon's constitution, says Forshufvud, is now attacked by the use of tartar emetic (a salt of antimony) and a lethal cocktail of orgeat and bitter almonds. Forshufvud considered this to be a key time. 'In the classic method of poisoning', he said. 'Tartar emetic is used to prepare the final blow: *the killing of the weakened victim that leaves no trace of arsenic.*' It would corrode the mucous lining of the stomach

which now becomes unable (by inhibiting vomiting) to expel poison. The orgeat and bitter almonds was the *coup de grâce*, the next poisoning step being administered as a medication.

3 May   Napoleon given a purgative of calomel as he was suffering from constipation. This was against the advice of Antommarchi, but with the agreement of the English doctors present encouraged by Montholon. Calomel was deadly when combined with bitter almonds and Napoleon's system was unable to expel it.

4 May   Napoleon collapses completely.

5 May   A little before 6 p.m. Napoleon dies.

After the autopsy, Napoleon's body was treated with some sort of *liqueur aromatisée*. Then it was placed in a casket of tin. This was now encased in three more coffins, two of mahogany and one of lead, then the whole lifted into a type of stone sarcophagus inside a strongly-constructed vault of thick stone. Napoleon's cadaver was thence placed in a grave excavated from the lava and black rock in the windswept Geranium Valley, later to be called Valley of the Tomb.

In 1975 Forshufvud visited Napoleon's grave and studied the scene of the burial, and the exhumation of the body in October 1840, which was a consequence of King Louis-Philippe's wish to curry favour with the Bonapartists. When Napoleon's body was exhumed from its non-airtight tomb it was found to be in a good state of preservation. Even though the green uniform in which Napoleon had been buried was decayed and his boots had split, his body was not decayed. Forshufvud took this as further proof of arsenic poisoning because he knew that arsenic was a good preservative of living tissue.

Forshufvud now finished his researches and completed his quest. He was satisfied that he had identified Napoleon's murderer and proved how it was done. Yet, no modern autopsy is likely, Napoleon is entombed for ever in *Les Invalides* in Paris and no French government is ever likely to grant such an autopsy, so Forshufvud's theory remains just that, but it is the most plausible yet on the death of Napoleon.

9

The Mysterious Death of the Prince of Condé

DID THE ENGLISHWOMAN SOPHIA DAWES KILL THE
ROYAL NOBLEMAN BECAUSE HE WAS GOING TO
LEAVE HER?

The peasant-folk on the estate of Château de Saint Leu heard with much grief, on 27 August 1830, of the death of their beloved and kindly *seigneur*, the Duc de Bourbon, Prince of Condé. At first the estate gossips recounted how *M. le duc* had died of apoplexy; others added that he had died by his own hand because his beloved sovereign, Charles X (1757–1836), had been forced into exile by the current revolution which had followed his suspension of the French constitution. But, as they sat over their wine in the summer dusk, others suggested that he was more likely to have been murdered by the whore, Sophia, Baronne de Feuchères.

How did an Englishwoman with a French title come to be involved in the *mystère* of Saint Leu? The *Dictionary of National Biography* (1888) and the *Biographie Universelle* (1855) help to build up the scenario. Sophia Dawes, known to her acquaintances and friends as Sophie, was born in 1790, the illegitimate daughter of the fisherman Richard Dawes of St Helen's, Isle of Wight, and one Jane Callaway. Sophia and her three illegitimate siblings were forced to enter Newport Workhouse in 1796, when Richard Dawes drank all the money that was to go to their food and clothing. A workhouse child until 1805, Sophia then became a maid-servant to the family of a farmer called Cliff, who lived near Newport, but she ran away in 1807 to become a chambermaid at the George Hotel, Portsmouth. Some time later she went to London where she worked intermittently as a servant and in a milliner's shop, the sack from which reduced her to selling oranges Nell Gwynne-style in the city's theatreland. By now Sophia was something of a beauty; she was tall, big-breasted and had an attractive face with a straight nose, full, sensual lips and blue eyes under thick eyebrows, her black hair clustered in curls on her high forehead. Sophia turned many a head and it is said that her stunning looks won her some bit part work as an actress in Covent Garden and Drury Lane. At this time she became the concubine of an army officer, who, like many of his fellow officers, placed his young mistress in a villa in the then hamlet of Turnham Green, Chiswick, London. Sophia broke with her lover around 1808 but was able to extract a £50 annuity from him before she left, her first triumph as a courtesan.

Her sojourn with the army officer gave Sophia Dawes a taste for the good life, and she embarked on a project to make herself 'a real lady'. To this end she placed herself in a finishing school at Chelsea in 1809, financed by the soldier's annuity. In a short time though, her fellow students learned more about the joys of Priapus than she learned about education, and she was asked to leave. Having sold her annuity to fund her education as a lady, Sophia was again destitute and she took up domestic service again, this time in a bawdy house in Piccadilly. This, however, introduced her to the côterie of London's rakes and her favours were now honed to perfection on prizefighters, royal dukes and dandies, and there was even a whisper that HRH George Augustus Frederick, Prince of Wales, and soon to be Prince Regent, had enjoyed the hours of darkness once clasped to Sophia's ample bosom.

Among the patrons of the house in Piccadilly was Louis Henri Joseph, Duc de Bourbon, whose father the now aged Prince de Condé had waited in vain on the French frontier to escort Louis XVI and his family to safety during their flight to Varennes. Both the duke and the prince had fought with the allies in the French royalist cause, and after the Franco-Austrian Treaty of Campo-Formio of 1797, the prince had seen military service under Czar Paul I, and had subsequently gone into exile at Wanstead, London, where they waited in vain for the restoration of the Bourbons. At the age of 14 the Duc de Bourbon had married Princess Bathilde de Bourbon (great-granddaughter of the Regent, Duc d'Orléans), and his only son being dead, the now 55-year-old duke was the last heir to the celebrated royal House of Condé. In due course *M. le duc* was introduced to Sophia Dawes on the procurement of his valet, and the erstwhile servant-maid was launched on her notorious career.

Not long after their first meeting, Sophia Dawes was settled by the duke in a spacious house in Gloucester Street, off Queen's Square, Bloomsbury, London. Jane Callaway, Sophia's sexually careless mother was installed with Sophia as chaperone, whilst music masters, language tutors and dancing mistresses called regularly to enhance and expand Sophia's education and social graces. By now the duke had settled £800 a year on her for her costume and expenses in society, and she had her miniature painted by Heut-Villiers in 1812. This cosy arrangement lasted for over two years until the events of 1814 were to alter the fortunes of the House of Condé. Napoleon abdicated to be banished to Elba and Louis XVIII ascended the throne of his ancestors and the aged Prince de Condé was restored to his fortunes, his estates, the chateaux of Enghien and Chantilly, and the *Palais Bourbon* in Paris.

It seems that the Duc de Bourbon was now heavily involved with diplomatic missions for the French royal house and, leaving London, discarded the pushy Sophia, who lost no time in following him to France. Never lacking for male company and largesse, Sophia Dawes spent months in pursuit of the duke, but was turned away from the *Palais Bourbon* and had her letters unanswered. Her perseverance was rewarded, however, when the duke answered one of her letters and a reconciliation took place between Europe's wealthiest man and the low-born, coarse-tongued fisherman's daughter. In 1818 the senile Prince de Condé died and Louis Henri Joseph, Duc de Bourbon assumed the title of Prince of Condé, although he was generally known at his own request as the Duc de Bourbon. Sophia Dawes's star was once more in the ascendant.

The next step in Sophia's plan was to be presented at Court and for that she needed a respectable position. She realized that she needed to be married, and preferably to a French nobleman. The duke, whose devotion to Sophia was rekindled, even allowed her to state that she was his natural daughter and in 1818 she was married at St-Martin-in-the-Fields, Westminster, London, to Baron Adrian Victor de Feuchères, an officer in the *Garde Royale*. The duke bestowed 72,000 francs on the couple and made the baron his *aide-de-camp*. True to character Sophia falsified her status on her wedding certificate, reducing her age by three years and proclaiming herself to be the widow of one William Dawes.

Sophia, Baronne de Feuchères, now had the position she needed to be received at the French Court and be accepted as a leader of fashion. To enhance her respectability she became a Roman Catholic and installed her mother and sister Charlotte in the palace funded by the duke who was her declared *protecteur*. Everyone in society – except her husband – knew that Sophia was the duke's mistress, but after a while the baron found out and challenged her with her unfaithfulness. Persuaded by the duke to keep quiet, the baron left Sophia in 1822 and a judicial separation was secured. Feuchères made his indignation quite clear, however, to King Louis XVIII and consequently Sophia was excluded from the Court. For a while Sophia lived with her mother, but the Duc de Bourbon implored her to return to him with the sop of the revenues of the Château de St Leu during his lifetime and the promise of inheriting the estate on his death; his sister Louise Bourbon was furious and the duke showed scant regard for the feelings of the family in his lust for the carnally bovine Sophia. To secure her position, Sophia demanded that the duke turn out M. et Mme de Rully, his daughter and son-in-law; the duke complied.

Phase two of Sophia's plan was to surround herself with people devoted to her. On her suggestion her nephew and niece, James and Matilda Dawes travelled to Paris and the duke made this former hotel porter his equerry with the title of Baron de Flassons, with the estate of Flassons in the *département* of Var. Matilda, Sophia married off to the Marquis de Chabannes de la Palice, a colonel in the *Guarde Royale* and a nephew of a prominent regular guest to Sophia's dinner table, the celebrated diplomat and former Foreign Minister, Charles Maurice de Talleyrand-Périgord (1754–1838). Sister Charlotte was married in 1822 to Justin Thanaron, an officer in the French Army; and, all these marriages were funded by the besotted duke.

Sophia also built up her own *côterie* including General Baron de Lambot, secretary and *aide-de-camp* to the duke, and Abbé Briant, her own secretary and tutor. These creatures acted as her informers within the duke's circle, and it was at this time that rumours began to circulate that the muscular Sophia beat the duke if he did not comply with her wishes.

In 1824 Louis XVIII died and was succeeded by his brother the duke's old friend Charles X. Because of the influence of Madame Royale, Louis XVIII's daughter-in-law, Sophia was still barred from court. She did not give up her politicking though, but the gossips were to add more sinister activities. The duke was ageing and increasingly infirm with his right arm disabled by an old war wound. What would become of his vast property and money should he die? Sophia realized that she was not the sole heiress, but her influence on the duke could increase her own portion of any bequests and she could persuade the duke to bequeath a large amount of his wherewithal to a royal nominee. In this scheme Sophia set herself up as broker and persuaded the duke to make a will in favour of Charles X's grandchildren. Through General de Lambot she made her work known to the king who spurned her proposed return to Court with contempt. Thus rebuffed Sophia consulted her friend Talleyrand, who suggested that she cultivate the Duc d'Orléans.

Louis Philippe, Duc d'Orléans, had been born in 1773 and was the son of Louis XIV's cousin, who in turn had voted for that monarch's death during the revolution. D'Orléans was distrusted by the elder Bourbons but was tolerated at Court because of his royal birth, and although he was despised by the duke for his father's regicide, on Sophia's insistence he invited d'Orléans to St Leu and Chantilly. In time Sophia managed to get herself invited to the d'Orléans home and further persuaded the Duc de Bourbon to become godfather to the hated d'Orléans son, the Duc d'Aumale. It was a key facet of the next phase of Sophia's plan for advancement.

Sophia now transferred her proposal to the Duc d'Orléans, and after some horse-trading, d'Orléans agreed and a scheme was hatched to make the Duc d'Aumale the Duc de Bourbon's adopted son. Despite his advancing senility the duke greatly resisted the plan to make anyone from the hated House of Orléans any kind of heir to the Condé fortune. But, following tears, tantrums and beatings the duke relented and on 30 August 1829 he signed a will leaving two million francs in cash and estates worth eight million francs to Sophia and the rest of his property and vast fortune to the Duc d'Aumale. In exchange for achieving all this for the Orléans faction, Sophia was responsored at Court and was received in a friendly manner by Charles X, although she was still snubbed by Madame Royale.

Reigning as 'Queen of Chantilly', Sophia was now the centre of a glittering social circle which was soon to crumble. Unmindful of the fate of Louis XVI, Charles X suspended the constitution, was overthrown, and was forced into exile, and the Duc d'Orléans ascended the vacant throne as King Louis Philippe in 1830. Gritting his teeth the Duc de Bourbon recognized the new king. By now French society was humming with Sophia's loose behaviour and her capacity for meat and drink, and sex with high and low. She expanded her spies in the duke's circle by recruiting such as the lusty sergeant of *gen d'armes* (later known as M. 'X'), and a former hairdresser in La Rue de la Paix called Lecomte, who was one of the duke's valets.

Even so, the duke had his own devoted followers, people like Baron de Choulot, Baron de Surval his steward, his chaplain the Abbé de la Croix, and Manoury his body-servant, along with doctors Bonnie and Hostein his surgeon and dentist. For years his intimate friends had advised him to flee from the monstrous Sophia's clutches, but he had lacked the moral courage to do so. Yet, now that the hated Louis Philippe was king, he longed to be with his friend the erstwhile Charles X in exile, and this steeled him to plan an escape. It is said that he even prepared a new will leaving his fortune and estates to the grandchildren of Charles X.

Taking Baron de Surval into his confidence, the duke made his plans for flight. He secured the necessary funds for the journey and bought a new carriage and two post horses in Paris so that his means of flight was not recognizable to any of his friends, let alone the awful Sophia. Alas he needed a passport and was unable to obtain one, and by then Sophia had found out about the scheme, warning that if the duke did flee she would follow him; all this after beating the old man about the head leaving him with a black eye and several facial bruises. To her friends she explained that she had saved the senile duke from a suicide attempt in which he was hitting his head against a wall.

The duke, however, made new plans to escape, this time to Switzerland. The Baron de Choulot was entrusted with the arrangements and the ploy of dressing up an elderly retainer as the duke and getting him ready for dispatch to the coast as a decoy to draw off Sophia was all arranged and 27 August 1830 was fixed as the day of escape. Although it is certain that Sophia did not know of the second planned flight, she was suspicious of the duke's future plans. She reported these suspicions to the new king by letter and he replied post haste with the words: '*Empêché d'éloignement du prince a tout prix*' (Prevent the departure of the Prince at all cost).

On 26 August 1830 the duke retired early after several rubbers of whist with two gentlemen of the household, de Préjean and De la Villegontier. The duke's bedchamber at Château de St Leu was situated on the first floor of one of the wings. It was a commodious chamber with two sash-windows overlooking the parkland and had a low ceiling. Two doors led to an ante-room which opened at one end on to the grand gallery and the salon, and to a secret staircase leading to Sophia's apartments situated on the ground floor. The duke's large, heavy bed was set in an alcove.

Because the duke was crippled with the ailments of old age it took him a long time to prepare for bed. Assisted on that night by his surgeon, Dr Bonnie, who rubbed ointment into his legs and bandaged them, and by the valet Lecomte who dressed his master in his elaborate night attire, the duke was finally hoisted into bed. Candles were placed on the table beside the bed; a night-light burned in the empty fireplace and after the duke had bidden Lecomte to wake him at eight o'clock the next morning the old aristocrat was left to Morpheus.

At the prescribed hour Baron de Choulot arrived at the chateau and Dr Bonnie and Lecomte hammered on the duke's bedroom door to wake him to get ready for the flight. When no answer came they broke the door, which was never usually locked, and found the duke dead, his body resting against the north window. Once the curtains were drawn back the duke's predicament was more easily seen. Stiff and cold the duke's body was hanging from the *espagnolette* (cross-fastening) of the long window, suspended by two handkerchiefs passed one through the other, one being round the neck and the other, with the coronetted monogram 'B', tied to the window's cross-bar. The duke's knees were bent and his toes touched the ground; his arms hung at his side and his head was bent on his chest.

Strange to tell the handkerchief around the duke's neck was loose and had made no mark on the flesh; the duke's eyes were closed, but the tongue did not protrude from the mouth; a chair was overturned

by the window. Sophia made loud lamentation on discovering the
duke's death, but was kept out of the chamber of death, although the
servants, in their confusion, ran in and out of the room unhindered.
Baron de Choulot entered and viewed the body, and shortly
afterwards official examinations were undertaken. In fact there were
four examinations:

Procès verbal: This was carried out by the *maire* de St Leu, Pierre
Gervais Tailleur, with his assistant Leduc, in the presence of Dr
Letellier and Dr Bonnie. The two doctors issued a death certificate
citing suicide as the cause of death, but noted incorrectly that the
tongue was protruding from the mouth. They considered that the
duke had died at 2.00 a.m. having locked himself in his chamber.
Manoury the valet, however, noted that the door leading to the secret
staircase was unlocked when he entered the room, but had been later
bolted by an unknown hand before the investigation.

Procès corporal: This second examination was carried out by M. de la
Roussiliere Clouart, the magistrate from Enghein. He ordered that
the duke's body be cut down and placed on the bed. The two valets,
Manoury and Romanze found the knotted handkerchief difficult to
untie as they had been secured by a 'sailor's knot' (knots that a
fisherman's daughter might have tied, the gossips whispered!). The
duke's chamber was now sealed in the presence of Clouart and two
other magistrates from Pontoise, M. Foret de Boisbrunet and M.
Dinit. Two further doctors from Pontoise examined the body and
agreed with the suicide verdict.

Procès royal: When King Louis Philippe heard of the supposed
suicide of the Prince de Condé, he was greatly perturbed. As his son
was now chief heir to the Condé fortune, the whole episode would
have to be thoroughly investigated, authenticated and made public.
He dispatched the eminent jurist and President of the Chamber of
Peers, Baron Pasquier, and the chief of police and royal *aide-de-camp*,
Col de Rumigny, to investigate. The royal investigators and their
entourage arrived at St Leu on 28 August 1830. They were met by
the examining magistrate and that afternoon Baron Pasquier wrote to
the king that the circumstances of the duke's death were so
extraordinary that they needed 'a most careful enquiry'.

Post mortem: Baron Pasquier was assisted in the fourth examination
by the eminent Dr Charles Chrétien Henri Marc (1771–1841), of the

Academie de Medicine, and Jean Nicholas Marjolin (1780–1850), also of the *Academie*, and surgeon of the Hôtel Dieu. The two doctors carried out a post-mortem in the presence of Dr Bonnie and Col de Rumigny and were able to affirm that death was due to strangulation. As there was no sign of a struggle the doctors confirmed that the duke had committed suicide; indeed they held that the scratches and bruises observed on the body were due to the duke's cadaver being knocked against the window or the chair from which the duke had launched himself into eternity and knocked over. Later Dr Bonnie noted that he had asked Marc and Marjolin to record officially that the duke's right arm was incapacitated and that he was very lame; the doctors refused considering these factors to be irrelevant.

To this post-mortem was added an inquiry into the duke's previous state of mind, by M. Dupon, the Minister of Justice, and M. Bernard, the Attorney-General. The witnesses interviewed were all of the Sophia Dawes 'set' and they all attested that since the fall of Charles X, the duke had been depressed saying that he had lived too long. No one was interviewed who told them of the duke's planned flight from Sophia, or his well-known aversion to suicide.

During his examination the Attorney-General discovered some fragments of torn paper in the duke's writing in the fireplace of the murder chamber. On piecing them together he found them to read '*Je suis seulement à mourir*' (I have only to die), and expressing the wish that he desired to be buried at Vincennes near to his son. The Attorney-General was confirmed by the fragments in his belief that the duke had resolved to end his life and entered the fragments as *témoignage supplémentaire* (additional evidence). In his *Les Secrets de St Leu* (1831), the historian De Belleville, considered the fragments to be 'a plant' as did A. Chano in *L'Espangnolette de St Leu* (1841).

On 6 September 1830, after lying in state for six days, the Prince de Condé, Duc de Bourbon, was buried in the vaults of the Abbey de St Denis with his ancestors, in the presence of the wholly royal assembly including the eight-year-old Duc d'Aumale.

Hardly had the duke been sealed in the tomb than the gossips began to further speculate on the death. The most popular verdict was that Sophia Dawes, still known to them as Madame de Feuchères, had murdered the old man with the assistance of Sergeant 'X', who by then had disappeared under mysterious circumstances.

Others added to this that the king himself had instigated the murder; in fact, the death of the duke hung over Louis Philippe for the rest of his reign. For following the proving of the duke's will, the king took possession of the Condé fortune and estates on behalf of his son, the Duc d'Aumale, and Sophia received St Leu, Enghien and Mont-morency and two million francs. So the gossips believed that this alone was motive enough for murder.

The rumours about Sophia Dawes built up. The Abbé de la Croix sent a petition to Louis Philippe asking for an audience at which he might reveal 'the truth of the horrible murder committed on the person of the king's unfortunate relative'; a memo on the subject was also sent to the queen. The king side-stepped the audience and referred the Abbé to the Attorney-General who noted the Abbé's comments, but took no action. Next, the priest published a pamphlet alleging that the duke had revoked his will and had made another leaving his entire fortune and estates to the grandchildren of Charles X, the Duc de Bordeaux and his sister. All the while Sophia Dawes brazened the sneers of the nobility and appeared regularly at Court with the permission of the king.

Another combatant entered the wrangle over the dead duke's fortune. His cousin, the Prince Louis de Rohan, was angered that he had received nothing from the will, and he brought a private action in the civil court at Pontoise to have the duke's will annulled, on the grounds that the old man had had undue influence exerted on him by Sophia Dawes and her creatures. The judicial inquiry laid bare the sordid relationship the duke had had with Sophia, but the Prince Louis doubted the integrity of the presiding magistrates at Pontoise and had the case transferred to the Royal Court at Paris. This meant that the whole evidence had to be heard again before the elderly judge Antoine Edmé de la Huproye. The judge was thorough in his accumulation of the evidence. He subjected Sophia Dawes to searching interrogations in which she defended herself with a mixture of skill and audacity emphasizing the duke's supposed suicidal tendencies.

After a minute study of the evidence Judge de la Huproye recommended that Sophia be arrested and charged with the murder of the duke with the assistance of Sergeant 'X' and the Abbé Briant. King Louis Philippe was horrified; the arrest of Sophia could rock his throne as he was implicated in the financial dealings which had brought his son the Condé fortune, which would be forfeit if Sophia was convicted. By various means Louis Philippe forced the judge to resign and his report was suppressed; the Prince de Rohan's case was heard in camera in the Court of Accusation by judges who owed their position to the king. On 21 June 1831 the presiding judge ruled that there were no valid grounds on which to accuse Sophia. But the Prince de Rohan was not satisfied; an appeal was quashed as was his action to have the duke's will invalidated, so he wrote and published his broadside *Observations a mèsure que les vérites de la mort du duc de Bourbon, prince de Condé* (Observations as to the truth of the death of the Duke of Bourbon, Prince of Condé). In this he exposed Sophia Dawes's origins, her intrigues, and her terrorizing of the duke. He emphasized too with more than implication that she had been the duke's murderess. Sophia sued the prince for libel and won; he was fined and sentenced to two months imprisonment, while the copies of his broadsheet were ordered to be destroyed. The prince sought refuge in Bohemia and died in 1836.

During 1832 there occurred an event of great embarrassment to Sophia and her set. Sophia's nephew, James Dawes, Baron de Flassons, boasted that he was not in Paris on the night of the duke's death, and consequently he could not be accused of the duke's death as was his aunt; he also disputed with Sophia over an allowance she had given him. Sophia and James went to London and on their return James Dawes was taken ill at Calais and died within a few hours. Sophia had him buried at St Helens, Isle of Wight, and meanwhile in Paris the gossips accused her of murdering James to silence him as a dangerously loquacious accomplice. Indeed Sophia was to be arrested on the suspicion of murder and once again Louis Philippe intervened, and steps were taken to shun her in court circles.

Her position now undermined, Sophia Dawes sold most of her French property; the Chateau de St Leu was demolished and the estate used for building sites. Sophia now sailed for London with her niece, Sophia Thanaron, and her 90-year-old mother who was placed in a convent in Hammersmith where she was shortly to die. With the capital she had Sophia Dawes bought the large estate of Bure Homage, Christchurch, Bournemouth, and built a mansion thereon. She now became a lady bountiful to the local community and donated large sums of money to charity. In 1840 Sophia Dawes developed dropsy and she became a patient of the celebrated surgeon, Sir Astley Cooper (1768–1841), but she died of a heart attack in London on 15 December 1840.

Sophia Dawes, Madame de Feuchères, bequeathed most of her fortune to her now adopted child, her niece Sophia Thanaron. Her will, because she had given a false description in her marriage certificate, caused much litigation over certain charitable bequests but her papers and letters, which had been relevant to herself and the House of Orléans were returned to Louis Philippe; they included the compromising letter in which the king had urged Sophia to prevent the flight of the duke *à tout prix*. The correspondence was eventually published in a book written by Alexandre Lasalle in 1853, but the incriminating letter had disappeared long before the book was subsequently suppressed.

Years later the Sophia Dawes scandal was revived when Lecomte the valet was alleged to have made a deathbed confession in which he said that he had seen Sophia, accompanied by Sergeant 'X', entering the duke's ante-room on the night of the 26–27 August 1830. Again when General de Lambot died he is said to have left behind some papers docketed 'Material to explain the murder of M. le duc de Bourbon, Prince de Condé'. These papers were supposed to implicate Sophia as instigator of the crime with Sergeant 'X' as the actual murderer assisted by Lecomte. The scandal relating to Louis Philippe's plot with Sophia Dawes and the duke's murder was kept alive by the de Rohans and the French Press during the whole of Louis Philippe's reign.

In the 1950s, the distinguished clinical physician Sir Arthur Salusbury MacNalty (1880–1969) made a study of the Sophia Dawes case with regard to his study of the work of J. Glaister in *Medical Jurisprudence, Toxicology and Public Health* (1902) and C. C. H. Marc *Examen medico-legal des causes de la mort de Son Altesse Royale le prince de Condé* (1831). He noted that all the physicians who had examined the duke's body had confirmed the verdict of self-stangulation, but had grave doubts that this was so. In his papers Sir Arthur noted:

In strangulation death is caused by the constricting force being applied circularly round the neck. Usually the ligature is so tight as to produce a groove round the neck where it has been applied. *This does not seem to have occurred in the duke's case, for the knotted handkerchiefs were loose round the neck*. (It was considered, however, by Dr Marc and M. Marjolin that the age and impaired health of the duke contributed to his death by suspension, even though the handkerchief was loose).

In strangulation the proximate cause of death is asphyxia, or, as forensic medical experts have termed it, 'comato-asphyxia'. The internal *post-mortem* signs are those of asphyxia, and sub-pleural punctiform haemorrhages may be present. The face is usually pale, but may be dusky. The lips are blue and so may be the tongue. The eyes may be closed or partly open; the tongue may be either in the mouth or protruded. The appearance is usually peaceful. Professor Ogston stated that in 21 cases the features had a look of calmness and placidity, while in only one suicidal case had they the appearance of anxiety.' *In the Duke of Bourbon's case the face of the corpse was pale,* the eyes were closed, the tongue did not protrude from the lips, although *the procès verbal erroneously stated it did, and the face was placid.* In the course of the inquiry at Pontoise and afterwards in the investigation in the Royal Court of Paris, certain doctors, called as witnesses by Prince Louis de Rohan said the fact that the tongue was not protruding negatived suicide. This was a common medical belief then but not today. Another point about which great play was made by de Rohan's doctors was that because the tips of the toes rested upon the carpet the case was therefore, probably, one of homicide rather than of suicide. Formerly this was taught, but it is not confirmed by experienced authorities like Tardieu, Ogston, Casper, Glaister and others. Glaister's experience was that in every case observed by him some portion of the body was found resting on the ground. The amount of the body so resting may vary in extent from the major portion of the trunk downwards to merely the tips of the toes, exactly as the Duke of Bourbon's corpse was found. . . .

Certain of de Rohan's witnesses – both medical and non-medical – stated that the Duke's physical disabilities, especially his injured right arm, would have rendered him unable to make the complicated knots in the handkerchiefs. Dr Marc and M. Marjolin had not the opportunity of examining these knots, for they seem to have been untied when the body was cut down. Their existence depends on hearsay. It was also said that the Duke was incapable of tying a secure knot, but the handkerchief was loose round the neck, and the mere suspension, as the royal physician and royal surgeon both declared, might have strangled the Duke.

Sir Arthur believed that Louis Philippe was not implicated in the murder, but went on:

> But one cannot exonerate him from making a disgraceful compact with a low-born adventuress to secure the bulk of the Duke's fortune, and for advising that the Duke should be restrained from leaving France. The King certainly had a proper and fairly impartial investigation made of the tragedy, but he did wrong in interfering to prevent the arrest of Sophia. Political reasons and fears for the stability of his new throne mainly influenced him, and behind these considerations lurked the apprehension that he might have to yield the Condé fortune to the de Rohans.

Sir Arthur summed up:

> From the medical viewpoint, therefore, we can agree with the experts that the appearances of the Duke of Bourbon's body after death were consistent with self-inflicted strangulation. *It is the antecedent circumstances that are so suspicious.* The persistent fleecing of the Duke by the rapacious Sophia over so many years, the compact between Louis Philippe and Sophia to secure the wealth of the Condés for his son, the price being a share of the spoils and her readmission to Court; the introduction into the Condé household of Sophia's creatures and spies; the intimidation and even physical violence inflicted by Sophia on the old man; the meditated flight of the Duke from Sophia's clutches, with the prospect of a new will made in favour of Charles X's grandchildren; and, finally, Louis Philippe's compromising letter to Sophia saying that Bourbon was to be restrained from flight at any cost, *which Sophia may have taken as an authorization to dispose of him.* Although these circumstances did suggest a possibility of murder, a possibility which was enhanced by the communication between the Duke's bedroom

and Sophia's apartments; by the unbolting and subsequent bolting of the door to the secret staircase; and by the disappearance of the mysterious Sergeant X, who was alleged to have been smuggled out of St. Leu in Sophia's carriage and taken by her to Paris.

It is undoubted that the duke led a dissipated life, and his appetite for lowlife sex may have cost him his life, averred Sir Arthur, who continued: 'certain non-medical evidence suggested a possible murder in which Sophia Dawes was implicated'. If so another royal duke was murdered for expediency at which his fellow royals averted their eyes.

10

To Kill a Queen

Queen Victoria's assumption of sovereignty of Great Britain and Ireland was a great novelty. For far longer than people could remember, the throne had been occupied by a series of old, eccentric men, whose appearance was as unsavoury as their habits, and who had, to a man, inspired indifference, derision, pity and distaste in equal portions. Victoria, however, began her reign at the age of nineteen on a wave of romance.

As a historical signpost the Victorian Age began at twelve minutes past two on the morning of 20 June 1837, when the last fitful spark of life was finally extinguished from the body of HRH Prince William Henry, the third son of George III and Queen Charlotte, who had ruled for seven years as King William IV. He was succeeded by his niece, Georgina Charlotte Augusta Alexandrina Victoria, the only daughter of HRH Prince Edward, Duke of Kent, and his wife, Her Serene Highness Mary Louisa Victoria of Saxe-Coburg-Saalfeld. The last of the Hanoverian monarchs, Victoria's pedigree was not impressive. The poet Percy Bysshe Shelley had described William IV and his brothers – whom Victoria called her 'wicked uncles' – as 'the dregs of their dull race' and posterity was not to rescue them from that opinion. Yet if all other monarchs are forgotten, posterity will remember Victoria. Her reign was to last for sixty-four years.

Queen Victoria was a person of great character contradictions. She fell heir to the Hanoverian traits of inconsiderateness, bluntness, hardness, deviousness and excitablity; yet, she could be unselfish, tactful, sympathetic, direct and patient in a most un-Hanoverian way. And, importantly, when the chips were down she had great strength of character and showed enormous courage when threatened by assassination.

The first attempt on her life took place on 10 June 1840, a few months after her marriage to Prince Albert of Saxe-Coburg-Gotha. At six o'clock on that day the queen and the prince were setting off for a drive to visit Victoria's mother, the Duchess of Kent, in the queen's new low phaeton, up Constitution Hill. In attendance were Her Majesty's equerries, Col Buckley and Sir Edward Bowater. Suddenly she heard an explosion as a young man called Edward Oxford was seen to snatch a pistol from his breast pocket and fire at the royal party from a range of about six yards. The queen recorded in her *Journal* that Albert had exclaimed: 'My God! Don't be alarmed!' She had smiled at his excitement and the next instant saw 'a little man on the footpath with his arms folded over his breast, a pistol in each hand.' Prince Albert was most protective as Victoria was four month's pregnant.

Edward Oxford aimed at the queen again, but Victoria ducked. Then a Mr John William Millais (the father of the future artist John Everett Millais) on the footpath, seized Oxford and the royal attendants closed in. The crowd shouted 'Kill him! Kill him!' as Victoria and Albert sped up the hill to the Duchess of Kent's home in Belgrave Square, at the centre of a hubbub of gentry who had been riding in Green Park and now formed up into a spontaneous escort. Oxford was committed to Newgate prison.

Later, Prince Albert showed Victoria the pistols Edward Oxford had used and which, she recorded 'might have *finished me off*'. The pistols themselves were to give rise to a mystery. The pieces were silver mounted with the monogram 'ER'. The initials resurrected the old chestnut about the Duke of Cumberland, King of Hanover. The monogram was interpreted by the gossips as being for *Ernestus Rex*. The rumour had long gone round Victoria's circle that Cumberland had wished to have Victoria removed from the throne and replace her himself. Victoria always hotly denied that Cumberland was opposed to her.

Baron Stockmar, King Leopold's agent, however, in a conversation with George Anson, Prince Albert's treasurer and secretary – who had incidentally, visited Oxford in prison – averred that he 'did not think the King of Hanover would be likely to be implicated in the affair, for tho' a wicked man and possessed of a conscience callous to the perpetration of most crimes – he had a peculiar feeling about those which were contrary to his notion of a gentlemanlike crime – conniving at the murder of his own family, would come under a class which he would not be guilty of. . . .'

In high places though the attempt was taken very much to heart. The 2nd Viscount Melbourne, her Prime Minister and the Marquis of Normanby, her Home Secretary, took the crime very seriously. Even the Clerk to the Privy Council, C. C. F. Greville – not given to pronouncements of a pro-Victoria nature – considered that she had acted with 'perfect courage and self-possession and exceeding propriety'.

The Press had been excluded from Oxford's initial examination at the Home Office. The under-secretary of state, Fox Maule, collected data on the case for the Prime Minister and from this data Oxford, an undersized youth, was held for trial on a charge of high treason. This trial was duly conducted on 9 July 1840 at the Central Criminal Court before Lord Denman.

Edward Oxford's defence was one of insanity, and his behaviour in court went a long way to substantiate the case during the trial. In court he appeared completely indifferent to what was going on and seemed more interested in the notoriety he had caused. When he was placed at the Bar, to plead to the indictment, he enquired of the warder next to him if there was anyone present of great social distinction. Oxford was seen to smile a great deal during the case and he frequently laughed out loud when the indictment was being read. Not the sordid, brutal villain of the usual murder trail, Edward Oxford was a slight, delicate young man with a sensitive face and large eyes.

The prosecution team was lead by the Attorney-General, Sir John Campbell, and the Solicitor-General, Sir Thomas Wilde, who were matched against Mr Sidney Taylor and Mr Bodkin for the defence. Taylor and Bodkin had a very difficult task. They had to prove that Oxford was not responsible for his actions and thus win a judgment that would substitute a life sentence for that of execution. There was no doubt of the guilt of their client; he made no pretence of innocence and readily admitted to the crime.

Sir John Campbell opened the case with comments on the nature of high treason with which Edward Oxford was charged. He then began a potted history of the accused and a description of the events which had led up to the assassination attempt. Edward Oxford had been born at Birmingham on 9 April 1822, and had been brought to London while still very young and had been sent to school in the Borough of Lambeth. On completing his education, Edward Oxford had worked in several hostelries as a barman, but never stayed in one place of employment very long. When he was planning his assassination of Queen Victoria, Oxford was living in lodgings at 6 West Place, West Square , Lambeth, not far from the Elephant & Castle.

From witnesses' testimonies it was established that Oxford had bought a pair of pistols for £2 from a person called Hayes of Blackfriars Road on 4 May 1840. At the same time he had purchased a flask of gunpowder; later he was to obtain percussion caps from an old school friend called Grey and procured some bullets from an unknown source. To tone up his skill at pistol firing he soon became a well-known figure at the shooting galleries which were then to be found in the Strand and Leicester Square. Having practised to his satisfaction Oxford then set forth to carry out the queen's assassination.

On the afternoon of Wednesday 10 June, about four o'clock, Edward Oxford entered Green Park. He watched Prince Albert returning home from an engagement at Woolwich, and was well aware that the prince and the queen would soon emerge for their evening drive. As their route invariably included Constitution Hill, Oxford took up his position there. A short while later the outriders appeared and the little procession proceeded in the direction of Hyde Park Corner, with the prince riding on Queen Victoria's right.

Oxford was now located some 120 yards from Buckingham Palace, and his behaviour was beginning to look a little odd. He was nervously pacing up and down with his arms under the lapels of his coat. No one interpreted the eccentric behaviour as a prelude to an assassination attempt.

As the royal carriage passed him, Edward Oxford fired one pistol. He missed, and now taking his second pistol out he fired again; once more he missed and the bullet struck the wall on the opposite side of the road. It seems that the crowd thought that the pistols had been fired by someone else as Victoria's carriage sped away and to make quite clear to all that he had done the deed Oxford shouted 'It was I'.

After his removal to custody the police searched Oxford's rooms and came across a locked box, which contained a remarkable collection of militaria, from a sword and scabbard to a bullet mould. With them was a series of notebooks and strange documents which indicated that Edward Oxford was mentally unbalanced. One document told of a totally fictitious military group called 'Young England' (not to be confused with the group of the same name set up by George Smythe and John Manners to revolt against parliamentary discipline).

Along with the documents in the box were letters purporting to be orders addressed to Oxford by one A. W. Smith, 'Secretary' to the 'Young England' group. One letter added to the mystery of the monogram 'ER' on the pistols; it read: 'Sir, You are requested to attend to-night, as there is an extraordinary meeting to be holden, in consequence of having received some communications of an important nature from Hanover. You must attend, and if your master will not give you leave, you must come in defiance of him – A. W. Smith, Secretary.

Mr Oxford, at Mr Robinson's, 'Hog-in-the-Pound', Oxford Street.'

The authorities were satisfied that Oxford had no connection with continental revolutionaries or political factions and the 'Hanover letter' was suppressed (probably at Queen Victoria's insistence because of the Cumberland implications).

Indeed, it was clear that Oxford had lived in a fantasy world inspired by the famous Cato Street Conspiracy of 1820 when a group of men under the leadership of Arthur Thistlewood had plotted to murder all the ministers in the Earl of Liverpool's Cabinet.

All these facts were related in court by the Attorney-General.

Sidney Taylor then addressed the jury on behalf of the prisoner and underlined the 'bad record' of the Oxford family. Oxford's grandfather, testified his grandmother Sophia Oxford, had been a seaman who had died in Greenwich Hospital, and had been a 'coloured man and had been addicted to large outbursts of intemperance'; Oxford's father, 'a mulatto jeweller', had also been an 'unbalanced person' who 'acted with the greatest cruelty to his wife' Hannah Oxford; in court this Hannah Oxford attested to how her husband had tried to murder her with poison 'several times'. Taylor showed too that Edward Oxford had suffered from 'fits of depression', and 'a marked craving' for notoriety. A plea of insanity was entered backed by evidence supplied by Dr Connolly of Hanwell Lunatic Asylum.

The jury found Edward Oxford 'guilty, but insane'. He was ordered to be detained 'during Her Majesty's pleasure' and was removed to Bethlehem Royal Hospital, Moorfields, and placed in the block for the criminally insane. The Rev. E. O'Donoghue noted in his *The Story of the Bethlehem Hospital* (T. Fisher Unwin 1914) that Oxford had as neighbours, James Hadfield, the lunatic ex-soldier in the 15th Light Dragoons, who had fired two pistol shots at George III while the king was visiting Drury Lane Theatre on 15 May 1800; and also Margaret Nicholson, who claimed to be the rightful monarch of Britain and who had stabbed the king on 2 August 1786.

In time Oxford was also detained at Broadmoor, and was released twenty-seven years later and went under surveillance to Australia, where he remained until he died. In her *Journal* for 22 September 1867, Queen Victoria noted Oxford's release and commented that he had expressed 'deep grief' at his offence.

The second attempt on Queen Victoria's life took place in 1842. According to her *Journal* on 29 May, when riding in The Mall, Prince Albert had noticed 'a little swarthy, ill-looking rascal' who pointed a pistol, fired, but missed at a distance of two paces. The would-be assassin then slipped away into the crowd. Queen Victoria was certain that the man would try again. Saying that she could not endure being 'shut up for days' in the palace with an assassination threat hanging over her, she insisted that they drive out the next day as if nothing had happened. So on Sunday 30 May at 6.30 p.m., the queen and Prince Albert proceeded down Constitution Hill with her Equerry-in-Waiting, Col Arbuthnot leading the escort, with Col Wylde also flanking the carriage. Contrary to tradition, Queen Victoria had that day dispensed with her lady-in-waiting, Emma, Lady Portman, having to be in attendance. Baroness Bunsen remembered Victoria saying, 'I must expose the lives of my gentlemen, but I will not those of my ladies.' Lady Portman stayed behind and sulked.

Some 300 yards from Buckingham Palace the man Prince Albert had seen appeared and fired at the royal party whose pace had now increased on Col Arbuthnot's orders. Once more the bullet flew harmlessly between the carriage wheels, as it rattled on to safety. The smoke from the pistol though, covered the face of Col Wylde. Prince Albert later wrote thus to his father, Duke Ernest of Saxe-Coburg-Saalfeld: 'It was at the same spot where Oxford fired at us, two years ago, with the difference only, that Oxford was standing on our left with his back to the garden wall. The shot must have passed under the carriage, for he lowered his hand. . . .'

The Times recorded that 'before the miscreant could have time to put [in] fresh priming, a soldier of the 2nd battalion of Scotch Fusilier Guards, quartered at Portman Street barracks, and who happened to be casually passing "pinned" him. . . .' First, the assassin was taken to Gardner's Lane police station and thence to the Home Office for questioning. *The Times* went on: 'He is 20 years of age, his height five feet five inches. His person somewhat corpulent; bearing notwith-standing the latter circumstances a very strong resemblance to Oxford. He was dressed in a dark frock coat rather too large for him, a light waistcoat, black stock, with a pin in it, drab trousers, boots, and a wide-brimmed hat . . . one particular circumstance observable in the prisoner's appearance is, that he has a peculiar rolling eye . . . several of his relations and acquaintances describe him as being of a very quarrelsome disposition.'

The prisoner turned out to be one John Francis of Great Tichfield Street, a journeyman carpenter. He was tried for high treason. Francis was found guilty and sentenced to be hanged, drawn and quartered.

Queen Victoria was anxious that the death penalty should not be carried out and discussed the matter with her judges. She ultimately decided to reprieve Francis whose punishment was altered to one of transportation for life, to Norfolk Island, a volcanic isle in the Pacific. Francis was released in 1867 on 'ticket-of-leave', the old licence to be at large before expiry of sentence.

On the day after Queen Victoria's clemency towards John Francis was made known, the third attempt on her life took place as she drove to the Chapel Royal, St James's, on Sunday 3 July 1842, with Leopold, King of the Belgians. This time the assassin was 'a deformed lad' called John William Bean of St James's Buildings, Clerkenwell. His gun misfired and Victoria knew nothing of the attempt until her return to Buckingham Palace.

In due time Queen Victoria told her advisers that such attacks on her life would continue as long as they were treated by the law as acts of high treason. She averred that the law gave the crimes too much romance and glamour, and suggested that the offenders should be given a good whipping and a stiff term of imprisonment; in this way she was convinced the attempts would stop. On her advice the Cabinet brought in a Bill making such attacks on the sovereign 'high misdemeanours', punishable by transportation for seven years, or imprisonment with or without a term of hard labour and a court option of whipping. The Bill became law on 16 July 1842 and Bean was sentenced to eighteen months imprisonment on 25 August.

The law had some effect as Queen Victoria had the respite of seven years before the next attempt on her life. The fourth attempt took place on 19 May 1849, some three months before her planned Irish visit, by a mad Irishman called William Hamilton. From her comments it is clear that she was more aware of her attacker being Irish than insane. It seems, according to the examination made by Mr Hall, Chief Metropolitan Magistrate at the Home Office, Downing Street, that William Hamilton, an unemployed man from Adare, Co. Limerick, had had a madcap idea of frightening the English Queen with a home-made pistol. In the event he borrowed his landlady's pistol and lay in wait for the queen to return from her birthday celebrations.

Since there was no bullet in the pistol, Hamilton was transported for seven years under Sir Robert Peel's new law. With Hanoverian directness, the three-year-old Princess Helena summed up the royal household's attitude: 'Man shot, tried to shoot dear mama, must be punished.'

On the 27 June 1850, as she was leaving Cambridge House, after visiting her dying uncle, Adolphus, Duke of Cambridge, Victoria was approached by a well-dressed young man. Suddenly, and before the police could intervene, he struck her with a cane, crushing her bonnet over her forehead and leaving a weal across her cheek. The Queen was riding with Prince Albert and the Princess of Prussia, and the Prince of Wales, Prince Alice and Prince Alfred. There was no escort, only a lady-in-waiting, Fanny Jocelyn. This, the queen's fifth assailant, was Robert Pate of Duke St, St James's, a retired lieutenant of the 10th Hussars. He was seized and manhandled by the crowd.

Victoria retained her presence of mind and after being revived by Fanny Jocelyn, called to her footman riding behind to 'Go on, I am unhurt'. Her vulnerability without an escort made the queen think 'more than usually' of the attempts on her life. Victoria had been hurt, only the deep brim of her bonnet had saved from worse than a black eye and a headache. The evening she went to the Royal Opera House where she received a five-minute standing ovation and a rendition of 'God Save The Queen' from the Italian cast. One of her Lords-in-waiting, the Earl of Hardwick, suggested to her that her battering was almost worthwhile for the popular affection it had elicited. She was not amused, and wrote in her *Journal*:

> Certainly it is very hard & very horrid, that I, a woman – a defenceless young woman [*Victoria was thirty-one and had recently given birth to her seventh child, Arthur, Duke of Connaught*] & surrounded by my children, should be exposed to insults of this kind, & be unable to go out quietly for a drive . . . for a man to strike *any woman* is most brutal, & I, as well as everyone else, think this *far* worse than any attempt to shoot, which, wicked as it is, is at least more comprehensible & more courageous.

Pate was tried for assault and sentenced to seven years transportation; the whipping was remitted.

Two decades were to pass before the sixth attempt on Queen Victoria's life, two days after the Thanksgiving Service at St Paul's Cathedral for the recovery of the Prince of Wales from typhoid, 27 February 1872. Of all the outrages during her lifetime this was to frighten Queen Victoria more than the other attempts because of its unexpectedness. The incident occurred as the Queen was returning to Buckingham Palace after a drive through Regent's Park. The perpetrator one Arthur O'Connor of Church Row, Houndsditch, a clerk for an oil and colour manufacturer was an undersized, scrofulous youth of eighteen armed with a flintlock pistol, who had watched the Queen leave the palace at 4.30 p.m. in her open landau with Lady Jane Churchill at her side and Prince Arthur and Prince Leopold sitting opposite. Her Highland Servant, John Brown, was on the box and two equerries, General Sir Arthur Hardinge and Lord Charles Fitzroy, rode on either side of the carriage. The smartly turned-out equipage was completed with outriders in front and grooms at the rear.

As the Queen completed her drive, Arthur O'Connor scaled the ten-foot high railing, unobserved and racing across the courtyard took up position at the garden entrance to the palace to intercept the carriage. The Queen's *Journal* takes up the story:

> Brown had just got down to let down the steps, and Jane C. was just getting out when suddenly someone appeared at my side, whom I at first imagined was a footman, going to lift off the wrapper. Then I perceived that it was someone unknown, peering above the carriage door. . . . Involuntarily, in a terrible fright, I threw myself over Jane C., calling out 'Save me,' and heard a scuffle and voices! I soon recovered myself sufficiently to stand up and turn around, when I saw Brown holding a young man tightly. . . . Brown kept hold of him till several of the police came in. All turned and asked if I was hurt, and I said 'Not at all.'

O'Connor had brandished his flintlock in front of Victoria's face with the intention of frightening the Queen into releasing Fenian prisoners. The Fenians were a secret society of Irishmen whose aims were to bring about the separation of Ireland from England and establish an Irish Republic. These Irish-American revolutionaries had been active since their establishment as the Irish Republican Brotherhood by James Stephens in 1858.

Prince Arthur tried to jump over the carriage but was too slow; John Brown seized O'Connor and held him until help came. It transpired that O'Connor had intended to present his petition for the release of the Fenians, then held by the British government, to the Queen as she knelt at prayer at St Paul's. He had attempted to hide in the cathedral on the eve of the Thanksgiving, but had been discovered and removed by the verger.

At his examination it was shown that Arthur O'Connor's great-uncle had been the Chartist leader, Feargus O'Connor, and that the lad had confused Chartism (a movement of the late 1830s demanding parliamentary reform) with Fenianism; it was clear that he had hero-worshipped the fiery Irish Chartist. Arthur O'Connor came from a family 'in reduced circumstances', but which had been able to send him to the church school of St-Dunstans-in-the-East, Fleet St, and had obtained for him an indenture to a law stationer. O'Connor had had a history of ill-health from tuberculosis to mental derangement. The day before the Thanksgiving service he had bought a flintlock at a pawnshop in Southwark for four shillings (20p), but it had proved utterly useless. Instead of ammunition O'Connor had stuffed the barrel with wads of paper and bits of leather.

Queen Victoria rewarded John Brown for his quick action. She gave him a gold medal and a £25 annuity, much to the Prince of Wales's disgust; HRH complained that Prince Arthur had behaved just as gallantly but received nothing but a gold tie-pin. Queen Victoria paid no heed and exhibited her strategic deafness when assessing the Prince of Wales's opinions.

Playing to the gallery in his broad Scots accent, John Brown appeared at Bow Street Court as the chief witness in the O'Connor trial which was heard before the chief magistrate Sir Thomas Henry. Prince Leopold also appeared to give testimony before the grand jury. In time the case came for trial at the Central Criminal Court and O'Connor (against his counsel's advice) pleaded guilty. Dr Harrington Tuke, of the lunatic asylum at Chiswick (where O'Connor's great-uncle Feargus O'Connor had been a patient) testified to hereditary insanity. Nevertheless the jury found O'Connor 'perfectly sane' and fit to plead and the judge, Sir Anthony Cleasby, sentenced him to one year's imprisonment at hard labour, with twenty strokes of the birch.

Queen Victoria fumed at her prime minister, W. E. Gladstone, at the 'extreme leniency' of the sentence and implored him to have O'Connor transported lest he try to assault her again. The Queen was right. After he had served his sentence O'Connor was persuaded to go to Australia, but he returned to England soon after. On 5 May 1874 he was arrested while loitering with intent outside Buckingham Palace. This time he was committed by court order to Hanwell Lunatic Asylum.

During 2 March 1882, a crowd of boys from Eton were grouped at Windsor Station to cheer Queen Victoria and Princess Beatrice when they arrived by train from London at 5.30 p.m. Once settled in the carriage by the Queen's Private Secretary, Sir Henry Ponsonby, the royal party set off for Windsor Castle with the faithful John Brown on the box. They had hardly gone a couple of dozen yards when Victoria heard an explosion which she thought had come from a locomotive. In fact another attempt, the seventh and final one, had been made on her life. This time the weapon was a six-chambered rapid-fire revolver.

The bullet missed and before the assassin could fire again two Eton boys rushed forward and belaboured him with their umbrellas. This time John Brown was upstaged and seemed bemused by the whole affair. On the way to the police station, the culprit revealed to Superintendent George Hayes, of the Windsor police that he was Roderick Maclean, a starving Scottish poet. On 5 May 1882 Queen Victoria recieved 900 Eton boys in the Quadrangle and addressed her 'protectors' personally.

Maclean was tried at Reading Assizes, Berkshire, for high treason. Two letters had been found in his effects which had relevance to the case. The first related to some verses that Maclean had sent to the queen. On Buckingham Palace stationary the letter read: 'Lady Biddulph is obliged to return Mr Maclean his verses. The Queen never accepts manuscript poetry.' The other letter summed up his grievances: 'I should not have done this crime,' Her Majesty's Government was addressed, 'had you, as you should have done, allowed me the 10s [*50p*] per week instead of offering the insultingly small sum of 6s [*30p – probably parish relief*] per week and expecting me to live on it. So you perceive the great good a little money might have done, had you not treated me as a fool and set me more than ever against those bloated aristocrats ruled by the old lady, Mrs Vic, who is a licensed robber in all senses. Roderick Maclean. March 2nd, 1882. Waiting Room, G.W.R.'

Never before had a poet taken such drastic measures. It appeared too that Maclean had suffered from a brain injury after a fall in 1866, and had been discharged from the Bath and Somerset Lunatic Asylum in 1881.

Maclean appeared in court in a green greatcoat with a worn velvet collar, and a flowing black tie partially concealing a frayed shirt. His defending counsel, Montague Williams QC, recalled later: 'With a vacant, imbecile, expression he kept glancing hither and thither about the crowded Court'. The defendant was found 'not guilty on the ground of insanity' and was ordered to be detained. Once again Victoria was furious at the verdict. 'If that is the law,' she stormed at the hapless W. E. Gladstone, 'the law must be altered.' Victoria's influence on her ministers prevailed and the law was altered in 1883 which substituted the verdict 'guilty but insane'. This law remained on the statute books until 1964 when Parliament restored the original statutory verdict of 'not guilty on the ground of insanity.'

The seven attacks on Queen Victoria always had a decided effect on the public. As a correspondent in the *Spectator* wrote on 4 June 1842:

> The Queen and People were drawn into more intimate communion. Compassion for the woman – young, a mother, and present to the view in all the most engaging relations of life – thus exposed to senseless perils, from which no general loyalty, no guards, and scarcely any precautions might be able to shield her . . . all these considerations prompted a display of popular feeling that had a deeper seat than mere 'loyalty' or attachment to the office of the Sovereign.

Although republicanism had periods of flourishing – particularly during Victoria's self-inflicted remoteness as the 'Widow of Windsor' – the nation was deeply shocked by the outrages. None of the attempts was associated with bloody revolution, although they all had features in common. With one exception, none of the Queen's assailants was of mature years, and all showed signs of mental derangement. Roderick Maclean was clearly insane as was Robert Pate and Edward Oxford, but the others were more of the 'half-baked loner' than the raving lunatic, and joined the ranks of such solitary regicides as the fanatical Dominican monk, Jacques Clement who stabbed Henry III of France in 1589, and Francois Ravaillac who assassinated Henry IV of France in 1610.

11

The Death of
King Ludwig of Bavaria

MODERN RESEARCH SUGGESTS THAT THE KING DID
NOT COMMIT SUICIDE

Queen Victoria was always adamant about the subject: King
Ludwig II of Bavaria, although he had once talked to her with his
eyes tightly shut, was not mad ... just eccentric, like all the
melancholic Wittelsbachs. But in his own kingdom these 'eccentrici-
ties' and his neurotic shyness were being assessed in a different light.
The king must be mad ... look at the way he spent vast sums on his
magnificent castles. Then there were his private performances of the
Wagner operas; and the unmarried King was becoming more and
more of a recluse. So it was decided that the 40-year-old King, the son
of Maximillian II of Bavaria and his wife Marie of Prussia, would be
investigated for insanity. A case would be prepared by Germany's
renowned psychiatrist Dr Bernard von Gudden, to be presented to
Ludwig's uncle and the potential Regent, HRH Prince Luitpold von
Bayern (Ludwig's brother Otto was insane, and ultimately only
became king in a nominal sense).

Von Gudden built up his case from both court witnesses and
backstairs gossip and his document, the *Arstliches Gutachten*, was
handed over to Prince Luitpold. Later the Prusso-German diplomat
and statesman Prince Otto von Bismarck was to describe the
document as 'rakings from the King's wastepaper basket and
cupboards'. Nevertheless the document was accepted by Luitpold
who considered his actions quite legal; according to the Bavarian

constitution a monarch could be deposed if he had been incapable of governing for more than a year. Ludwig had neglected his duties consistently so was believed to be unfit to rule. So, on Wednesday 9 June 1886, Prince Luitpold prepared a proclamation which declared that his royal nephew was no longer king; Luitpold declared himself Regent. Ludwig was not to receive the proclamation.

A state Commission headed by the Baron von Crailsheim, Foreign Minister and Minister of the Household, set out for the Schloss Neuschwanstein on 9 June to interview the King. On arrival at the castle they found the gates barred against them. After huffing and puffing at the gates and a humiliating parley amongst themselves at the nearby village of Hohenschwangau they returned to Munich. In England Queen Victoria was to note that 'they had bungled it'.

On 11 June a second Commission set out under guard and on this occasion Dr von Gudden and his medical warders had no difficulty in gaining access to the castle, and entering the King's private apartments. As the King was informed of their arrival, von Gudden, who had taken the precaution of having a strait-jacket with him and a bottle of chloroform, expected trouble. But, the six-foot tall King entered in a state of complete calmness. Immediately von Gudden stepped forward and delivered a prepared speech: 'Your Majesty, this is the saddest duty of my life that I hereby have to inform Your Majesty that a proclamation has been issued by HRH Prince Luitpold which declares that forthwith he is taking over the regency of Bavaria due to your Majesty's mental health being in question.'

Von Gudden assured the King that he 'would improve greatly . . . in time'. Ludwig challenged the doctor that he could not declare him insane as he had not examined him, nor had he seen him since 1872. Von Gudden produced the *Gutachten* and on its 'evidence' King Ludwig II became a virtual prisoner of the doctors.

Ludwig was informed by von Gudden at four o'clock on the morning of 12 June that three coaches were waiting in the courtyard of Schloss Neuschwanstein to take them to Schloss Berg on Lake Starnberg. The King knew the castle well, he had spent a great deal of his youth there and those memories were overlaid with romantic thoughts about his favourite and beautiful cousin, Empress Elizabeth of Austria, wife of the Emperor Franz Joseph. Inside the coach Ludwig could not fail to note that the doors were locked and made to be unlocked from the outside only. A glance through the window too would reveal that his coach was the centre of three and that the cortège was heavily guarded by outriders. Thus Ludwig left his beloved Schloss where he had said he had now passed through the 'saddest hours' of his life, never to return.

The royal party arrived at Schloss Berg at midday. Ludwig commented on the new grilles being fitted to the windows to prevent his escape and the peepholes being bored in the doors so that he could be constantly observed. Dr von Grashey, von Gudden's son-in-law, had been instructed to prepare for a mental patient. Tired, Ludwig retired to bed early and was kept there until 8 a.m. on the morning of 13 June 1886, Whit Sunday, the date marked out by fate for his death.

Accompanied by Dr von Gudden, Ludwig set off for a walk about 11 a.m. and they made their way through the grounds and the woods by the lakeside; warders and police followed at a discreet distance. They were to report later that the king and his doctor paused to sit on a wooden bench and chat. They returned to the Schloss between noon and 1 p.m. for lunch which the king ate alone. While lunching with his young assistant, Dr Franz Carl von Mueller, von Gudden remarked that he and the king were to walk again that evening, but this time the warders and the gendarmes would not be needed. Von Mueller demurred but the older man said: 'The king is but a child', and that neither would be in any danger. The afternoon of Whit Sunday passed uneventfully with domestic and recreational activities, and around five o'clock Ludwig was served with a substantial snack and settled down to consume a large quantity of alcohol.

By 6.45 p.m. the king and his doctor were setting out for their walk; both had coats, hats and umbrellas. Von Gudden informed the castle staff that they would be back by 8 o'clock for supper. They never returned alive.

Historic tradition tells us that when the couple had not returned by 8 p.m. a search was undertaken on the orders of the Chief Gendarme, Johann Lauterbach. He noted that he had seen Ludwig and von Gudden make for the lake at 6.45 p.m. and to underline his statement he said he had 'heard the local clock strike 6.45'. Lauterbach's gendarmes searched and re-searched the grounds but found nothing. By 10.30 p.m. it was raining heavily and windy. Then the searchers' guttering lanterns picked out two coats and hats and umbrellas, the very ones belonging to Ludwig and the doctor, by the side of the lake. Dr von Mueller and the Schloss Administrator, von Hurber, then saw two large black objects 'swimming' on the surface of the lake. Investigations showed that they were the cadavers of the king and the doctor. Taken to the side of the lake artificial respiration was carried out for an hour; but at midnight Dr von Mueller declared: 'His Majesty King Ludwig II of Bavaria is dead, and likewise his doctor'.

For ten years or so from 1975, Jeanne Handzic, a legal proofreader in the City of London, and an amateur historian, studied the demise of Ludwig and was more and more suspicious of the testimony that had been presented at the inquiry following the discovery of the bodies. In 1985 she called to question this testimony of the 'witnesses' and particularly commented on the watch which witnesses had said was hanging out of Ludwig's waistcoat when he was fished out of the water.

The watch had stopped it was said at 6.54 p.m. From this it was inferred that the king had died at that precise time (von Gudden's watch had stopped at 8.10 p.m.). But, said Ms Handzic, it would take at least two minutes for the watch to stop. So if the Chief Gendarme had been correct and Ludwig left the Schloss at 6.45 p.m., or so, he must have been dead around 6.52 p.m. Based on a personal examination of the grounds Ms Handzic averred that it was 'physically impossible for the two men to have walked the 800 metres from the Schloss to the point where their bodies were found in the lake' in just seven minutes.

Historic tradition shows that von Gudden is likely to have been drowned too because he was either, trying to stop Ludwig from committing suicide, or from escaping his custody. It had been noted by one of the king's suite, Count Freiherr von Washington, that there had been several people on board boats on the lake and that they might have been in readiness to effect the king's escape; indeed it was suggested that the Empress Elizabeth had planned an escape to her own family residence a mile and a half across the lake. And what about the coats? Tradition takes care of them too; either the doctor pulled off the king's coat in a struggle, or he had taken it off himself prior to swimming out to an escape boat. It was suggested too that the king had strangled the 62-year-old doctor and had then had a heart attack and drowned. This was backed up by 'witnesses' who averred

(*Above*) William II, bynamed Rufus (r. 1087–1100), was shot dead in the New Forest during a hunting expedition.

(*Above*) Edward II (r. 1307–27) was cruelly murdered at Berkeley Castle, Gloucestershire, and buried near the high altar of the cathedral of St Peter and the Holy Trinity, Gloucester.

(*Right*) Richard III (r. 1483–85) was the victim of vicious Tudor propaganda. His supposed murder of King Henry VI, his own brother, his wife and two nephews remains unproven in every instance.

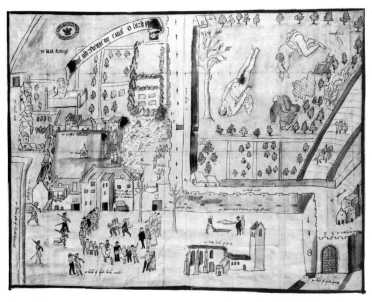

Scene at Kirk o'Field after the murder of Henry Stewart, Lord Darnley, in 1567.

The gallant *Eagle*, soaring vp on high:
Beares in his beake, *Treasons* discouery.
MOVNT, noble EAGLE, with thy happy prey,
And thy rich *Prize* to th'*King* with speed conuay.

This woodcut from Vicar's *Mischeefes Mystery* (1617) cartoons the incredible receipt of the letter warning James VI & I of the Gunpowder Plot by Robert Cecil via Lord Mounteagle (lampooned by the eagle in flight).

The assassination of Henry VI, King of France, on 14 May 1610, by François Ravaillac.

Louis XVI says farewell to his soon to be executed wife Marie Antoinette and his family before his own execution in 1793. His son, the Dauphin Louis Charles, who clings to him, may have escaped from the regicides of the French Revolution.

HRH Ernest, Duke of Cumberland, King of Hanover 1771–1851, one of Queen
Victoria's 'wicked uncles' accused of all kinds of human baseness by public gossip.

(*Left*) Edward Oxford, sketched by T. P. Wilson in the dock at the Old Bailey, Monday, 22 June 1840. Oxford had attempted to assassinate Queen Victoria as she travelled in a carriage up London's Constitution Hill.

(*Above*) John Francis, sketched from life at the Old Bailey. Francis had made his attempt on Victoria's life on 30 May 1842.

(*Left*) Ludwig II, King of Bavaria, died at Schloss Berg in 1886 under suspicious circumstances. Scholars have always doubted the official accounts of the monarch's death, suggesting that Ludwig was murdered.

Crown Prince Rudolph died in tragic circumstances in January 1889. The official records suggest suicide, others believe his death was ordered by a senior politician.

(*Above*) The mistress of Crown Prince Rudolph of Austria, Baroness Marie von Vetsera, was a part of the supposed suicide pact of 1889 at Mayerling. This photograph was found in a locket on Rudolph's cadaver.

(*Right*) Elizabeth, Princess of Wittelsbach, Empress of Austria, assassinated on 10 September 1898 by the anarchist Luigi Lucheni on the Montblanc quay, Geneva.

The House of Windsor was criticised by both Russian and British monarchists for their apparent inaction to help the eventually murdered Russian Imperial Family. Here at Bernstorf, September 1896, the future Queen Alexandra of Britain (first left standing) poses with Emperor Nicholas II (fourth left); in front Empress Alexandra is seated with Grand Duchess Olga on her knee.

Archduke Franz Ferdinand and his wife the Czech Countess Sophie Chotek pose with their children. Both the archduke and his wife were assassinated at Sarajevo on 28 January 1914 by the Serbian fanatic Gavrilo Princip.

(*Above*) Recent research points to the probability that Bulgarian King Boris III was assassinated by the Nazis in 1943. Here Boris, with his General Staff, takes the salute at a march past in Sofia.

(*Right*) Carlos I of Portugal, *en route* for Lisbon from Villa Vicosa, was murdered with his heir Luis Filipe by republican assassins on 1 February 1908.

to having seen the king's footsteps in the mud beside the lake, showing that the king had waded out into the water alone; and all this in seven minutes from the Schloss door some eight hundred metres away.

The two bodies were taken to the Schloss and certified dead by the authorities. No cause of death was entered on the king's death certificate, but on Dr von Gudden's the words 'drowning and strangulation' were entered. An autopsy took place only on the king.

Ms Handzic summed up her own conclusions about the events at Lake Starnberg as follows: 'The bodies were not, and cannot have been, in the water from shortly before 7 p.m. They were assuredly placed there by assassins unknown after fall of darkness; these assassins having laid in wait and waylaid the king and doctor far nearer to Schloss Berg itself, where indeed there was at least one boathouse, from which boats were later that night commandeered for assistance. It is alleged, although I have no evidence but equally, when stated, it is never denied, that the boathouse was pulled down "by orders from Munich" on 14 June 1886. Inevitably, the assassins would have had no alternative but to have murdered the doctor as well as the king, because he was a prime witness to their deeds and could never have been relied upon to "keep quiet" had he been allowed to return to the castle alone, the king being dead. Indeed, he would, without doubt, have been lynched by the populace.'

Certainly there *were* conspiracies to depose Ludwig – the *Gutachten* conspiracy stage-managed by Freiherr von Lutz, Minister of Justice, was a constitutional one – but others believe that there was a more sinister plot to eliminate Ludwig altogether. Maybe the king realized that the plots were real and that madness was to be a cover-up. The whole thing was very suspicious and on 16 June 1886 *The Times* voiced public doubts: '. . . the exact manner of the king's death still remains uncertain and cannot now be ascertained. It is not at all likely that any further light will be cast upon this unique tragedy.'

12

The Mayerling Tragedy

ROYAL MURDER IN A SEALED ROOM

It was as if the Hapsburg family had wanted to sweep away forever that place of violence and grief. Today the room in the hunting lodge at the village of Mayerling, near Baden, where Crown Prince Rudolph of Austria, son and heir of the humourless and conservative Emperor Franz Joseph and his beautiful wife, Elizabeth, Princess of Wittelsbach, was found dead on 30 January 1889, is replaced by an ornate chapel, the centre of a silent order of Carmelite nuns. The first accounts of Rudolph's death came from a government that had panicked and stated that he had suffered from a heart attack; but, shortly afterwards it was reported that he had committed suicide. Even so, it was a royal death which was surrounded with mystery and whose consequences were to destroy Europe.

Some time later it was officially revealed that with Rudolph had died his mistress, the Baroness Marie Vetsera, and that her body had been smuggled out of the lodge. Both had been shot through the head. The clever, rash and pleasure-loving Rudolph – who, two years before his death had been treated for syphilis – had married the Belgian princess Stephanie, the daughter of Leopold of Belgium; the marriage was a failure and Rudolph consorted sexually with women both of high society and those of the *demi-monde*. Seventeen-year-old Marie Vetsera was from the minor Austrian nobility and had met the Crown Prince at the races at Freudenau. Only months later the girl who had been groomed by her promiscuous mother, Baroness Helene Vetsera, a well-known society whore, lay naked and dead in a storeroom.

Rudolph did not see eye to eye with his father the Emperor concerning the future rôle of the imperial monarchy. The Crown Prince was the author of volumes of travel memoirs, and was a political pamphleteer. He had made enemies because of his Hungarian sympathies, so much so that he was being constantly watched by the police for he associated with state political 'undesirables'. Again, Rudolph was contemplating divorce – an unheard of process for the heir to the House of Hapsburg; so there were many undercurrents which might have led to the Crown Prince's death, and modern historians have toyed with the idea that Rudolph and his young mistress were murdered, victims of political plotting. One such story was believed and promulgated by no less a personage than HIM the Empress Zita, wife of Emperor Karl I, the last of the Hapsburg monarchs.

Although she was not a witness to the Mayerling events, the ex-Empress Zita was an intimate of the Imperial circle and her testimony forms one of the most bizarre royal stories of modern history. Dying a nonagenarian in exile in Switzerland, and latterly too ill to publicize the details of the story, Zita's narrative was recorded for her by the Austrian political author Erich Feigl. Zita averred that Rudolph was murdered by the direct order of the iercely anti-German mayor of Paris – and later Prime Minister of France – Georges Clemenceau. The murder she attested was carried out on Clemenceau's behalf by one Dr Cornelius Hertz, an American businessman who operated in Europe and who had close links with French politicians. Hertz said Zita, hired a gang of professional killers who tracked down Rudolph at Mayerling, and there shot him and his mistress.

Clemenceau's motive in all this was believed to be the German-Austrian alliance which was being cemented between Kaiser Wilhelm II of Germany and Franz Joseph; Clemenceau wished to scupper that alliance. As a part of his plan Clemenceau wished to cultivate the Archduke Rudolph who, his agents had assured him, was opposed to his father on most political issues; towards this end Clemenceau instructed his brother-in-law – a friend of Rudolph – to develop the friendship. What Clemenceau proposed, said Zita, was interpreted by Rudolph as treason and he baulked at working directly against his imperial father. Because he knew so much about the French plans, Zita further noted, Rudolph had to die. Thus was he murdered at Mayerling by the agents of France. If true, the assassination was the most outrageous piece of political chicanery of the time; but how does Zita's testimony stand up against the events?

The official version of the events at Mayerling were prepared via a royal commission headed by the Emperor's trusted court physician, Dr Widerhofer. When the doctor arrived at Mayerling he unlocked the door of the Crown Prince's room, opened the shutters and surveyed the scene. The candles still guttered from the night before, and the revolver presumed used in the deaths was lying on the floor. Widerhofer examined Rudolph's perforated skull and glanced at Marie Vetsera's body, her long hair covering her nakedness and a rose clutched in her hand. She too had a bullet hole in the temple. It was Dr Widerhofer's opinion that Marie had been dead some six to eight hours *before* Rupolph, who the doctor was convinced had committed suicide. Before his death Rudolph had written six letters, one, to his mother, said: 'I have no right to live, for I have killed'.

Matters had to be dealt with discreetly. The Emperor had to be informed in full of what had been discovered. The letter implied that the Crown Prince had murdered and, if he had then committed suicide, it would be difficult for the heir apparent to His Apostolic and Catholic Majesty to be given a Christian burial with his ancestors in the gloomy Hapsburg crypt of the Capucines' monastery on the Neuemarkt. Indeed Cardinal Mariano Rampolla objected to a Christian burial on these grounds.

After the body of Marie Vetsera had been identified by her uncles Alexander Baltazzi and Count Stockau, a burial was arranged; an interment which was as shocking in its conduct as the callousness of its rapidity. Late on Thursday 31 January 1889, the body of Marie Vetsera was dressed in a fur coat and hat, to hide the head wound, and was propped up in a closed carriage and seated between her two uncles. It was then driven to the monastery of Heiligenkreuz, and permission having been granted by the abbot, the beautiful Marie was perfunctorily buried as an outcast, following a half-hearted service. All part of a plan concocted by the Minister-President, Count Edouard Taaffe to maintain the public lie that the Crown Prince had died of heart failure. Even so Dr Widerhofer in his report, and subsequent post-mortem, noted that 'certain conditions in [*the Crown Prince's*] brain denoted pathological disturbances, which justified the supposition that His Imperial Highness shot himself in a moment of mental derangement'. Although several priests refused to take part in subsequent public masses for the Crown Prince's soul, Pope Leo XIII allowed a Christian burial.

The various versions of the death of Crown Prince Rudolph, who was 31 at the time of his death, may be built up from the *Stattsarchiv* in Vienna. Private journals and diaries of the Austrian nobility related how Rudolph drank a lot, how he was addicted to morphine (for his migraine) and how he had become moody and unpredictable; all showing how he had become unstable and hinting at mental unbalance.

Then there were the rumours about his 'suicide pact' with various of his mistresses. According to one bedmate, Mitzi Kasper, Rudolph had talked of a suicide pact – if she loved him, Rudolph had said, she would unite with him in a joint death – and she had warned Baron Alfred von Kraus, President of the Imperial Police, of the Crown Prince's wild talk. The police, who always dogged Rudolph's steps, had noted too that he was becoming very clumsy with firearms; on one occasion at the imperial shoots at Murzteg in 1888, Rudolph had nearly shot his father.

Stage-managed by the Emperor and aided and abetted by the Hapsburg 'aunts' it was circulated that Rudolph and Marie were hopelessly in love and wanted to marry. As Rudolph was married to Stephanie, and a divorce was out of the question, neither wished to break off the relationship so they both chose to die together rather than face a separation . . . or dishonour. In truth it is just not credible that Rudolph killed himself because he could not give up Marie. The Minister of Commerce, Marquis Oliver Bacquehem, notes Werner Richter in *Kronprinz Rudolf von Osterreich* (1941), attested that Rudolph was tired of Marie and wanted to get rid of her.

Slowly the events at Mayerling were assessed. On 28 January 1889, Rudolph had furtively left the Hofburg Palace in Vienna and travelled via Baden (two hours away from Vienna by train) to the *Roter Stadl* (Red Shack) where he met Marie. Together they drove by way of a back road – probably to try and throw off any police who had been following – to Mayerling. There in Rudolph's room at the hunting lodge Marie was secreted. Rudolph's shooting companions, Count Hoyos and Prince Philip of Coburg, did not stay at Mayerling, and were unaware of Marie's presence. In fact only four people knew she was there; the driver of the cab which brought them; Loschek, Rudolph's faithful valet; a maid; and a cook.

At 6.30 on 30 January 1889, Crown Prince Rudolph appeared and ordered breakfast. He was never seen alive again. At 8.30 after being called repeatedly, and the door of the death room having been pounded hard, the portal was broken open and the bodies found. Rudolph was discovered half-sitting on the edge of the bed with Marie beside him; on the floor was a revolver and a mirror (which it is thought Rudolph had used in the suicide firing).

From this point on both the testimony and the artefacts were either distorted or manipulated. The revolver (probably an 8mm cavalry revolver) disappeared and the testimony – although truthfully told to the Emperor and his agents by Hoyos and Loschek – was tampered with.

Historians today generally discount Empress Zita's theory of murder by French agents as Hapsburg gossip, totally unprovable. But she is not the only one to hint at murder. In the *New York Times Magazine* (26 January 1964) Robert Payne in his article 'Mayerling Remains a Mystery' put forward the idea that Rudolph's murder was arranged by Count Taaffe.

The difficulty for anyone trying to prove the murder theory is that the two victims left farewell letters. It is possible however that Rudolph's death was a political execution, resulting from the police discovery of his treasonable activities. If Rudolph himself – when offered the opportunity of dying by his own hand – had refused he might have been dispatched by someone acting for the government. There are four distinct factors supporting this conjecture:

In his letters (attested as genuine by handwriting experts from Scotland Yard) Rudolph stressed that he chose death to save his honour.

Rudolph left no message for his father, who he may have believed ordered his death.

In Richter's *Kronprinz Rudolf* there is accredited testimony that Rudolph's cousin Countess Marie Larisch, daughter of Duke Ludwig of Bavaria, had been told by him that by going to Mayerling he would be in mortal danger because of his political activities, and that his father was a part of that danger.

Rudolph's skull was so shattered that possibly a revolver was not used, but that as Albert Freicherr von Margutti says in *Vom Alten Kaiser*, Rudolph was killed by a blow with a heavy object (like a champagne bottle or a rifle butt).

While Empress Zita's theory is totally groundless and Payne's suggestion cannot be proved, that Rudolph's death *was* ordered by a high authority cannot be ruled out. The Emperor Franz Joseph entrusted all the documents concerning the case to Count Taaffe with the order that they should never be disclosed under any circumstances. This suggests that there was a dark secret therein . . . a secret that was more important than just suicide, for the Pope had agreed to the Christian burial. Franz Joseph knew that his state papers about Rudolph and Marie would be on view one day, so he wanted to make sure that the truth about them should never be known. He succeeded because Taaffe took the papers to his castle of Ellischau in Bohemia and there they were said to have been burned. Thus ensuring that the most mysterious of all Hapsburg mysteries will forever remain unsolved.

NB: *Former Empress Zita died on 14 March 1989 and featured in two Austrian television programmes on the 100th anniversary of the Mayerling shooting. In them she maintained her stance that Crown Prince Rudolph was murdered.*

Postscript:

Assassination attempt on Emperor Franz Joseph

On 18 February 1853, a young Hungarian journeyman tailor Janos Libenyi made an attempt on the Emperor's life. Franz Joseph had been strolling on the Vienna city walls, accompanied by his Adjutant, Count Maximilian O'Donnell. As they paused to watch soldiers drilling below, outside the city walls, Libenyi rushed the Emperor from the rear and struck the back of his neck with a knife. Alerted by a cry from a woman nearby, Franz Joseph span round and avoided the full impact of the assassin's thrust. O'Donnell pounced on the attacker and subdued him. In the meantime Libenyi had shouted

Eljen Kossuth (Hail Kossuth) in token of his support of Louis Kossuth the Hungarian patriot who in 1848 had led a rising of his countrymen against the Hapsburg dynasty. Libenyi was hanged a few days later and Franz Joseph soon recovered from his injury. A large new church, the Votivkirche, was built in Vienna to commemorate the Emperor's deliverance.

The Murder of the Empress Elizabeth

On 10 September 1898, Crown Prince Rudolph's mother, the ageing Empress Elizabeth – whose final years had been spent wandering over Europe – was herself assassinated with a sharpened file, by the anarchist Luigi Lucheni on the Montblanc quay, Geneva, *en route* for Territet. Her lady-in-waiting Countess Irma Sztàray, attested that as they hurried to the quay a man collided with them. The man raised his fist at the Empress and knocked her white parasol out of her hand; the blow had been enough to knock over the Empress who fell backwards hitting her head on the pavement. The Empress was helped to her feet and taken aboard the Territet boat and she collapsed on deck. Only when her clothes were loosened was a bloodstain on her chest seen, and did her lady-in-waiting realize that the Empress had been stabbed.

As the stab-wound was so small, the Empress's demise was slow, and she died a short time after receiving the last rites at the Hotel Beau-Rivage, Geneva. It was the uncanny granting of her own wish: 'I would like to die alone, far from my loved ones, and for death to take me unawares'.

Her assassin, Luigi Lucheni, had been a foundling brought up at the hospital of Saint Antoine. His background had left him with a grudge against society and to expiate what he perceived society had done to him he vowed that he would kill the first royal personage he met. Lucheni was quickly captured after his attack on the Empress and he was sentenced to life imprisonment; later he hanged himself in jail.

13

The Bullet that Changed the Map of Europe

ON 28 JUNE 1914 AT SARAJEVO, A BOSNIAN SLAV
STUDENT MURDERED A ROYAL ARCHDUKE, HEIR TO
THE THRONE OF AUSTRO-HUNGARY

Archduke Franz Ferdinand came from a happy family, which was in itself an unusual thing amongst European royalty. Yet, the eldest son of Emperor Franz Joseph I's brother Archduke Karl Ludwig of Hapsburg-Lorraine, and Maria Annuncida, daughter of King Ferdinand II, of the Two Sicilies, born on 18 December 1863, had the Hapsburg traits of acquisitiveness and excelling in excesses. From a young age Franz Ferdinand was a natural sharpshooter and shooting was to be his lifelong passion; ironically it was a well-aimed bullet that was to cause his death.

Third in line to the throne, Franz Ferdinand pursued a military career but spent much of his time at the Imperial Court or in Vienna enjoying the *gemütlich* social life. The death of his cousin Crown Prince Rudolph on the night of 29–30 January 1889 at Mayerling moved Franz Ferdinand one place up the succession list, but his father was only three years younger than Emperor Franz Joseph, so Franz Ferdinand was talked of as successor to his uncle as Emperor of Austria, King of Jerusalem, Apostolic King of Hungary, King of Bohemia, Galicia, Lodomeria, Illyria and Croatia. Because of Rudolph's death too, Franz Ferdinand became more involved in state occasions. In 1890 the Emperor promoted him to Colonel of the 9th Hussars, stationed at Odenburg, in an attempt to encourage his non-academic nephew to learn more about the Hungarians. Franz Ferdinand's state affairs increased too and during the winter of 1891–92 he went to Russia to deliver a letter of friendship from his uncle to Czar Alexander III; but he learned little diplomacy and was often heard in private making anti-Hungarian remarks and promoting his ideas for dividing Hungary into national units.

Franz Ferdinand's proposals were unpopular in Hungary and when the archduke was diagnosed as having tuberculosis in 1895, the pro-Budapest newspaper *Magyar Hirlap* commented that if the archduke died of his illness they hoped that 'there would be no mourning in Hungary'. Franz Ferdinand was furious, but his mind was taken off his illness and his annoyance by tragedy being heaped upon tragedy for the Hapsburgs. In 1896 his father Archduke Karl Ludwig died and in September 1898 the Empress Elizabeth was assassinated in Switzerland. Karl Ludwig's death made Franz Ferdinand the ageing Emperor Franz Joseph's heir.

Franz Ferdinand's position had long made him a candidate for a good dynastic marriage, and he was now 37; but he defied his family's wishes and married morganatically Countess Sophie Chotec von Chotkwa und Wognin, at which ceremony only three of his close relatives attended. As a sop to rank, however, the Emperor conferred the title of Princess of Hohenberg on the new Archduchess Sophie. By the autumn of 1904 Franz Ferdinand and Sophie had a son and two daughters, and, because of court protocol humiliatingly placing Sophie after the youngest archduchess, the couple spent less and less time at court and lived on their country estates or went travelling. Even taking into consideration his royal and military duties, Franz Ferdinand was rarely away from home for more than a week at a time. Despite being little known by the general public, Franz Ferdinand kept up his hostility to the Hungarians who wanted more and more autonomy from Vienna. Franz Ferdinand felt that the emperor had 'gone soft' on Hungary and continued to voice his scorn for Hungarian nationalism and the ambitions of the South Slavs and Serbia.

Until 1914 the Hapsburg monarchy ruled not only Austria and Hungary, but the Adriatic provinces of Dalmatia, Bosnia and Herzegovina. So it is true to say that from 1900 to around 1906 the threat posed to the unity of the Hapsburg monarchy and the army by the demands of the Hungarians absorbed a great deal of governmental time in Vienna; and the increased dissatisfaction amongst the ethnic South Slavs, the Slovenes, Croats and Serbs, between the Danube and the Adriatic, was building up more political pressure. Each group was fiercely jealous of its national history. They all disagreed too as to how their future destiny be formed; for instance the Croats saw the establishment of an autonomous South Slav kingdom within the Hapsburg monarchy, whereas the Serbians wanted a South Slav state, with them as leaders, outside the monarchy. These political fragmentations were exploited by the Hungarians who pursued a divide and rule policy.

A prime target for Greater Serbian propaganda were the Serb and Croat inhabitants of the ancient Christian Kingdom of Bosnia and the Duchy of Herzegovina, which had been overrun by the Turks in the fifteenth century; still legally Turkish citizens the Serbs and Croats were *de facto* under Hungarian rule. Herein was a complicated interplay of politics and the majority of people were poor peasants, of which a typical Serb family were the Princips of the Grahovo Valley. Petar Princip and his wife Nina won a hard living from the fertile red earth, with Nina toiling in the fields while Petar supplemented their income by acting as a carter; but as Serb *kmets* (peasants) they had to hand over one third of their produce to their Turkish Muslim landlord. On 13 July 1894 Nina Princip gave birth to a sickly boy, who as he had been born on St Gabriel's Day, was called Gavrilo to protect him through childhood illnesses. Indeed, destiny had already put her hand on Gavrilo Princip to give him an international notoriety that would last as long as there are historical records.

Gavrilo Princip grew up in an atmosphere of radical propaganda fed by the uproar of resentment in Serbia – among the Catholic Croats, the Orthodox Serbs and the Muslims – for the award, in 1908, to the Austrians of the mandate to occupy Bosnia and Herzegovina. Archduke Franz Ferdinand thoroughly agreed with his uncle's *fait accompli* annexation, to him, 'Austria must rule Bosnia, not Hungary'.

Backed by the newspapers and the Christian church, the Greater Serbia party propaganda – from its base in northern Serbia – flourished to find fault with everything that the Austrian administrators did. Austria banned all political parties and permitted the inhabitants of Bosnia and Herzegovina no say in their government, thus resentment spilled out in national feeling. Nevertheless despite the restrictions, young Gavrilo Princip obtained a good schooling with the help of his elder brother Jovo who was milking the prevailing system as an entepreneur near Sarajevo, and joined an illegal students' group who met regularly to discuss ethics, politics, and literature. Gavrilo Princip also began to read the socialist and anarchist pamphlets that were passed from hand to hand among the students and by the time he was 13 he was a firm believer in the erstwhile Italian dictator Giuseppe Mazzini's dictum that 'a country must be liberated by its youth, self-denying crusaders prepared to sacrifice their lives for liberty and justice.'

During 1910 it was suggested that loyalty to the Crown would undoubtedly be strengthened if a member of the Imperial Family should visit Bosnia and Herzegovina, and at the beginning of March it was announced that the Emperor himself would visit on 30 May to 5 June. By the end of May the authorities got wind of two assassination plots against Franz Joseph. One tip-off came from the Austrian Embassy in Paris quoting an American student who spoke of a South Slav anarchist plot, while the other came from the embassy in Sophia, whose ambassador told of a plot by the Serbian nationalist association the *Slovenski Jug*. Both plots were aimed at killing Franz Joseph while he was in Mostar, the capital of Herzegovina. No action was taken after an investigation was carried out by the authorities in Mostar, and the Emperor, because of his age, was not informed.

Strict security precautions were in force for the visit and no assassination attempts were made, although a few days later an unsuccessful attempt was made on the Governor of Sarajevo, Feldzeugmeister Mariyan Varesanin, by a Serbian law student Bogdan Zerajic, who committed suicide minutes after his bullets had missed the Governor as he drove back from the opening of parliament.

Zerajic's action captured the imagination of the young radicals, several of whom sought out the unmarked grave of the Serbian student and paid homage with flowers and bowed heads. One to pay homage and be inspired was Gavrilo Princip who decided to emulate the 'martyred' Zerajic. In 1912 a new governor was appointed in Baron Slavko von Cuvaj, and new restrictions were set in motion against political meetings, strikes and demonstrations. One of the boys expelled from Sarajevo for striking from their studies as a protest against Cuvaj's measures was Gavrilo Princip who exiled himself by walking to Belgrade.

At the time there were many young Bosnians in Belgrade, most were poor, many slept rough, and all, including Gavrilo Princip, were hungry. The young congregated at cheap cafés where a cup of coffee could be made to last for hours while they talked anarchy and of the dream they had to live in an independent South Slav state as free citizens. Princip frequented the café *Zeleni Venac* (Green Garland) and through his contacts made it known that he wished to join the *komitadjis* revolutionaries who were planning an advance into Macedonia under the leadership of Major Vojin Tankosic, a regicide of the 1903 coup against King Alexander. Princip appeared before Tankosic who declared him unfit. Princip returned to Bosnia in a state of abject misery and demoralization.

Across the winter of 1912–13 Princip stayed with his brother at Hadziu, outside Sarajevo, and there he monitored the advance of the Serbian army for now war had broken out and Montenegro, Bulgaria, and Greece had attacked Turkey. The military disturbances gave all kinds of anarchist groups in Bosnia and Herzegovina good cover to plot revenge on the House of Hapsburg. All the time Princip seethed about Tankosic's rejection of him and the desire to be a national hero grew daily. He returned to Belgrade and the war ended on 30 May 1913, but because the apportioning of the spoils of war gave Bulgaria the lion's share of Macedonia, war broke out again, to be short lived; by the Peace of Bucharest, Serbia was given a huge part of Macedonia. The ceding gave the revolutionaries a great fillip.

All these jockeyings excited Gavrilo Princip who returned to Bosnia to see the province now under a harsh 'military-police regime' which restricted Serbian movements in particular. Students still gathered to plot assassination with the new governor, Feldzeugmeister Oskar Potiorek as a prime target; but no assassination was attempted.

In 1913 the Emperor appointed Franz Ferdinand Inspector General of the army which made him responsible for the administration, equipping, morale, and training of the imperial soldiery, and straight away Franz Ferdinand decided to make a visit to the troops in Bosnia. Arrangements were now made for the archduke and his wife to visit troop manoeuvres in Bosnia during 25–27 June 1914, and a call at Sarajevo was also arranged for Sunday 28 June. This date was known as Vivodan, an emotive day in the Serbian calendar, the anniversary of the annihilation of the Serbian army by the Turks at Kosovo in 1389. One historian described the brashness of the visit as foolhardy as if 'King George V had decided to visit Dublin on St Patrick's Day in 1917.' It was a day that the Serbs might select on which to try assassinations; if Franz Ferdinand was warned of this by his staff at this stage he chose to ignore it. It seems that Franz Ferdinand was himself indifferent to assassinations, even though there had been six attempts on Hapsburg dignitaries during 1910–14. Franz Ferdinand had publicly declared: 'Security measures? . . . I do not care the tiniest bit about them. Everywhere one is in God's hands. Look, out of this bush, here at the right, some chap could jump at me. . . . Fears and precautions paralyse one's life. To fear is always a dangerous business.'

In particular the Austro-Hungarian imperial secret service was monitoring the activities of the *Ujedinjenji ili Smrt* (Union or Death), a terrorist organization generally known as the *Crna Ruka* (the Black Hand). By 1914 their membership was growing in Belgrade and their propaganda machine was being honed to pefection; this formed the background to the arrival of Gavrilo Princip to lodge in Belgrade at a house occupied by young Bosnians. As the news of Franz Ferdinand's trip to Bosnia became public knowledge, Princip resolved to attempt an assassination and invited a 19-year-old Serb friend Nedeljko Cabrinovic to assist him. They shook hands on the deal and were soon joined by another compatriot Trifko Grabez the son of a Serb Orthodox priest. One of Princip's friends of his student days, Danilo Ilic was to supply weapons. Ironically Major Vojin Tankosic, who had turned down Princip for active service, was instumental in supplying the youths with Browning pistols and nail bombs through the good offices of Milan Ciganovic a member of the guerilla *komitadjis*.

Princip, Cabrinovic and Grabez set out for Sarajevo on 29 May and were smuggled safely over the River Drina into Bosnia with the help of Captain Rade Popovic, the frontier gendarmerie commandant. They made a slow journey across the countryside and as they neared Sarajevo they noted increased police checks on the road and trains as a prelude to Franz Ferdinand's visit. When they arrived at Sarajevo the conspirators split up, Princip making his base at his brother's house at Hadzice. In the meantime Danilo Ilic, who had supplied the weapons, had gathered a back-up team of would-be assassins. By 6 June Princip had moved into Ilic's mother's house and seven assassins were now assembled: Princip, Cabrinovic, Grabez, Ilic, a fanatical Serb nationalist Muslim Muhamed Mehmedbasic, a student Vaso Cubrilovic, and his friend Cventko Popovic. It was now common knowledge that Franz Ferdinand would stay at Ilidze and move on to Sarajevo on Sunday 28 July, but the conspirators had to wait until His Imperial Highness's itinerary in Sarajevo was made public.

On 24 June Franz Ferdinand and Archduchess Sophie's programme was announced and Princip and the assassination team got down to planning the actual murder. The programme was set for Franz Ferdinand to arrive in Sarajevo from Ilidze by train at 9.50 a.m. The plan was for the archduke and archduchess to be in Sarajevo for four hours at which he would visit the town hall (10.10–10.30 a.m.); open and tour a new museum (10.40–11.40 a.m.); lunch with Feldzeugmeister Oskar Potiorek at the Konak (noon to 2 p.m.), and then return to Ilidze. Studying this programme the conspirators decided that it would be best to attempt the assassination while Franz Ferdinand was driving through Sarajevo and the six conspirators could line the route at different points to enhance the chances of success. On 26 June the pistols and bombs were distributed among the seven, each of whom received a small packet of cyanide for the mass suicide they planned immediately after Franz Ferdinand was dead.

During the imperial party's visit there were to be no soldiers patrolling the streets, and known 'suspected citizens' were not shadowed or rounded up as would have been the normal practice. To their credit though, the police administrators did warn Governor Potiorek that the archduke was in danger from the Black Hand and the Young Bosnia groups in particular. The governor rebuked the advisers for 'having a fear of children'. All in all there were only 120 local police to 'turn their faces towards the crowd during the passage of the imperial party' along the four-mile route, the local press was to report.

Sunday 28 June 1914 dawned a splendid summer day. It seems that some of the conspirators, like Cabrinovic and Grabez, were having second thoughts about the assassination, but Princip was all geared up for his entry into the rôle of Serbian hero. Franz Ferdinand and Archduchess Sophie left Ilidze a little behind schedule and were greeted by Feldzeugmeister Potiorek at Sarajevo station. The crowds got their first glimpse of the imperial couple as the archduke inspected a guard of honour; Franz Ferdinand was dressed in the full dress uniform of a cavalry general, a pale blue tunic with a deep gold braid collar and gold braided cuffs, a sash with a large gilt tassel, black trousers with a double red stripe, and a hat adorned with green plumes. Sophie wore a long white silk dress with red sash, and had a large picture hat with feathers and carried a parasol. The seven imperial cars then set off for Sarajevo town hall. Franz Ferdinand was seated in a car belonging to Count Franz Harrach with Sophie on his right; Potiorek and Harrach faced them on folding seats. The car's hood was folded back and was preceded by a front car full of police, and then the car containing the Mayor and Dr Edmund Gerde, a senior civil servant responsible for the police department. Behind came the four cars containing the archduke's suite, Potiorek's adjutant Giuseppe Merizzi and Sophie's lady-in-waiting Countess Lanjus.

As Franz Ferdinand left the station all the conspirators were ranged along the Appel Quay, which ran parallel with the Miljacka river, and each would-be assassin covered the three bridges across the river: Mehmedbasic, Cubrilovic and Cabrinovic in the vicinity of the Cumurja Bridge, Princip at the Lateiner Bridge, Grabez at the Kaiser Bridge, while the other two were on the side of the Appel Quay opposite the Cumurja Bridge.

Soon the imperial cars came into view travelling slowly. The archduke's car, with its black and yellow imperial standard, passed Mehmedbasic and Cubrilovic who seemed to lose their nerve and did nothing. As the car passed his position, Cabrinovic threw his bomb, but missed and it landed to explode on the road. Fumbling for his cyanide, and spilling most of it, Cabrinovic jumped over the quay into the river; Mehmedbasic, Cubrilovic and Popovic panicked and ran away, while Ilic just disappeared.

Franz Ferdinand reacted as any senior officer would, he ordered his car to stop while he sent the Count to find out if anyone had been killed. Count Alexander Boos-Waldeck's car had taken the worst of the explosion and Boos-Waldeck had been grazed by splinters; Merizzi was streaming blood from a head wound which was being mopped up by Countess Lanjus, the other members of the suite were unhurt and ran to see if the imperial couple were safe. Meanwhile Cabrinovic had been caught by the police in the shallows of the river and was taken to the police station.

Unable to see what was happening Princip was in a state of confused agitation. He had heard the bomb explode and as the front cars had stopped he thought that the assassination had been successful. As the cars started again Princip saw Franz Ferdinand and Sophie and realized all had failed; to his right by the Kaiser Bridge, Grabez also saw the archduke and duchess pass, but made no attempt to throw his bomb. Simultaneously Grabez and Princip decided to wait around for the imperial couple to return.

Franz Ferdinand carried out his official duties as planned, but insisted on making one change; instead of visiting the museum he would call on the wounded Giuseppe Merizzi at the hospital. Although they had tried to persuade Sophie to wait for the archduke's return she insisted on not leaving her husband's side while he was in Sarajevo. As the entourage drove away from the town hall on its way to the hospital, Count Harrach positioned himself on the running board of the car to shield Franz Ferdinand with his own body. The cars proceeded down the Appel Quay and were monitored by Grabez who did nothing. All the other assassins had now dispersed and Franz Ferdinand would have been safe if fate had not taken a perverse turn.

For a reason that was never officially explained, Dr Edmund Gerde's car, instead of going straight down the Appel Quay to the hospital, turned into the Franz Joseph Strasse on the route to the museum. Count Harrach's chauffeur Loyka, who had not been told of the cancelling of the museum trip followed Gerde's car. Almost immediately Potiorek told Loyka to stop and go back. Loyka braked and made to reverse the car. The limousine was now outside Moritz Schiller's delicatessen shop into whose window Gavrilo Princip was gazing. The imperial car was now some five feet away from him. Princip raised his pistol and fired two shots; one went through the right-hand door of the car and hit Sophie, the second hit Franz Ferdinand in the neck.

Potiorek shouted to Loyka to drive over the river to the Konak, both realizing that the imperial couple were injured; Potiorek thought that the mortally wounded archduke, who still sat upright and was supporting the archduchess across his knees as she had fainted, was only slightly wounded. Meanwhile Count Harrach was still on the running board and later he made this deposition quoted by Theodor von Sosnosky in his *Franz Ferdinand* (1929):

As the car quickly reversed a thin stream of blood spurted out of His Imperial Highness's mouth on to my right cheek. With one hand I got out my handkerchief to wipe the blood from the Archduke's face, and as I did so Her Highness called out 'In God's name what has happened to you?' Then she collapsed, her face between the Archduke's knees. I had no idea that she was hit and thought she had fainted from fear. His Imperial Highness then said 'Sopherl! Sopherl! Don't die! Live for my children'. I took hold of the collar of his tunic in order to prevent his head sinking forward and asked him 'Is Your Imperial Highness in great pain?' He answered distinctly 'It is nothing'. Then he turned his face a little to one side and said six or seven times, more faintly as he began to lose consciousness, 'It's nothing'. There was a very brief pause, then the bleeding made him choke violently, but this stopped when we reached the Konak.

Archduchess Sophie was found to be dead on arrival at the Konak and Franz Ferdinand died a few minutes later. Gavrilo Princip was arrested immediately, and the cyanide he swallowed had only made him sick; he was alive and taken away to be interrogated.

The assassination at Sarajevo was undoubtedly one of the most amateurish royal murders of modern history; it succeeded only because of the negligence of the authorities and sheer luck. The consequences of the assassination though, were devastating for the whole of Europe. Austria declared war on Serbia and the Russians mobilized. The Germans declared war on Russia and France, and on 4 August 1914 Great Britain declared war on Germany and World War I was enacted.

Despite the mobilizations an investigation into the assassination was begun. All the assassins had been arrested, except Mehmedbasic, who had escaped to Montenegro. The material on the assassination was gathered and assessed by Judge Leo Pfeffer an undistinguished and totally incompetent investigator. He dismissed Ilic as small fry, after Ilic had voluntarily supplied a great deal of information on the plot; so Pfeffer had concentrated on Grabez, Princip, and Cabrinovic.

The state trial began on 12 October 1914 with twenty-five accused standing trial. They included those who had helped Princip and Grabez across Bosnia and several others who had known about the plot but had said nothing to the authorities. The youngest was 16 and about half of the indicted were under 20. All pleaded guilty except Princip who declared: 'I am not a criminal because I have killed a man who has done wrong; I think I have done right'.

Grabez's testimony was based on the fact that he believed that Franz Ferdinand was personally responsible for all the wrong that Bosnia had suffered; he emphasized that as Franz Ferdinand was Inspector General of the army he was the natural enemy of all Slavs and that the South Slavs could never have political liberty while he lived. He said though that if he had known that the assassination would precipitate war then he would not have taken part. Cabrinovic's testimony was along the same lines. That war had been declared did not concern Princip, he said, and his only remorse was that he had killed Archduchess Sophie; his second bullet had been meant for Potiorek. The basis of his testimony was that as a peasant his aim had been to avenge the peasants who had suffered so much under the Hapsburgs.

It took the Sarajevo court three days to arrive at a verdict. All the five youths who had taken the main roles in the assassination were found guilty of treason and murder. But, as they were being judged under Austrian law, they could not be executed as they were under 20 years of age. Instead Princip, Cabrinovic and Grabez were sentenced to twenty years imprisonment, while Cubrilovic and Popovic were given sixteen and thirteen years respectively. Being over 20, Ilic was sentenced to death along with the others . . . several of the small fry were acquitted.

Princip, Carbrinovic and Grabez were sent to the military prison at the fortress of Theresienstadt in Bohemia, and there all three died of tuberculosis; Cabrinovic and Grabez in 1916 and Princip in 1918 the year that the war that he had precipitated had come to an end.

14

The Case of the Missing Imperial Corpses

WHAT HAPPENED TO CZAR NICHOLAS II AND HIS
FAMILY? WERE THEY MURDERED, OR SPIRITED
AWAY?

Perhaps the most merciless female anarchist ever to defy the might of the Czarist regime was Vera Figner. Coming from a well-to-do background, Vera Figner, born in 1852, enjoyed all the privileges of pre-Soviet Russian middle-class life. As women were not allowed to study medicine in Czarist Russia, Vera Figner studied the subject in Switzerland, but in 1873 she became so fired with the cause of bloody revolution that she gave up her training as a physician to aid the revolution and the proletariat as a general nurse. Around 1877 she joined a terrorist group called the People's Will who had condemned to death Alexander II, the ruling Czar of All the Russias, who was ironically dubbed the 'Czar Liberator'. Bent on helping to overthrow the Czarist system, Vera Figner descended to the political maelstrom of secret police interrogations, deceptions and treasons. Between 1879 and 1881 she was privy to the several plots to assassinate Czar Alexander.

Alexander II had been attacked in 1866, for instance, by a disaffected student, and was assaulted again in 1867 while visiting Paris. Foolishly he weakened the *Troisième Bureau* (secret police), and gave anarchists like Vera Figner much needed elbow room. Disguised as a society lady, Vera Figner infiltrated an agent into the South Western Railroad. He was to monitor the movements of imperial trains from his base at Odessa. A fanatical leader of the People's Will,

Zhelyabov, now planned to mine the Czar's train as it entered Kharkov, but the dynamite failed to explode. The terrorists persisted and two attempts later they blew up what they thought to be the imperial train and killed twenty people; Alexander was not on board.

During September of 1879 Stepanoff, of the People's Will, managed to secure a job at the Winter Palace, at St Petersburg, and despite the tight security there, smuggled in a quantity of dynamite which he stored in his kit in a basement. On 5 February 1880 the conspirator lit a slow fuse and quit the palace. The resultant explosion only slightly damaged the dining room leaving Czar Alexander and his family unscathed.

In the spring of 1880, Vera Figner kept her hand in by planning the assassination of Regional-general Paniutin, but this attempted murder was abandoned when another attempt on the Czar's life was given top priority. This plan involved an attack on Alexander as he passed through Odessa on his way to the Crimea, but, as with other attempts, the plan was marred by a series of accidents. But progress was made in a plot to assassinate the Czar as he passed a cheese shop on his Sunday visit to a cavalry barracks. Tunnelling from the cheese shop out into the street was begun in January 1881, but work was abandoned when they struck a sewer. At last the terrorists obtained news that the Czar was to take an alternative route, and Vera Figner helped to fill the bombs to be used. On 13 March 1881 the terrorists were successful in St Petersburg. One bomb destroyed the back of the Czar's carriage and he stepped out of it to thank God that he had been delivered only to be killed by a second bomb.

So, thanks to the activities of Vera Figner – who survived until 1942 to die at the age of 90 – Nicholas Alexandrovich Romanov, the last Czar of All the Russias, was provided at the age of 13 in that fateful year of 1881 with a terrible reminder of that danger that he and his family were always in. For a few hours after the terrorists' bomb had killed the Czar, young Nicholas surveyed the mangled body of his grandfather at the Winter Palace.

Educated as an autocrat, Nicholas Romanov succeeded his father Alexander III in 1894 as Nicholas II and the same year married Queen Victoria's granddaughter the beautiful Princess Alix of Hess-Darmstadt. They were to have four daughters, Olga, Tatiana, Marie and Anastasia, and a haemophiliac son, Alexis. The outbreak of

World War I was to accelerate the demise of the House of Romanov. By March 1917 the Czar's authority crumbled around him and the war-weary nation demanded sweeping changes in how they were ruled. Within a year the world's richest and most powerful monarch was to totally vanish without trace.

The timetable leading up to the disappearance of the imperial family was rapid. On the advice of his generals, Nicholas II abdicated in his private railway carriage on the evening of 15 March 1917. Nicholas also abdicated on behalf of his haemophiliac son Alexis and handed over his inheritance to his brother, the Grand Duke Michael Alexandrovich. A day later Michael II abdicated too and the 304-year-old House of Romanov was swept away. Technically the Grand Duke Michael was the 'last Czar of All the Russias', but he had never been crowned, and he was shot by the Bolsheviks at Perm on 10 July 1918.

Nicholas, his family and a few close courtiers became prisoners in the palace of Tsarskoe Selo (now Pushkin), near St Petersburg. All round the extremists were calling for Nicholas's blood, and the two revolutionaries Lenin and Trotsky preached the overthrow of the new Provisional Government. The Russian prime minister, Alexander Kerensky, warned of the coming bloodshed and 'for their own safety' the imperial family were moved to Tobolsk in Siberia. When the October Revolution brought Lenin to power, the Czar and his wife were moved to the two-storey Ipatiev House overlooking Voznesensky Avenue, in the mining town of Ekaterinburg (now Sverdlovsk) in the Ural mountains; their children followed three weeks later, their journey having been delayed by the ex-Czarevich Alexis's most recent haemophilic attack. The new Communist rulers now dubbed the old house built by the merchant N. N. Ipatiev, 'The House of Special Purpose'.

By 14 July 1918 the White Russian army was approaching Ekaterinburg, and what to do with the Romanovs was a pressing matter on the Ural Soviet. To this point in time history is clear and accepted, but the events close to the supposed murder of the imperial family soon became the subject of conjecture.

The fate of the Romanovs, as accepted by historians, is built up from data supplied by Communist sources alone. Highlighted was the testimony of one Comrade Fydor Gorshkov given to Alexander

Kutuzov, the Public Prosecutor at Ekaterinburg. Gorshkov testified: 'The whole of the imperial family was assembled in the dining-room where they were informed that they were going to be shot, and shortly after this the Letts fired at the imperial family, and they all fell down on the floor. After this, the Letts began to make sure that they were all killed, and discovered that the Grand Duchess Anastasia Nikolayevna was still alive, and when they touched her, she screamed dreadfully; she was hit on the head with a rifle butt, and stabbed thirty-two times with bayonets.' The Letts mentioned were soldiers from the Baltic provinces of north Russia serving with the Bolshevik army.

At best the testimony was third-hand and down the decades historians have regurgitated the version with extraordinary naivety. The story has been embroidered from a number of sources and was accepted hook, line and sinker by such celebrated historians as Robert K. Massie in his *Nicholas & Alexandra*, where he has the imperial family's jailer at Ekaterinburg, Comrade Yankel Yurovsky, saying to his men: 'Tonight, we will shoot the whole family, everybody'. Massie recounts how the deed was accomplished in the cellar of the Ipatiev House some time after midnight on 17 July 1918. With them, Massie further wrote, died the family's personal physician Dr Yevgeny Botkin, their footman Alexei Trupp, their cook Ivan Kharitonov, and the Czarina's maid Anna Demidova.

The story of the death of the Czar (but not what actually happened) was communicated to the diplomatic corps through a statement made by chairman Yankel Sverdlov, of the Soviet Central Executive Committee, and consequently the first Communist head of state, on the 18 July 1918. Sverdlov noted that 'the wife and son of Nicholas had been 'sent to a safe place'; the fate of the former Emperor's daughters was not mentioned. This was the first of a long line of contradictory statements about the imperial family which were put out by the Soviet official sources. It was not until 1924 that the Soviets released officially the story that *the whole* family had been massacred at Ekaterinburg; a story to which they have stuck rigidly for almost seventy years.

A number of official and unofficial investigations – a few White Russian soldiers and some civilians played detective – into the fate of the imperial family took place very soon after they had vanished. On

25 July 1918 Ekaterinburg was captured from the Bolsheviks by the White Russians and on 30 July the first civilian inquiry was conducted by Alexander Nametkin, Examining Magistrate for Important Cases at Ekaterinburg, on behalf of the Public Prosecutor of Ekaterinburg, Alexander Kutuzov.

Nametkin made a minute assessment of the Ipatiev House and the remaining domestic *bric-à-brac* of the Romanovs. Accompanied by a patrol of White soldiers he also investigated the story that the bodies of the imperial family had been taken to a wooded mining area to the north-west of Ekaterinburg; an area known as the 'Four Brothers' because of a clump of lone pine trees. There the bodies were said to have been burned and related artefacts crushed, and the whole remains thrown down a mine shaft. On 7 August 1918 Nametkin was sacked from the inquiry and very soon after he was to die violently. The White Russian version was that he had been 'caught by the Bolsheviks [*who still had skirmishers in the wood around Ekaterinburg*] and executed for investigating the murder of the Czar and his family'. It is interesting to note that at the time of his death Nametkin was investigating the possibility that the imperial family had actually left Ekaterinburg alive.

The next phase of the investigation was conducted for the civilian court by Judge Ivan Sergeyev. He set about collecting material evidence and interviewed dozens of witnesses. Sergeyev looked closely at the 'murder cellar' (really a semi-basement) at the Ipatiev House. Herein he is alleged to have found bullet holes in the walls of the room and actual spent bullets in the plaster. He noted too that the room had been washed after the bullets had been fired, but 'stains of reddish colour' in the room were not inconclusively established as blood. He concluded that people unknown had been shot in the sinister room.

Meanwhile an Officers' Commission was busy at work at the Four Brothers mine, and collected a quantity of human and animal remains and fragments of clothes. All of these were carefully collated by Sergeyev. Pieces of jewellery found at the mine were formally identified as belonging to the imperial family by the former tutors of the imperial children, Pierre Gilliard and Sydney Gibbes, who had by now arrived in Ekaterinburg. Of the human remains – one man's finger, two pieces of human skin, and some artificial teeth – Dr

Vladimir Derevenko, who had been a physician to the Czarevich, attested that the finger was the forefinger of his former colleague Dr Botkin.

Yet, despite several weeks of searching at the mine, no evidence of any Romanov corpses were ever found; and Sergeyev had a growing file of reports that the imperial family had been transferred from Ekaterinburg alive under heavy disguise.

Acting for the British government, there now arrived in Ekaterinburg, Sir Charles Eliot, the British high commissioner and consul-general for Siberia. He had discussions with Judge Sergeyev and prepared for the British Foreign Secretary, A. J. Balfour, an official report; a document which was of particular interest to the Czar's cousin, King George V. Therein Eliot recounted his findings on the captivity of the imperial family, his personal impressions of the Ipatiev House, the murder room, and concluded with some very interesting observations:

> On 17 July a train with the blinds down left Ekaterinburg for an
> unknown destination and it is believed that the surviving
> members of the imperial family were in it. It is the general
> opinion in Ekaterinburg that the empress, her son and four
> daughters were not murdered but were dispatched on 17 July to
> the north or west. It therefore seems probable that the imperial
> family were disguised before their removal.

So already a short while after the official Soviet communiqué, the investigators came across a welter of inconsistencies.

Sir Charles believed that at least the Romanov women were disguised and taken from Ekaterinburg. A quantity of hair found in the Ipatiev House was later identified by the Czar's valet, Terenty Chemodurov, as coming from the four daughters, and may have been cut off as part of the disguise.

On 23 January 1919, Judge Sergeyev was fired from his post by General Mikhail Diterikhs, staff officer in the White Russian regime, who was conducting the 'Romanov Inquiry'. Sergeyev disappeared and was deemed 'executed by the Bolsheviks'. The judge's dismissal was a direct military interference in a civilian investigation, but complaints were brushed aside. Sergeyev disappeared as Nametkin had, at the point when he began to believe that the imperial family had escaped or considered at the very least that only the Czar and Dr Botkin had been executed in the 'murder room'.

For a time the investigation was carried out by a new official prosecutor, Valery Jordansky; he did not last long, and he was deemed killed by the Bolsheviks too. All the time, the White Army were disseminating stories that the Czar and his family were dead. They had two main reasons for doing so. First, such a fact would show that the Bolsheviks were vicious murderers, and second, it elevated the Romanovs to the position of martyrs. These were far stronger propaganda points than having the Romanovs alive as a rallying point for a counter-revolution.

What the White Army really needed now was an investigation to prove the death of the Romanovs. So the White authorities appointed Nikolai Alexeyvich Sokolov to carry out investigations to establish this fact.

Sokolov was a career lawyer then attached as a court investigator for specially important cases of the Omsk Regional Court. In his investigations Sokolov was assisted by another committed czarist, Captain Pavel Bulygin, who had been the commander of the personal guard of Nicholas's mother, the Dowager Empress Marie (she had left Russia in April 1919 on a British warship sent for her by George V); also in Sokolov's team was Robert Wilton of *The Times*, an undercover British agent pledged to prove 'The-Czar-was-assassinated-by-the-vile-Bolsheviks' theory (his articles in *The Times* in 1920 put forward this theory). Though Sokolov carried out his investigations with legal thoroughness he too was committed to prove that the Czar had been murdered. He began his work in the spring of 1919 and his book *Ubiistvo tsarskoi sem'i* ('The Murder of the Imperial Family') which appeared in 1924, is still the basis of 'proof' used by suceeding generations of historians that the imperial family were massacred at Ekaterinburg.

The basis of Sokolov's conclusions that the imperial family had been massacred by the Bolsheviks was founded on four main premises:

First was a captured coded telegram of 9.00 p.m. on 17 July 1918 from the chairman of the Regional Soviet, Alexander Beloborodov to Nikolai Gorbunov, secretary of the Council of People's Commissars, stating: PEREDAITE   SVERDLOVU   CHTO   VSYO

SEMEISTSVO POSTIGLA TA ZHE UCHAST CHTO I GLAVU
OFITSIALNO SEMYA POGIBNET PRI EVAKUATSII. ('Tell
Sverdlov family suffered same fate as head officially family will die in
evacuation'). The telegram had been found in Ekaterinburg Post
Office by the White Army, and was interpreted as proof positive that
the 'Sverdlov' family (code name for the Romanovs) had been
executed. Modern scholarship assessing both the code and accom-
panying signature (which give the impression of being prepared and
written at a date later than 1919) opines that the telegram is forged,
and left to be deliberately found to back up the massacre 'evidence'.

Then there is the testimony of an 'eye witness' who said that he saw
the imperial family dead only minutes after the execution. The
witness was identified as Pavel Medvedev, the former leader of the
Russian exterior guard at the Ipatiev House. He had given himself up
to the White authorities. He was the only person who testified to
having seen the bodies of the imperial family. Medvedev is recorded
as having died of typhoid, but it is likely that he was liquidated by the
Whites before Sokolov arrived at Ekaterinburg. Why would such a
wanted man, indeed, give himself up to the Whites in any case? He
would know that he would be executed for regicide, or complicity
therein. But his testimony was a plank in the Sokolov case.

Thirdly, Sokolov ordered a detailed examination of the terrain and
mineshafts at the Four Brothers mine. Altogether he made 65 finds of
bric-à-brac which had belonged to the imperial family; charred
fragments of jewellery, scorched pieces of clothing, burned metal
clasps, and clothes fasteners were all examined by those who had
served with the Czar and his family and identified as belonging to
them. With the fragments were found a number of bones. Sokolov
concluded that the corpses of the imperial family had been stripped at
the mine – with some of their personal jewellery trampled into the
mud – and then chopped in pieces and destroyed by acid and fire. But
the bones could not be inconclusively considered to be of human
origin, and no skulls or teeth (both very difficult to destroy) were ever
located.

Finally, Sokolov's main premise noted that the body of the Grand
Duchess Tatiana's dog, Jemmy, was dredged up from the mine. But it
was odd to opine, as Sokolov did, that a slaughtered dog was proof
that the family with which it lived had been slaughtered too, and none

of the witnesses who had described the 'murder room' had even mentioned a dog.

Sokolov's case was an extremely tenuous one. The witnesses were contradictory, the testimony was conflicting and so many of the items found could so easily have been planted. Indeed it is a strong supposition that the dog's cadaver was a deliberate plant by Sokolov to help prove his case; another of the imperial children's dogs had been found at Ekaterinburg and had been adopted by soldiers. Throughout it is clear that Sokolov made the evidence fit his theories. For as he worked he continually came across witnesses who claimed that the imperial family was still alive; as their testimony did not fit his brief, Sokolov discarded or suppressed it.

Nikolai Sokolov left Ekaterinburg in July 1919 and the dossier and the relics amassed were handed over (reluctantly) to General Mikhail Diterikhs. At this point Sokolov bows out of the main investigation, although he did do some further interviews with those who knew something about the case. By 1921 he was in Paris with Captain Bulygin, Pierre Gilliard and Robert Wilton. All of them were subsequently to write books with their own versions of the 'massacre'. Sokolov died in November 1924.

Over the years the official Soviet 'historical re-write' department has issued various versions of what happened to the Romanovs, but all emphasize the Ipatiev house murder of *all* the imperial family.

Because of the inconclusiveness of the evidence, since 1924 many, many stories have circulated that somehow the imperial family did escape and lived out their lives in secret exile. Many too, accepted the mysterious Anna Anderson, who died in 1984, as the Grand Duchess Anastasia, the youngest daughter of Nicholas and Alexandra. Mrs Anderson, who married Maryland University professor, Dr John Manahan, spent sixty years trying to prove her claim to be the Czar's daughter. And many influential royals went out of their way to refute Mrs Anderson's claims; one such was the late Lord Louis Mountbatten. In his biography *Mountbatten*, Philip Ziegler points out that Mountbatten pressed the BBC not to give Anna Anderson's backers a platform.

Why Mountbatten should spend large amounts of his own money to counter Mrs Anderson's claims still remains a mystery; indeed he never ever tried to meet her himself and expose her as a fraud. Even today the Royal Family remains tightlipped about the Romanovs, following George V's obvious opposition to any proposal to offer asylum to the Romanovs in Britain in 1917–18. In the book *Tutor to the Tzarevich*, J. C. Trevin, who prepared 'an intimate portrait of the last days of the Russian Imperial Family' from the papers of Charles Sydney Gibbes, notes that a letter was sent to a Miss Margaret Jackson (who had acted as a governess to the Czarina when she was a girl) with the hope that its contents would be passed on to George V; the letter was a coded appeal for help. The letter went unanswered and has now disappeared from the Royal Archives.

HM Government too, has been consistently unwilling to admit any knowledge of the real fate of the Romanovs, and any question in the House of Commons on the subject has been fobbed off. For instance, a question asked by Baroness Ward of North Tyneside in 1976 was fudged over by Lord Goronwy-Roberts, Minister of State at the Foreign Office.

The 1960s were particularly good for the 'Romanov industry' and the American journalist Guy Richards produced three books which were particularly fanciful, *Imperial Agent*, *The Hunt for the Czar*, and *The Rescue of the Romanovs*, none of which were based on authenticated documentation and gave very far-fetched accounts of the 'rescue' of the imperial family.

By far the most meticulous examination of the disappearance of the imperial family was the investigation conducted by the television journalists Anthony Summers and Tom Mangold and published in 1976 as *The File on the Tsar*. Their carefully argued assessment of the case began with the re-discovery of the seven-volume record which Nikolai Sokolov had brought out of Russia. The journalists found the dossier in Paris in 1962 along with photographs taken during the 1919 investigations at Ekaterinburg. Closely examining the dossier and sifting through the data that Sokolov had never published they built up the basis for their belief 'that the Romanovs were not all massacred in the Ipatiev House'. They further conducted a world-wide investigation which lasted for four years; they talked to relatives of the imperial family and had all of the evidence available assessed by historians, pathologists, code-breakers and scientists. Their conclusions ran thus:

Summers and Mangold believe that the 'massacre' at the Ipatiev

House was a hoax to cover the disappearance of the imperial family. They also believe that the Czar's other imperial cousin, Kaiser Wilhelm II, had a hand in what really happened at Ekaterinburg, although the two nations had been at war since 1914. Like the Czarina, Wilhelm was a grandchild of Queen Victoria, and teutonic blood is thicker than most when it comes to family ties. Certainly by the summer of 1918 cables were exchanged between Moscow and Berlin on how to assist the German-born Czarina leave Russia. There is documentary evidence on file that Moscow and Berlin were negotiating for the 'women of the imperial family' to be 'permitted to leave the country'. Such a plan made sense for Russia's new leader Vladimir Ulyanov Lenin, who planned to use the imperial family as pawns. Indeed Summers and Mangold show that Karl Radek, head of the European Department of the Bolshevik Foreign Commissariat, was negotiating the release of the Romanovs *six weeks after* they disappeared at Ekaterinburg 16–17 July 1918. Lenin wanted the Romanovs alive as a matter of priority to use as an exchange for his friend Karl Liebknecht, 'one of the most important revolutionary politicians in Europe', who was a captive of the Germans. An assassination attack on Lenin in August 1918 changed the course of events, but Moscow was still bartering with Berlin on 10 September. As German intelligence in the Urals was strong, the Bolsheviks dare not risk lying about the lives of the Romanovs. Indeed on 27 September 1918 the Czarina's sister, Victoria, Marchioness of Milford Haven, received a telegram from Victoria the Crown Princess of Sweden that the imperial family were still alive; information which had come via the Czarina's brother, the Grand Duke Ernst Ludwig of Hesse and emanating from those very German intelligence sources.

The two journalists cited the report written in December 1918 by Carl Ackerman of the *New York Times* as being the most accurate about what really happened at Ekaterinburg. Ackerman, whose informant was one Domin (who the two journalists believed was a pseudonym for the Czar's valet, Terenty Chemodurov) told how the Czar was tried by a kangaroo court and shot on the night of 16 July 1918 by soldiers of the Red Army. Chemodurov later recounted the same story to more than one person and added that Botkin, Demidova and Trupp had been shot on the same occasion. Summers and Mangold were able to compare Ackerman's report with several other similar contemporary accounts which were written from Bolshevik sources before the Communist Party re-write teams could suppress them.

Summers and Mangold believe that the Czar *was* shot at Ekaterinburg and probably the Czarevich because he was heir. So that left the Czarina and her daughters; what really happened to them? The two journalists aver that they left Ekaterinburg *alive*.

Already there were clues on how the transfer might have been achieved. The clothes found at the Four Brothers mine were undoubtedly those of the imperial women – clothes discarded as a part of the disguise, to be replaced by workmen's clothes. Chemodurov said that the imperial women were 'obliged to put on soldiers' uniforms'. Then there were the hair clippings found; haircuts would be deemed an important part of the disguise. So disguised the imperial women were moved from Ekaterinburg by train. Remember, Sir Charles Eliot's papers had included the comment: 'On 17 July, a train with the blinds down left Ekaterinburg for an unknown destination, and it is believed that the surviving members of the imperial family were in it.'

The two journalists produced testimony – suppressed by Sokolov –that the imperial women were moved from Ekaterinburg to Perm, 200 miles north west, guarded by the Communists of the Regional Soviet. The testimony verified on oath by one Natalya Mutnykh, a nurse from Perm, stated that the women remained in Perm until December 1918.

Perm fell to the White Army at Christmas 1918 and from the dossiers of the victorious General Rudolf Gaida, Summers and Mangold were able to take their investigations further. Gaida's investigators, members of the *Ugolovny Rozysk* (CID), found witnesses to testify that the imperial women had been held at 'Berezin's rooms on Obvinskaya Street'. Summers and Mangold also uncovered evidence that one of the Czarina's daughters (probably the Grand Duchess Anastasia) tried to escape; she was found, arrested and taken to Cheka HQ. Having been beaten during her recapture Anastasia was treated at the secret police headquarters by Dr Pavel Ivanovich Utkin; this was now 10 December 1918.

It appears that the imperial women were then moved to a convent in Perm and as the White Army approached Perm they were moved through Kazan, on the railway line to Moscow. That they were in Perm and were evacuated in 1919 was attested by Alexander Kirsta, assistant head of the White Military Control at Perm.

To sum up, Summers and Mangold have provided authenticated evidence that the previously held belief that the imperial family were massacred at Ekaterinburg is false and that the following hypothesis can be put forward: Czar Nicholas II and his son were probably executed in the area of Ekaterinburg around 16 July 1918 and the Romanov women were transferred to Perm and were moved by railway towards Kazan in December 1918. At Kazan the trail petered out. So what happened then?

Summers and Mangold note: 'All the signs are sinister'. January 1919 was the date when the Czarina and her daughters were last seen alive. But there is no proof that they died in Bolshevik captivity. By 1919 Lenin had no reason to keep the imperial family alive, for Germany had lost. He may have ordered their execution, or he may have let them just succumb to their natural fate. So maybe, Anastasia Nicholaievna did escape to become Mrs Anna Anderson-Manahan.

Right up to today the Anna Anderson story, which inspired two films – one starring Ingrid Bergman and the other Lilli Palmer – is alive; for to the end at the age of 82 she claimed to be the sole survivor of the supposed massacre of 1918. For thirty-seven years Anna Anderson fought her case before the German courts and her plea for recognition was found unproven. The final verdict though on 17 February 1970 was inconclusive, it noted: 'We have not decided that the plaintiff is not Anastasia, but only that the Hamburg court made its judgment without errors'.

In 1988 the author Michael Thornton made public his belief that Anna Anderson – Mrs Anderson-Manahan – was finally murdered. She died in hospital in Charlottesville, Virginia, USA, in 1984 of old age and the after-effects of a stroke the public were told. But Thornton averred: 'She did not die from natural causes. Somebody disconnected her oxygen tube. Her husband Dr John Manahan there when she died told me about it.' Thornton went on to explain: 'Anna's husband had left the hospital room for a minute; when he returned the oxygen tube had been wrenched out of the machine and she died from oxygen starvation. Anna was too weak to have done it herself and the staff at Martha Jefferson hospital are too professional to have such an occurrence happen.' The hospital held an inquiry and her death certificate (not available to anyone except the family under the laws of Virginia) states she died of 'cerebrovascular accident'. But the Commonwealth of Virginia Death Certificate lists her as Anastasia Nikolaevna Manahan, born at Peterhof 1901 the daughter of Czar Nikolai and Alex of Hesse-Darmstadt.

As part of a Press statement in July 1988, Thornton, who had her power of attorney in England said: 'She lived in fear of being assassinated all through her life. She had many death threats. Her very existence was a challenge to accepted Soviet history. I think that somebody feared that she would reveal what had happened at Ekaterinburg. Were they raped before they were murdered? The French Secret Service say they were sexually assaulted. Did more than one of them escape? Her existence was a reminder of the most sensitive part of Russian history. Even now, they can't bear to speak of it. It's dismissed in one sentence in Soviet encyclopaedias.'

As a footnote to the story, in 1977 Dr Moritz Furtmayr, one of Germany's leading forensic experts was comparing photographs of Anastasia and Anna using the PIK process (which compares points of the skull, and was used as an identification process in the Demjanjuk 'Beast of Treblinka' trial) when she found that there had been earlier studies of the real Anastasia's right ear. Dr Furtmayr found that the original study showed that it compared with Anna's ear to an extent that any court of law would accept. So had the Grand Duchess Anastasia really survived the Bolsheviks' murderous bullets of sixty-six years before?

A recent postscript to the murdered Romanovs story evolved thus. Reuter's Moscow correspondent filed the story that the remains of the Romanovs had been found in 1979 by Soviet policeman Geli Ryabov. Reporting Ryabov, the *Moscow News* stated that the Romanovs had been shot by the Cheka (Lenin's secret police of 1917–22) at Ekaterinburg, and not by the local Bolsheviks. Ryabov said to Soviet reporters: 'The bodies were . . . loaded onto a Fiat truck and the terrible hearse started on its journey back [*the executioners, said Ryabov, had decided not to bury the bodies at the mine as noted in the 'official story'*], but the truck got caught in a swamp and it was decided to dump the

bodies there.' Ryabov went on – here there is a snag for supporters of
the Anastasia story – and found eleven bodies, which would make up
the full complement of the seven royals and four retainers! In reality
though, Ryabov's story runs contrary to the official story and totally
runs contrary too, to Diterikhs and Sokolov's eyewitness testimony. It
remains a curious fact, that even today the story of a long dead
monarch and his family is still presented to the world in the form of
official lies.

15

A Quintet of Assassination

 ### Murder of the King of Italy

In the eleventh century, Savoy, now a part of France, was a country within the Holy Roman Empire, and the Savoy dynasty quickly acquired a large chunk of land in north western Italy and Piedmont. By the fifteenth century the dynasty's lands became a duchy and their territory stretched as far as Nice. In 1720 Victor Amadeus, Duke of Savoy, who had reigned as King of Sicily for seven years, obtained the throne of Sardinia, and although the family were expelled from the mainland during the Napoleonic era, their lands were restored after Napoleon's fall and they returned triumphantly more powerful. In 1861, Victor Emanuel II, who had become King of Sardinia in 1849, succeeded as sovereign of a united Italy and was himself succeeded by his son Umberto I.

Umberto was to contribute an enormous amount to the decline in the prestige of the House of Savoy because of his reactionary attitudes and his blind insistence on dwelling almost exclusively within a narrow court circle. His amours also contributed to public scandal. In 1882 he entered into a triple alliance with Germany and Austria in the hope of gaining stability, but his dreams of empire proved hollow with the first Italian expedition to Ethiopia ending in disaster. Umberto's reign was a time of great anarchistic movement in Italy, indeed the country was a nursery of potential assassination, with France – because of the Franco-Italian rivalry in North Africa – keeping the pot boiling with outside aid. It was Italy's interests in Ethiopia and French intrusion therein, which had Francesco Crispi, the Italian Minister of the Interior, writing in his diary that he had heard from the King of Portugal in August 1888 that the French were plotting Umberto's assassination during his visit to Romagna for the military manoeuvres. The French had been stirring up the socialist leaders in Romagna but in the event there was no plot from that quarter but it led to the Italian police increasing surveillance on known agitators.

The record of the Italian police in gathering data on plots and intrigues was probably the worst in Europe. They had been totally wrong-footed in November 1878 when the first attempt on Umberto's life had been made. King Umberto and Queen Margherita had been driving in Naples during a state visit when an anarchist named Giovanni Passanante made a lunge at Umberto who was protected in his carriage by Prime Minister Benedetto Cairoli throwing himself over the king and thus sustaining a dagger wound in his thigh. Umberto pardoned his assailant, but it took the police ten years and the assassination of Empress Elizabeth by an Italian to put their support behind a conference on international assassination in Rome. There were few practical results of this 1898 meeting and two years later the anarchists were to triumph.

On 29 July 1900 Umberto was on his way home from presiding over an exhibition of gymnastic sports when the assassin struck. Umberto liked to give the impression that he was a man of the people when it suited him and he had gone walkabout among the young gymnasts at Monza, near Milan. He had just got back into his carriage when out of the crowd rushed the Tuscan Gaetano Bresci who fired at the king at point blank range. Umberto died immediately. Bresci, a skilled workman from Patterson, New Jersey, had been sent by an anarchist group in that city to kill Umberto with the intent of precipitating a revolution. In the event Umberto's death was to lead to a period of greater constitutional achievement which was only overthrown when the Italian people chose Fascism as their political credo.

A king and his heir die in Portugal

Portugal's monarchy in the twentieth century, heirs to the great rulers like Prince Henry the Navigator and John II, fell foul of the country's increasing humiliation in Africa. The British government, backing Cecil Rhodes's expansion policy in Central Africa, had demanded Portugal's withdrawal from Nyasaland and Mashonaland in 1890. Already in 1889 the Portuguese Emperor of Brazil had been overthrown. At home the ruling house of Braganza was continually being ridiculed and resented for their 'financial extravagance and uninspiring deportment'. They were looked upon as complete foreigners by many Portuguese. In 1640 Portugal had revolted against the rule of the Spanish Hapsburgs under John, Duke of Braganza, and the male line of the Braganzas was of the German Wettin dynasty. The prominence of foreign banks and financiers in Portuguese affairs underlined for the Portuguese people that their royal family was of a foreign dynasty. In 1891 a body of mutinous troops seized the city hall at Oporto, and although quickly suppressed the attempt coup was a significant bubble to overboil the political pot. By 1900 Portugal was over £177m in debt and the stout Germanic looking monarch, King Carlos I, was deemed by the more fanatical republicans to be responsible for much of the indebtedness.

By 1906 the anti-monarchist movement had grown rapidly, and there were mutinies on the warships *Don Carlos* and *Vasco da Gama*; monthly the monarchists lost ground politically and were constantly being thrown by financial scandals. In November 1906 it was revealed that 'illegal financial advances' had been made to King Carlos by the Portuguese Treasury without the consent of the parliament, the Cortes. During May 1907 the monarchist Prime Minister, Joao Franco, dissolved the Cortes and announced to the world that he would thereafter rule by decree. King Carlos supported this open dictatorship and consequently lost the support of the monarchist cadres who deplored despotic rule. On 6 January 1908 the Portuguese royal family left Lisbon for their palace at Villa Vicosa and there Carlos was informed of the details of the now planned republican uprising communicated to him by Franco. The Prime Minister arrested the republican leaders and drew up a decree applying the penalty of transportation for life for such plotting. As

Carlos signed the decree and decided to return to Lisbon the secret
political societies, of which there were dozens, assembled in their
different secret sessions to watch for an opportunity to unleash bloody
revolution.

On Saturday 1 February 1908, the Portuguese royal family – King
Carlos, Queen Amelia, daughter of the French pretender the Count of
Paris, and their two sons Crown Prince Luis Filipe and Prince
Emanuel – set off for Lisbon from Villa Vicosa. The royal family was
due in Lisbon at 4.15, but owing to a railway breakdown the ferryboat
Dom Luiz, in which the party were to cross from Barreiro to Terreiro
do Paco, was late. As the delay upset the security plans, King Carlos
was anxious for his family's safety in driving through the Lisbon
streets; but assured by the dictator Joao Franco that all was under
control the party continued in a two-horse open carriage for the drive
to the Necessidades Palace.

Among the crowd were ranged various political fanatics, each quite
separate and acting independently, but most were armed with loaded
firearms waiting in an opportunistic way to assault any of the royal
family they could. As the carriage was about to turn into the Praca do
Commercio, a young man sprang behind the carriage and shot King
Carlos in the neck. At once Queen Amelia tried to knock the man off
the back of the carriage with a bouquet with which she had been
presented, but the man fired again and this time dispatched the king.
The assassin was killed by a police bullet. Then another assassin, an
ex-cavalry sergeant and failed schoolteacher called Buica joined the
assault, and fired at the Crown Prince whom his mother tried to
protect with her body; Buica too was killed by the police. As the
carriage drove to the safety of the palace the king and his heir were
dead. Although Prince Emanuel was wounded, he survived to reign
for two years as Emanuel II, whereafter Portugal became a republic.

Hellenic homicide of the founder of the Greek royal family

When Otto I, King of the Hellenes, abdicated in 1862, the Greeks
wanted to invite Alfred, Duke of Edinburgh, the son of Queen
Victoria as their king. Yet, the Great Powers (who had chosen Otto
Wittlesbach to rule as the first king of the independent state) selected
Prince William of Denmark – son of Charles IX, and brother-in-law

of Edward VII – to be constitutional ruler of Greece as George I. King George I had a great rapport with the British royal family and he exchanged warm letters with his nephew George, Prince of Wales, in which family endearments like 'my dear old pickled pork' and 'my dear old sausage' were used.

George I, born in 1864, proved himself to be a capable monarch within a democratic constitution which allowed the monarch far more power than his relations in Britain. Yet, military power and its influence in politics was too strong, thus in 1909 the Military League, a powerful military organization forced the resignation of the Greek government and obliged King George to dismiss all his sons from their military posts. The Military League dissolved itself in 1910 and new constitutional amendments were formulated in 1911 to reinstate the powers of the monarchy to be much as they were before.

In keeping with the informality of his court – the king and his family roller-skated in the ballroom of the German-Grecian palace King Otto had built in Athens – George I lived a simple life. Throughout his fifty-year reign he survived many setbacks to be caught up by fate in 1913.

In the Balkan war the Greek army took possession of Samos on 15 March 1913 and the Turks were defeated. Following the capitulation of Salonica, King George established his headquarters there, and on 18 March took his customary afternoon stroll with a single *aide-de-camp*. On their way home a badly-dressed man fired two shots from a revolver and King George fell; he expired shortly afterwards in hospital without uttering a word. Two Cretan policemen seized his assassin who turned out to be a Greek half-wit called Schinas, to whom George had refused to give money.

Massacres in the land of assassinations

The outside world heard of one of the most bloody regicides in history from the telegram dispatched to the *Neue Freie Presse* at Vienna from Semlin on 11 June 1903. Confirmed by telegrams to the *Neues Wiener Tagblatt*, it told of the assassination of King Alexander of Servia, his Queen Draga, the king's brother-in-law and two sisters-in-law, a general, an *aide-de-camp*, and twelve men of the palace guard. *The Times* of 12 June 1903 noted of 'no parallel [to] be found in recent

European history for such wholesale extirpation of a reigning family and of its partisans. . . .'

The assassination surprised no one, for, the superstitious said, it had been forecast many years before, by the clairvoyant peasant Mata of Kremna. In 1868 this peasant had prophesied the violent deaths and assassination attempts of members of the Obrenovich family. During the nineteenth century two families disputed the rule of Servia, the Karageorgevichi and the Obrenovichi, both families having revolted against the Turkish suzerainty. The throne of Servia, which was only a principality until 1882 when it became a kingdom, changed hands between the two families several times. Mata of Kremna forecast correctly the death of Prince Michael Obrenovich IV, murdered in 1868 in the Kashnootnyak (Deer Park) near Belgrade; and the attempted assassination on 21 June 1899 on the life of ex-King Milan while driving in his carriage from the Citadel of Belgrade. The latter attempt was by a paid assassin, one Knezevich, aided and abetted by two czarist colonels. So when King Milan had abdicated in 1889 in favour of his son, the superstitious counted the years for the whole prophesy to be enacted with the death of the new King Alexander Obrenovich who was to be the last of his line to rule. Mata of Kremna's prophesies were recorded as he told them in 1868 by Alexander Popovich, Deputy of Ujitza.

Alexander Obrenovich, who ruled as King Alexander I, was born in 1876 the son of King Milan IV and was consequently 27 years old when his father abdicated in his favour. In 1900, Alexander married his mistress the widow of Svetozar Mashin, one Draga Mashin, a domineering and unpopular woman who had been a lady of honour to Alexander's mother, the Bessarabian beauty, Queen Nathalie. Queen Draga was to be one of the main reasons why Alexander met such a violent death.

Writing in 1906 one of the regicides wrote of the *principales causes qui amenèrent la fin tragique du Roi* to Chedomille Mijatovich erstwhile Servian Minister to the Court of St James. These reasons included conspiracy against the government; flouting the law that had exiled his father; the suspension of the constitution in 1897; the arrest of members of the government opposition; the unconstitutional marriage of his barren mistress against the wishes of his government and with the politicking of the Czar of Russia; collusion with Russia;

and the rise of the queen's relatives by nepotism – for instance her brother Nikodiyé Lunyevitza was elevated to become heir apparent.

From the beginning of 1901 the Servian secret service were aware of rumours regarding the proposed assassination of King Alexander, and there were several groups who toyed with the idea of replacing King Alexander with Prince Peter Karageorgevich. By the autumn of 1902 a definite conspiracy was afoot to assassinate the royal family, led for the army by Col Alexander Mashin (Queen Draga's brother-in-law) and his principal coadjutors Lt.-Col Domyan Popovich and Lt.-Col Mishich, and for the civilian conspirators by ex-Home Minister Genchich. Their declared intention was to annihilate the Obrenovich dynasty and replace it with that of the Karageorgevich.

A number of plans were laid to murder the royal couple but these came to nought, until on 10 June 1903 the conspirators were all in places of advantage. The equerry on duty at the palace, Lt.-Col Mika Naoumovich, who acted as main conspirator on the spot, monitored the king's movements throughout the day. He ordered cases of strong wine to be sent to the officers' mess at the palace, where it was drugged by 2nd Lt of the Palace Guard, Peter Zivkovich, who was to make sure that the commander of the Palace Guard, Capt. Peter Panayotovich, received a large share. Elsewhere in Belgrade the conspirators gathered, Lt.-Col Peter Mishich at the Kolaratz Restaurant, others at the Servian Crown Hotel and more at the Officers' Club.

Before midnight Col Mishich went to the Palilula Barracks where the King's Own VIIth Regiment of Infantry were quartered, and took over as commander. The troops were moved out to the Royal palace which they encircled by 12.30 p.m. The police monitored the troop movements, but following a series of telephone blunders, the palace was not warned. Soon the soldiers were in place within the palace precincts and the officers made for the royal quarters in the Old Palace, whose main door was blown by dynamite. By 12.35 p.m. the officers had gained access to the inner rooms of the palace and were soon at the front door of the royal apartments.

The sound of the exploding dynamite roused the gendarmerie from the Teraziya quarter of Belgrade who fired on the ring of soldiers. Very soon though all opposition was countered by the encircling soldiers. The explosion had cut the electric power lines and the palace was now in darkness. Using candles to light their way a group of officers led by Capt. Dragutin Dimitriyevich, began to search the royal apartments. Meanwhile the royal couple had found a safe hiding place in a small alcove reached by a secret door from the royal bedroom. In the alcove was a window overlooking the Imperial Russian Embassy, to which the royal couple now looked for signs of life. In the window they saw the Russian Minister Tcharikoff staring at them impassively. Tcharikoff, who had known of the conspiracy for some days was monitoring the situation for his government. The Russians had welcomed and supported Alexander's marriage to Draga knowing full well that it was unpopular and would help fire regicide; the Russians had decided that Peter Karageorgevich on the throne would better serve their purpose in the Balkans.

Having received no reaction to their waving the royal couple now saw in the garden below the figure of Capt. Luba Kostich of the Royal Guard. Queen Draga opened the window and shouted: 'Your King is in danger! For God's sake, to the rescue, to the rescue!' Kostich replied by emptying his pistol in the direction of the queen, and Draga slammed shut the window shutters.

Kostich ran up the staircase and led the conspirators in the direction of the king and queen's location. The king's *aide-de-camp*, General Petrovich, who had been wounded during the attack was brought to the scene and was hectored into revealing the secret door leading into the windowed alcove. Stupidly believing a promise that the king and queen would be unharmed, Petrovich indicated the door and encouraged the royal couple to reveal themselves. Slowly the king opened the door and there stood the couple in their night attire. 'What is it you want? And what of your oath of fidelity to me?' asked Alexander. His reply was a volley of revolver shots which did not dispatch the royal couple. The soldiers now attacked them with slashing swords – the hated Queen Draga received the worst of it and was soon dead, but the king rolled around in agony.

Shouting '*Ziveo Kralj Petar*' (Long live King Peter) the soldiers threw the now naked bodies of the king and queen out of the window –Alexander was still alive as he was hoisted over the window-ledge. The fingers of the dying king made a grab for the sill, to be hacked off by one of the brave young officers. For two hours the naked bodies lay in the garden in the rain where they were inspected by the Russian Minister Tcharikoff who gave the order that they be wrapped and taken to the palace. Inside was a scene of diabolical merriment as the soldiers sang and danced, whooped and pillaged through the royal apartments pocketing anything of value.

On the orders of Col Mashin, Queen Draga's young brothers Captains Nikodiyé and Nicholas Lunyevitza were murdered by Lt Tankossich, while Capt. Michael Yosupovich killed the War Minister General Milovan Pavlovid and Lt Milosh Popovich killed the Minister of Home Affairs (Police) Velya Todorovich. The way was now clear to proclaim Peter Karageorgevich as King Peter I.

Created out of the peace treaties of 1919, the new Kingdom of Yugoslavia was officially called the Serb-Croat-Slovene Kingdom until 1929, and Peter I of Servia was elevated to the new throne of Yugoslavia after King Nicholas I of Montenegro had been strategically deposed.

In time Peter I was succeeded by his son Crown Prince Alexander who at first acted as Regent on his father's behalf and then ruled as king on his father's death in 1921. King Alexander fully intended to be a constitutional monarch, but his army training made him see all dissent to his wishes as mutiny and he made the mistake of favouring the Slovenes in his kingdom at the expense of the Croats. In June 1928 a Montenegran deputy of the Yugoslav government shot dead two Croatian Peasant Party members and wounded three others. Alexander was appalled and in trying to put things right dismantled the 1921 constitution, dissolved the extant political parties and muzzling the Press shared executive power with his council of ministers. In due time the royal dictatorship became unpopular and the brutalities of the police in persecuting the Peasants Party led to a welter of assassination plots. In 1934 King Alexander was murdered in Marseilles during a state visit to France; the French Foreign Minister, Louis Barthou, died with him. His assassin, Velucko Kerin a member of the pro-Communist International Macedonian Revolutionary Organization, one of a group of Croatian terrorists, had leaped onto the running board of the official car. Kerin was himself badly injured and died a few hours later.

Alexander paid the price of royal dictatorship, partiality and flirting with the new Nazi regime in Germany; he had been invited to

France mainly to ensure that he would support France rather than Germany.

And the royal killing game goes on. In April 1989 *The Times* reported that a Croatian nationalist organization leader was discovered to be in a plot to kill Crown Prince Alexander of Yugoslavia. The Crown Prince had turned down the possibility of being called king, on the death of his father in 1970, but is still referred to as King Alexander by Yugoslavia monarchists. Nationalist Slobodan Milosevic was reported in the trial of Vinko Sindici at Dunfermline, Scotland, to be plotting to kill King Alexander in London. Sindici, allegedly a major in Yugoslavia's dreaded secret police the SDB, was accused of attempting to murder Milosevic. So, still today, even exiled monarchs stripped of all political power, in their very personages are deemed dangerous symbols of nationalism and are constant targets for terrorist groups.

16

The Mysterious Death of Bulgaria's Doomed Monarch

WAS KING BORIS III KILLED BY THE GESTAPO ON HITLER'S ORDERS?

The last crowned King of Bulgaria was called Boris III. His father had had the nickname of 'Foxy Ferdinand', and was a cunningly competent ruler of a seething mass of Balkan nationals. Born in 1861, Ferdinand was the heir of Augustus, Prince of Saxe-Coburg-Gotha, who shared a grandfather with Queen Victoria. Frederick had been elected Prince of Bulgaria in 1886 to Queen Victoria's complete consternation on the forced abdication of the Bulgarian principality's ruler, Alexander of Battenburg. Victoria had wired her Prime Minister, Lord Salisbury, to inform him of her displeasure: 'He is totally unfit – delicate, eccentric and effeminate'. What worried her most was that Bulgaria would fall to Russia, who had cast rapacious eyes on Bulgaria ever since the country had achieved independence from Turkish rule in the 1877–78 war. Yet, Victoria need not have been so hysterical for Ferdinand had a successful reign by the standards of Balkan achievement, to die in exile at the age of 91 in 1950. Ferdinand presided over the successful reorganization of the Bulgarian army, updated the railways and renovated the capital of Sofia, and under his guidance the Bulgarian ship of state fended off any adversaries.

King Boris III was Frederick's heir by his first marriage to Princess Marie Louise of Bourbon-Parma, and Prince Boris of Tirnovo was 14 when his father proclaimed the principality of Bulgaria (technically still under Turkish suzerainty) an independent state in 1908, with him as 'Czar of All the Bulgarias'. As time went by Frederick's successes went sour and he lost territory as a consequence of the Balkan War of 1913, and because of his allying himself with Kaiser Wilhelm II's Germany, lost more territory during World War I. In September 1918 the army declared Bulgaria to be a republic and a brief civil war ensued. The old order won, however, but the monarchy was really saved by the abdication of Ferdinand in favour of his son as Boris III.

Boris soon had to face the remarkable premiership of Alexander Stamboliski, the peasant leader who, with the support of the Agrarian Party, was the country's virtual dictator from 1919 to 1923. When that party won an overwhelming majority in the *Sobranjie* (parliament), in 1923, Stamboliski made moves to have a referendum on the monarchy. Boris and the army launched a *coup d'état* which stirred up internal factionalism and Stamboliski was murdered the same year by terrorists of the Internal Macedonian Revolutionary Organization. Uprisings were quickly suppressed as the communists jockeyed for position to take advantage of the circumstances. On 14 April 1925 there was an unsuccessful attempt to assassinate Boris while he was driven to Sofia. Two days later a bomb concealed in the roof of the ancient cathedral of Sveta Nedelja exploded during the funeral service of an assassinated general. The bomb was hideously successful with 160 dead, but Boris escaped unhurt. The retribution assured that the communists remained an ineffective force in the Balkans for many years and left them with one more score to settle.

Macedonian terrorism continued, but the authoritarian regime which was established after the fall of the government in 1934 put an end to Macedonian terrorist activities. Boris skilfully rode the ensuing political storms and by 1936 he had established a royal dictatorship. Yet from 1936 to 1939 the country prospered, women were given the vote (although the old political parties were banned) and Boris remained reasonably popular with his people.

Even so Bulgaria's position was precarious as were all the independent states from the Baltic to the Black Sea and the Mediterranean. They had all arisen in their modern form from when the neighbouring empires collapsed, and their future looked grim as resurgence worked its way through Germany and a new dynamism stirred in the Soviet Union. To Boris the future lay between these two, and he chose to foster Germany. Despite his apparent sympathies with the aims of the National Socialists, Boris did his bit to get over to Hitler that to take on Britain would be a mistake. During his shooting trips with Field-Marshal Herman Goering at Schorfheide, Boris tried to help avert war.

When war did come, Boris endeavoured to keep his country neutral, but by early 1941 the king had to yield to Hitler's demands to give passage to German troops *en route* for the invasion of Greece. The Soviets rubbed their hands and the Russian-orientated leftists positioned themselves for action. Germany curried favour with the Bulgarians by inducing Rumania to surrender the province of the Southern Dobrudja, which had been her ill-gotten gain from Bulgaria in 1913. As time went by the Bulgarian Government, urged by Boris endeavoured to keep its neutrality, but pressure increased after the outbreak of the German-Soviet war. The government of Prime Minister Bogdan Filoff came under more and more German pressure and Bulgaria introduced anti-Jewish legislation, forbidding them, for instance, from living in Sofia and forcing them to wear the yellow star of David. It must be said though that it was Boris who succeeded in saving Bulgarian Jews from deportation to German concentration camps for extermination, by defying Hitler's insistence.

The beginning of 1943 saw the deterioration of Boris's relations with Hitler accelerating. The Führer was not impressed by Boris's attitude towards the Jews, and Boris deeply resented the activities of Gestapo agents in Bulgaria. He was incensed too by the National Socialists' persecution of his sister Nadezhda of Bulgaria, Duchess of Wurttemburg for bringing up her children as Roman Catholics (she died in 1958). Later the Nazis' brutal ill-treatment of Boris's sister-in-law, Princess Mafalda of Savoy led to her death in a German concentration camp in 1944.

In March 1943 Hitler invited Boris, and his chief of staff, General Konstantin Loukash, to talks at Berchtesgaden. Boris knew that because of the *Wehrmacht*'s defeat at Stalingrad that Hitler would be pressuring him to join the war. Various plans were discussed but no pressure was put on Boris to enter the war, though strong hints were made by Joachim von Ribbentrop, Hitler's foreign-affairs adviser, to make an asserted effort 'to help solve the Jewish problem' and escalate persecution of the Jews. Again in June, Hitler invited Boris to talks but no direct demand was made for Bulgarian troops to be sent to the Eastern Front. The Nazis, though, began to believe that Boris intended to distance himself from the Axis group and once more invited the king to secret talks with Hitler in August 1943.

Boris met Hitler that time at the Führer's headquarters on the Eastern Front near Rastenburg in East Prussia. These talks reduced Hitler and Boris to icy politeness, particularly after a private meeting the Führer had with the king over lunch at Hitler's personal headquarters at the bunker known as the *Wolfsschanze* ('Wolf's lair'). No one knew for sure what passed between them, but writing in 1957 in his book *The Sword and the Olive*, the former English Minister at Sofia, Sir George Rendel was able to add this comment:

> Some years later I was told by a foreign friend who had exceptionally close contacts in Bulgaria and whose story I am inclined to believe, that, at this point [*the summer of 1943*] Hitler demanded to summon Boris to Berlin. It seems that the king was injudicious enough to have a long telephone conversation with his unmarried sister, Princess Eudoxia [*Evdokia*], on the eve of his departure, and to have referred not only to his determination not to send Bulgarian troops against Russia, but also his intention, if King Victor Emmanuel should agree to an armistice with the Allies, of immediately trying to follow his example. The line seems to have been tapped by the Germans and the story runs that King Boris was greeted by Hitler with one of his hysterical bursts of fury. King Boris then arranged to return to Sophia by air.

This was later confirmed by Princess Evdokia in a handwritten testimony in which she noted that Boris had told his oldest adviser Strashimir Dobrovitch that at the private lunch 'Hitler went into a rage when [*Boris*] refused his demands .... Screaming like a madman, he attacked me and Bulgaria in a torrent of accusations and threats.' Boris had not given in.

On the flight back to Sophia, Boris, who was greatly interested in avionics, took the co-pilot's seat, and encouraged the pilot to increase altitude. To ease breathing the king and his staff inhaled an oxygen mixture. The flight was uneventful but the king was exhilarated by the trip. Yet, quite out of character, when he arrived at Sophia, Boris did not contact his wife, Queen Giovanna, nor talk by phone to his beloved children Princess Maria Luisa and Crown Prince Simeon at the Varna Palace.

During the ensuing weeks, Boris's behaviour became unusual. He would take spells of being suddenly pale and tired. He was examined by his friend the eye doctor Dimitar Bolabanov and the palace physician Dr Dragomir Alexandrov. When they left he said nothing to his aides but in a telephone conversation to his sister Evdokia, later that evening, Boris said: 'It's with "the ticker" . . . you'll see I'll die from angina pectoris.' Half an hour later after working with his trusted palace secretary Pavel Grouev, Boris's valets rushed in to his room at the sound of him vomiting violently. By the time Boris's brother Prince Kyril arrived next morning the king's condition had worsened and an urgent message was sent to Berlin to Dr Rudolph Sajitz, who had treated Boris for many years, to hasten him to the king's bedside. The Nazi authorities co-operated willingly and speedily in facilitating the doctor's transportation.

Palace doctors had diagnosed a severe gall-bladder attack, but as time passed it was clear that it was heart trouble rather than gall-bladder and there were symptoms of a thrombosis and coagulation of blood in the heart. Curiously, Queen Giovanna was not informed about the seriousness of the king's illness – indeed she was not told at all, and even the government were not told. That evening Prince Kyril drove to his sister Evdokia's house to inform her of their brother's illness. Evdokia's first reaction was: 'Could he have been poisoned? He has been [to see Hitler]'.

By now Dr Sajitz diagnosed an infarct, an embolism, but with complete rest for six months, the king was expected to recover. But he must not be disturbed by anything. Air alerts had become more frequent as British and American planes passed over Bulgaria to bomb the Rumanian airfields in Ploesti. So as not to alarm the king, Prince Kyril ordered that the Bulgarian Air Defence was not to sound the sirens unless an attack was definite. As a part of his treatment Boris was given medicines flown in from Germany and administered by his German doctors. This was looked upon with grave suspicion by his sister. When she visited her brother, Princess Evdokia asked the direct question: 'Has my brother been poisoned?'

She was assured by Boris's Bulgarian medical attendants that this was not the case.

Queen Giovanna had only now been informed of the king's illness, but was notified that she need not visit, but as Boris's condition worsened she was called to his bedside. Some time during the doctor's examinations and consultations, the courtier and architect Yorodan Sevov remembered Dr Daskalov, one of the palace physicians, expressing doubts that Boris was suffering from something other than thrombosis, and the word 'poison' was mentioned. Sevov discussed this poison comment with the now present Viennese liver specialist Dr Hans Eppinger (who was later to be involved in medical experiments on inmates of Nazi concentration camps) who confessed that it was a possibility. A short time later Eppinger – who had also been whisked to Boris's bedside by the Nazis – having thought of what he had said, denied the possibility.

By 28 August – the Assumption of Our Lady, an important religious holiday in Bulgaria – Boris slipped into a coma and at 4.22 he died 'in horrendous pain'. Immediately proclamations were prepared announcing the king's death and the accession to the throne of the seven-year-old Crown Prince Simeon. As the communiqués flashed from embassy to embassy, many people in Bulgaria were asking: 'Why was a normally healthy man in his prime (Boris was 49), now struck at such a momentous hour for the country?'

The official version of Boris's cause of death – coronary thrombosis complicated by an infarct – was widely circulated, but suspicion that all was not as it seemed was almost immediate. Most people in Sofia believed that the Nazis had killed Boris. By 29 August 1943, the German minister at Sofia, the Nazi SA Obergruppenführer Adolf-Heinz Beckerle was writing this secret report to von Ribbentrop:

Sophia 29 August 1943
Today, before their departure, I asked the German doctors de Crines, Eppinger, and Sajitz to come and see me. They told me that they were sorry that during all this time they were unable to get in touch with me. They felt that they were kept, so to speak, prisoners at the palace, in order to prevent any news from leaking out. Even yesterday, after the king's death, they had found it impossible to come here. They understood that

King Ferdinand and the Italian royal family had to be notified first. In addition, the entire diagnosis had been left to them. The Bulgarian doctors stayed in the background. Sajitz said that he had spoken to the king while he was still conscious. The king was aware of the gravity of his condition and believed that this time, 'that was it', and he would not live. The king thought that he had angina pectoris. He attributed it to the the strains of an excursion to Mount Moussala, which he had undertaken the previous Wednesday. Because of suspicions, I asked the gentleman if the illness and death could have been due to some outside cause (poison). The three doctors answered unanimously and immediately in the affirmative, invoking the similarity of the symptoms. Eppinger spoke of a *typical Balkan death*. But could they say more? Could they reliably attribute death to such a cause? This could not be said with certainty; an autopsy would have been necessary for that. They have suggested at least a brain autopsy. At the beginning, it was denied altogether but, later, it was agreed to perform one after the embalming. At this point, it would be of no use, so they abstained from the decision of having it performed. I have the impression that, in spite of the limited scientific hard evidence, the doctors are privately convinced of a violent death. They told me that, because of professional secrecy, they will make this statement only to me; upon their return to Germany, they will have to restrict their statements to the general diagnosis of the illness.

In reality a partial autopsy had taken place on the region of the heart, but the results were never published.

If the report is genuine, and there is no reason to believe that it is not, then it is clear that if Boris was murdered, the Germans had nothing to do with it. In fact in the long run it was to their advantage that Boris stay alive.

The fact that the German doctors were able to speed to Boris's side in war-torn Europe has always suggested that someone important (probably Hitler) was interested in keeping Boris alive. The doctors may not have been in the know if Boris was being poisoned – Eppinger did mention his alternative diagnosis of poisoning which he later retracted – but it is known that Eppinger retained his suspicion. In a recorded meeting with Col Carl-August von Schoenebeck, the German air attaché at Sofia, Eppinger said, in the presence of Sajitz: 'I believe it is poisoning.' This irreproachable King has fallen victim of a most common murder. Sajitz added that the spots which had appeared on Boris's body before death indicated dispersion of poison. Eppinger quoted a similar case in the supposed murder of the Greek Prime Minister John Metaxes (official verdict blood poisoning and uremia following tonsillectomy). In his diary Schoenebeck insisted that Dr Eppinger remained highly suspicious of the cause of Boris's death and averred that the king had been poisoned by an 'Indian poison', extracted from a 'creeping plant or from a snake'. Eppinger's suspicions were never made public; ultimately Eppinger committed suicide.

Historians today ask two questions: Was Boris's death natural? If not, who murdered him? Different factions have put forward five culprit groups; the Nazis; the British; the Soviets; Bulgarian Communists; the Italians . . . or was it suicide? Both Hitler and Goebbels believed that Boris was poisoned and openly blamed the Italian royal family. This was undoubtedly a conseqence of Hitler's increasing anti-Italian rages. His hypothesis was that the hated Princess Malfada of Savoy (Boris's sister-in-law) was engineering Italian influence in Bulgaria and Boris had been resisting.

All in all only one group stood to gain from Boris's death and that was the Soviets. Stalin had already earmarked Bulgaria as one of his satellites when the war was over. The Communist terrorists had been carrying out systematic assassinations. Generals Christo Loukov, Atanas Pantev and Sotir Yanev had all been murdered; so was Boris their victim too?

What about the suggestion of suicide? Undoubtedly Boris was in a state of physical and mental exhaustion when he returned to Sofia from meeting Hitler for the last time, and his erratic behaviour (not calling his family) marked the state of his feelings. His Prime Minister Fitoff said that during the flight Boris had said: 'Today, during our flight back, I would that the enemy fighters had shot our plane down, so it would all be over'. Boris had achieved great things in opposing Hitler – he had managed to keep Bulgaria out of the war and had protected Bulgarian Jews from deportation. Yet events were escalating that even Boris could not halt, and to continue to oppose Hitler would mean German occupation of Bulgaria. Yet, to a deeply religious man like Boris, suicide was not an option. But was the thought of an occupied Bulgaria the extra stress and despair that would lead to a collapse of Boris's will to live? Also he was worried about his health. In public certainly Boris played the rôle of the man who did not care any more – he hunted vigorously despite the pains in his chest, he climbed at Moussala taking the most difficult and dangerous paths; and he neglected his family . . . all out of character.

No one knows for sure how Boris died and even today there is uncertainty about his grave. Because his original burial place at the Rila monastery became such a place of pilgrimage, his body was moved to Vrana where it was reburied in the palace park in 1946. Yet, after the royal family left Bulgaria stories tell of how the grave was defiled and the coffin removed. So no one knows where Boris's remains are today.

Following Boris's death, the six-year-old Simeon II ascended the throne of Bulgaria under the regency of Boris's brother Prince Kyril of Preslav and two others. On 5 September 1944 the Soviet Union attacked Bulgaria and the leftist cadres helped set up a Soviet satellite. Among their first victims was Prince Kyril who was shot during the night of 1 February 1945, preceded solely by the Soviet refinement of being made to dig his own grave. The exiled King Simeon II still lives in Spain; and Princess Evdokia died in 1985 still protesting that her brother had been killed by the Nazis. Queen Giovanna, it seems, never fully believed the official cause of her husband's death, and although Simeon and his sister always prefer to think the death was of natural causes they still have private doubts.

Select Bibliography

Chapter 1

Freeman E. A., *The Reign of William Rufus* (Oxford 1882).
William of Malmesbury, *Chronicle of the Kings of England*, (London 1887–89).
Savage, Anne, *The Anglo-Saxon Chronicle*, (Philips/Heinemann 1982).
Barlow F., *William Rufus*, (1983).

Chapter 2

More, Sir Thomas, *History of King Richard III* (Folio Society 1965).
Walpole, Horace, *Historic doubts on the life and reign of King Richard III*, (Folio Society 1965).
Seward, Desmond, *Richard III: England's Black Legend*, (Hamlyn 1983).
Kendall P. M., *Richard the Third*, (George Allen & Unwin 1955).

Chapter 3

Donaldson, Gordon, *The 1st Trial of Mary Queen of Scots*, (Batsford 1969).
Davidson M. H. A., *The Casket Letters*, (London 1965).
Fraser, Antonia, *Mary Queen of Scots*, (Weidenfeld & Nicolson 1969).

Chapter 4

Gerard J., *What was the Gunpowder Plot?*
Edwards F., *Guy Fawkes*, (1969).
Simons E. N., *The Devil in the Vault*, (1963).

Chapter 5

Mousnier R., *L'Assassinat d'Henri IV 14 Mai 1610,* (Paris 1964).

Chapter 6

Baschet G., *Un Louis XVII Colonial*, (1907).
Tuber C., *La Mort de Louis XVII*, (1958).
De Beauchesne M. A., *Louis XVII. Sa Vie, Son Agonie, Sa Mort*, (1853).
Lenôtre G., *The Dauphin*, (1922).
Sicotière De la, *Les Faux Louis XVII*, (1882).

Chapter 7

Van Thal, Herbert, *Ernest Augustus, Duke of Cumberland and King of Hanover*, (Arthur Barker 1936).
Jesse, John Heneage, *Memoirs of The Life and Reign of King George III*, (London 1867).
A Minute Detail of the Attempt to Assassinate HRH the Duke of Cumberland. (London 1810).

Chapter 8

Richardson Frank, *Napoleon's Death: An Inquest*, (1974).
Weider B., Hapgood D., *The Murder of Napoleon* (1982).

Chapter 9

Andre L., *La Mystérieuse Baronne de Feuchères*, (Paris 1925).
Bowen M., *The Scandal of Sophie Dawes*, (London 1934).
Montague V., *Sophie Dawes, Queen of Chantilly*, (London 1911).

Chapter 10

The Letters of Queen Victoria. Ed. A. C. Benson, Viscount Esher (Murray 1907).
The Annual Register. 1840, 1842, 1849, 1859, 1872, 1882.

Chapter 11

Tschudi Clara, *Ludwig The Second*, (Swan Sonnershein 1908).
Blunt Wilfred, *The Dream King*, (Hamish Hamilton 1970).

Chapter 12

Haslip Joan, *The Lonely Empress*, (Weidenfeld & Nicolson 1965).
Lonyay Carl, *Rudolf: The Tragedy at Mayerling*.
Gribble F., *The Life of the Emperor Franz Joseph*, (Nash 1914).

Chapter 13

Eisenmenger V., *Archduke Franz Ferdinand*, (1931).
Redlich J., *Emperor Franz Joseph of Austria*, (1929).
Cassels L., *The Archduke and the Assassin*, (1984).

Chapter 14

Summers A., Mangold T., *The File on the Tsar*, (Gollancz 1976).
O'Connor J. F., *The Sokolov Investigation*, (Souvenir Press 1971).
Trewin J. C. *Tutor to the Tsarevich*, (Macmillan 1975).

Chapter 15

King Umberto I of Italy

Crispi F., *Memoirs*, (1912).
Clark M., *Modern Italy 1871–1982* (1984).

King Carlos I of Portugal

Cunha V de B., *Eight centuries of Portuguese Monarchy* (1911).

Chapter 16

Heiber Helmut, *Der Tod des Zaren Boris*, (1964).
Groueff Stephane, *Crown of Thorns*, (1987).

Name Index